SONS OF OLYMPUS

BOOK 1

STORM CHASER

EDEN ROYALE

Copyright © 2022 by Royale Media Group Ltd

All rights reserved.

No portion of this book may be reproduced in any form without written permission from the publisher or author, except as permitted by copyright law.

Published by Royale Media Group Ltd

www.EdenRoyale.com

For Alex, and the start of our own adventure

Author's Letter

Dear Reader,

They say good things happen when you least expect it. And that was certainly true for the *Sons of Olympus*. At a time in my life when I was desperate for a new adventure, I suddenly found a group of hunky Greek demigods appeared in my mind, each with their own adventure to pursue and story to tell. And just like that, life suddenly got more interesting...

Many hours, coffees and perhaps one too many wines later, the Sons of Olympus had made the journey to the page, ready for me to share with the world. And it's my hope that by sharing their stories with you, they can add a sprinkle of magic to your day, too.

And what better way than starting with the descendant of the big man himself? Zeus, King of the Storms, and playboy of Olympus. The idea for *Storm Chaser* came to me when watching a storm brew on the beaches in Devon, England. As great black clouds descended and filled the sky with ominous thunder, inspiration struck (as did torrential rain, although I suppose that's an English summer for you). One by one, Zed and the Stormchasers swept me away on a great adventure - and I hope they do the same for you.

Now settle in, hold on tight, and get ready to meet the Sons of Olympus!

I hope you enjoy them as much as I have,

Eden Royale x

P.S. If you'd like to join Tempest and Zed on their next adventure, claim your **FREE** sequel book at **EdenRoyale.com**

Prologue

Zephyr groaned as the god's curses rang through the skies. If there was one thing worse than a lifetime of serving the Olympians, it was being at their beck and call for an eternity. As Hera's booming voice filled the heavens once more, he couldn't help but question whether immortality was such a good thing after all.

"Zephyr, get here this instant!"

With a grumble, he drifted along the winds, knowing that keeping the Queen of Olympus waiting was a worse idea than jumping into a Gorgon's lair. So much for his quiet evening of riding the breezes and trying to sneak into the Heroes Bar. He ascended to the peak of the mountain and braced himself as he entered the palace. For a goddess, the Queen of Olympus sure knew her fair share of blasphemous phrases.

"What took you so long, Zephyr?"

Hera's eyes burned with fury as she sat at her desk, working late as usual. Zephyr gulped, and reminded himself to tread carefully. Hera's curses were infamous, and the last thing he wanted was to be transformed into a cow. Or worse. A mortal.

1

"My queen, is something wrong?" Zephyr hovered around her uncertainly, trying to gauge the extent of her fury. "Has my lord been dallying with the mortals again? Or has Aphrodite been stealing your beauty cream?"

"It's far worse than that. Look."

Zephyr followed her eyeline to the hearth that stood in the center of the palace. His eyes narrowed, then widened in shock.

"It can't be..." He flew to the hearth and drew a startled breath. "The flames have died! But this means..."

"Olympus will fall, and the world will fade to darkness." Hera looked gloomily to the heavens above. "The signs have been there for centuries. The stars shine less brightly, troubles plague the world below, and hope is harder to find."

"Oh, this is terrible news. Would you like me to fetch the King?"

"The King is on vacation with his knuckle-headed brothers. And besides, what good would he do?"

Zephyr had to admit that she had a point. Zeus might be King, but everyone knew Hera was the real boss of Olympus. He drifted alongside her as she paced up and down the palace, the cogs whirring in her mind.

"No, this isn't a war we can fight with strength and might. This requires a delicate touch." She peered into the shadows of the hearth before turning to Zephyr. "Tell me, what's our best weapon against the darkness?"

Zephyr paused to think. It was times like this he wished he had Athena's brain.

"Um... a torch?"

"*Love*, Zephyr. It shines brighter than anything else. Love will always beat the darkness." Hera sifted through the ashes and let them fall through her fingers like grains of sand. "Love will reignite the flames of Olympus and save us all."

Zephyr groaned as Hera turned to him. "You already have a plan, don't you?"

The queen smiled, and handed him a photograph of a group of men.

"They call themselves the Sons of Olympus. They're gods amongst mortals, direct descendents of the Olympians. And they're our only hope."

Zephyr narrowed his eyes at the men in the photograph. He had a nose for smelling trouble among the gods. And these men had trouble written all over them.

"The Sons of Olympus are destined for great things. They're future leaders of their kind, protectors of the earth and the heavens. And their strength of heart can reignite the fires of Olympus."

Zephyr glanced at Hera suspiciously. "Why do I get the feeling there's a catch?"

"You're a fast learner. Despite the Sons of Olympus' strength, their hearts remain empty. They drift through life, squander their gifts, and leave a trail of chaos and destruction in their wake." Hera sighed, and gazed into the darkness of the hearth. "They forget what's truly important. Love."

"So you want me to play matchmaker?"

"I've consulted with Aphrodite and found the perfect match for each of them. Their equal in strength of heart. Their one true love." Hera handed Zephyr a list of names and locations. "If we

3

can bring them together, the strength of their love will restore the light of the world."

"Surely the Erotes would be better suited to this?" complained Zephyr. "Or I could ask the Romans if Cupid could help? It would only take a few arrows…"

"Cupid is an oversized baby in a diaper. And besides, we need real love, not something forced by magic." Hera shook her head and turned her gaze to Zephyr. "We can't allow the Sons of Olympus to know that we're interfering. No, this requires a gentle touch. It requires someone who can travel anywhere, without being seen. Someone who can bring these couples together without them even knowing it. It requires *you*."

Zephyr sighed. "You want me to meddle."

"All you need to do is give the Sons of Olympus a little nudge in the right direction. A gentle breeze, a change of tides, a whisper carried in the winds. Anything that sets them on the path to encounter their true love." Hera smiled knowingly. "Once they lay eyes on their mate, I have no doubt that their godly instincts will kick in. Even the gods are powerless to fight against the fates."

"Oh, I know all about the gods and their instincts. But it always ends in disaster. Like when Hades thought it would be a good idea to abduct Persephone, and caused global famine in the process. Or when Zeus turned his girlfriend into a cow…" Zephyr gulped as Hera's eyes narrowed. "My point is that times have changed. The Sons of Olympus can't lay claim to their mate like their ancestors did. There are laws against that kind of thing."

"You're right, Zephyr. For this to work, their mates must fall in love willingly, and without magic. It relies on the Sons of

Olympus overcoming the biggest challenge of all. Love." Hera flashed Zephyr another smile. "Thank the Fates we have you to help them."

"Hey, I haven't agreed to this yet." But Zephyr's heart sank, knowing there was no denying the Queen of Olympus. He glanced at the photo again. "Let's say I was to accept... which one of these Sons of Olympus would I start with?"

Hera pursed her lips while she ran her finger along the photograph. "Let's see. We could start with the descendent of Poseidon, although I hear he's busy being a recluse at the bottom of the ocean. Or perhaps Hephaestus' descendent. How do you feel about dragons?"

Zephyr shuddered and shook his head. "Maybe something where I won't be burned to a crisp. What about him?"

Zephyr pointed to another man in the photograph, whose eyes glimmered with golden sparks.

"An excellent choice. The descendant of Zeus, no less. The future King of the storms."

"Well, if he's anything like his ancestor, it shouldn't be any trouble getting him to fall for a woman." Zephyr gulped as Hera's scowl deepened. "No offense, my queen."

"The problem isn't his interest in women. It's getting him to stay in one place. The man drifts across the world like a storm, leaving a trail of broken hearts and destruction in his wake." Hera sighed. "I guess some things do run in the family. Last I heard, he and his Stormchasers were chasing a storm to the West."

"Stormchasers?"

"Supernatural biker gangs with a penchant for racing in highly dangerous storms on obnoxiously loud motorcycles. I could barely get a wink of sleep last time they raced through here."

Zephyr looked at the man in the photo once more. He certainly didn't remember Zeus riding a motorcycle. Then again, he supposed long flowing robes and big beards had gone out of fashion too.

"Times have changed."

"They have indeed, Zephyr. Still, it might do you some good to visit the earth. I fear you've grown far too used to your leisurely lifestyle of floating along the breezes." Hera clapped her hands, as if the matter was decided. "Well, you must be on your way. You have a storm to catch. Just follow the trail of destruction and you'll find Zeus' descendant."

"I'm not sure about this..."

"There'll be no arguing, Zephyr. Olympus needs you. The *world* needs you." Hera smiled sweetly, ignoring Zephyr's grumbles as she ushered him out of the palace. "You must find the Sons of Olympus and fill their hearts with the light of love. Only then will the light return to Olympus."

"Do I even have a say in the matter?"

"What would you rather do? Drift aimlessly along the breezes and dally with the Muses?" Hera rolled her eyes as Zephyr shot her a look that implied he'd much rather do such a thing. "You've lost your way, Zephyr. You need purpose and direction. This quest might just be the very thing you need."

"Purpose and direction are overrated. I prefer to drift through life." Zephyr glanced at the Heroes Bar as a peal of laughter echoed from within its curtain of clouds. "Besides, I have plans tonight."

"Trying to sneak into the Heroes Bar and flirt with the Muses once again? It won't work, Zephyr. They only admit heroes in there."

"An antiquated policy if ever there was one."

"Well, perhaps I can help." Hera gave him a scheming grin, and conjured a sheet of parchment in her hand. "A fitting reward for the hero who saves Olympus."

Zephyr peered at the parchment then blinked in surprise. "A hero's license? For me?"

"Think about it, Zephyr. You'd be the talk of Olympus. People would sing ballads in your honor. You'd be inundated with social invites." Hera followed his eyeline to the cloud-covered Heroes Bar, where delicate melodies drifted into the sky. "And I'm sure the Muses would want to thank you, in their own way..."

Zephyr gulped, having momentarily lost the ability to speak. He reached out for the hero's license eagerly.

"It's everything I've ever wanted..."

Hera smiled knowingly, but the hero's license disappeared in a puff of smoke.

"Well then, that's settled. You'll get your hero's license, *after* you complete your quest."

"But Hera..."

"The sooner you find the Sons of Olympus, the sooner you get what you want. Now hurry. You don't want to keep the Muses waiting." Zephyr glanced back to the Heroes Bar as a firm hand guided him out of the palace. "Go, Zephyr. The fate of the world depends on you."

Without another word, Hera shimmered in a golden light before arcing into the sky like a shooting star. Zephyr groaned and cursed Hera for her meddling. If there was one thing he'd learned, it was that the Olympians and love always ended in disaster. Something told him this wouldn't be as straightforward as the queen believed.

He looked at the Heroes Bar once more and sighed longingly. Zephyr didn't know who the Sons of Olympus were, but the sooner he found them, the sooner this would all be over. And Hera had a point. This could finally be the ticket to getting the Muses to notice him.

He glanced at the photograph of the Sons of Olympus, and to the man with eyes that gleamed with sparks.

"The King of the Storms, eh? Well, if it's storms you're after, that's something I can deliver."

Zephyr called to the winds that raced across the earth. He moved them ever so gently, plucking them like a weaver moving threads in a great tapestry, until all pointed to the same town below. He smiled to himself as the storms changed their course, and drifted through the highway he'd created. Hera had a point. Perhaps he was the best person for the job, after all.

He allowed himself a moment to marvel at his work, before pulling on his hood and drifting along the currents to the earth below.

The path had been set. He just hoped the King of the Storms would follow it.

1

The storm had raged for days.

Dark winds howled through the once-peaceful town, while black rain lashed the fleeing townsfolk as they ran for cover. As hanging flower baskets swayed wildly in the storm, one by one, the residents shuttered their windows, locked their doors, and huddled in the safety of their homes.

But there were those who peered through their windows and watched the storm that raged above. Those who knew what raced in the cloud-covered skies. Those who knew that the storm was the playground of the gods.

Zed revved his motorcycle, causing another ripple of thunder to echo through the skies. He roared with laughter at the pandemonium that spread through the town like wildfire. The mortals below would never know the thrill of riding the storm. They would never feel the heart-pounding sensation of racing through the sky. And they would never know the freedom of traveling with the storm, leaving nothing but devastation in their wake.

He pressed himself flat to his motorcycle and raced across the jetstream that formed the highway of the gods. The others followed his lead, filling the sky with the deafening roar of their engines. A streak of violet lightning sped alongside him, and he turned to see a woman emerge, her purple Mohawk withstanding the force of the storm.

"Race you to the finish line?"

A smile flickered across his lips. "What makes you think you can win this time?"

A bolt of turquoise electricity zoomed through the air as a long-haired youth joined them. He flashed Zed with a mischievous grin as his blue hair billowed in the wind.

"You just wait, Zed. I've got these bikes running at their best. You won't stand a chance."

The sound of revving engines filled the air as Ixion and Dash raced ahead, sparks shooting out of their exhausts. Between Ixion's skilled riding and Dash's engineering, they were a force to be reckoned with. The thrill of the ride sent sparks flying from Zed's fingers, as he revved his engine to chase after them. It had been far too long since he'd had a real challenge on the track.

Zed braced himself as he took a hairpin corner at full speed, gale force winds buffeting him as he steered his motorcycle along the narrow track. It was reckless, and for many, would mean a long fall to the earth below. But Zed had spent a lifetime riding the storms. This was in his blood. And while others were chained to the earth by their fears, Zed had made the skies his playground.

The jetstream branched out, and he veered away from Ixion and Dash as they soared through the skies. He watched them, momentarily spellbound by the beauty of the violet and turquoise lightning that wove playfully through the sky. It was a rare sight to see two Stormchasers ride so perfectly in-sync. And with Seth's leadership, such a sight was becoming rarer.

Zed gazed longingly at the bonded pair. Once it had been enough to follow the storm, to drift from town to town and never think about anything but the present. But now... now he wasn't so sure. The storms didn't hold the same thrill as they used to, the rides were too long, and the races had lost their luster. Something was missing. And for once, he couldn't ride away from his problems.

As Dash's cackle of glee filled the air, Zed shook the thought from his mind. He revved his engine, and focussed on the track before him. The storm was no place for his worries. And right now, he had a race to win.

Zed followed the jetstream, racing between flashes of lightning that struck the magical road. It took him beneath the thick storm clouds, and out across the open expanse of the windswept plains below. He basked in the frenzy of the storm, reveling in the rains that pelted the earth and the winds that tore through the valleys. The mortals could build their roads and cities, but they could never tame the true power of the storm.

As he basked in the chaos, a noise drifted from the valley below. He peered over the edge of his motorcycle and his eyes widened as a pair of headlights sped through the darkness. It was an earth-bound.

Zed watched the mortal as they rode through the storm. It was preposterous. The earth-bound should cower in fear in their brick houses, not intrude into the playground of the gods. He cast an eye to the storm above, knowing he should focus on the race. But someone needed to teach that foolish mortal a lesson.

He leaped onto another jetstream and drifted further below, towards the plains where the earth-bound raced. He sneered at their bike, knowing such a piece of junk would be an affront to Zeus himself. The air crackled as he gathered power, and formed a golden bolt of lightning in his hand. He'd show this earth-bound the true power of the storm.

Zed hurled the lightning towards the mortal. It struck the road before them, exploding into a shower of rock. He smiled to himself as clouds of rock dust drifted from the track. That should serve as a warning.

But his smile faded as the earth-bound continued to speed ahead, undeterred by his storm. Anger and indignation ran through him as he sent another lightning blast, followed by a sonic boom of thunder that shook the very foundations of the earth. But the rider below wove through each blast of lightning with ease, as if reveling in it.

Zed's anger gave way to intrigue, and a flicker of a smile crossed his lips. They were the first mortal he'd met who didn't flee in terror at his storms, and certainly the first to keep up with him in a race. Ixion and Dash might not be any competition for him, but this mortal had proved themselves to be a formidable opponent.

The storm drifted further into the mountains, filling the air with the roar of the Stormchaser's engines. Zed rode higher along the jetstream, the mortal racing beneath him, undeterred by the danger. They were a skilled rider, and could give most of his crew a run for their money. But there were some things that the earth-bound could never do.

Zed raced along the jetstream towards the center of the storm, where the lightning burned brightest and the storm blew strongest. He revved his engine, pushing it to its limits as he followed the curve of the track and sped into the center of the storm. He roared out in victory as he soared through the finish line. The storm filled with a dazzling light show of golden sparks, before he descended to the earth and skidded to a halt in a shower of rock and smoke.

A flash of violet lightning filled the air as Ixion landed next to him. Zed leaned against his motorcycle and raised an eyebrow at her.

"I thought you were going to give me some competition."

Ixion's usual scowl deepened, and sparks shot out from her violet Mohawk.

"We're supposed to ride above the storm clouds, Zed. What if the earth-bound had seen you?"

"Relax. All they would have seen was lightning."

Another flash, and Dash landed next to them, his turquoise hair billowing behind him in the wind. He banged his fist against his handlebars and cursed.

"Dammit, I thought I was going to win this time. My bike's still too slow." He looked out at the valley beyond and shook his head. "I'd have been faster if it hadn't been for that earth-bound getting in the way."

"A likely story."

At the mention of the earth-bound, Zed turned to where the storm raged. The rider continued to race towards the storm, climbing higher up the mountain roads.

"Are they insane? They'll ride off the top of the mountain if they're not careful. And it's a long way down."

But Zed's eyes widened as he realized what the earth-bound planned. He pointed to the mountain peak, its curve forming the perfect ramp into the sky.

"They're not planning on falling. They're planning on leaping into the storm."

Ixion's frown deepened. "Impossible. No mortal could make that jump. It would be suicide."

Zed's heart quickened as the earth-bound raced higher into the mountain. It was dangerous, it was reckless, and yet the sight of it set his heart alight.

"Zed, you have to stop them. If they make the leap..."

He knew Ixion was right. He reluctantly gathered electricity in his hands, knowing it was his duty to protect the Stormchasers' secret. But as he watched the earth-bound, a strange sensation swept through him. It stirred the very core of his being and made him feel more alive than the wildest of his rides.

"Stop them. Now!"

Zed knew he should act. He knew his duty to the Stormchasers should come first. But the strange feeling swept through him, stronger than any storm, until he was powerless to fight it.

"Zed!"

The electricity in his palms fizzled into sparks, and the mortal rode deeper into the storm. Ixion turned to him with a scowl that reached new depths of disapproval.

"They're an earth-bound, Zed. If Seth finds out..."

"That earth-bound nearly outraced us all. They deserve a chance."

Ixion's scowl deepened, but a wide grin spread across Dash's face.

"You know, I think they might be crazy enough to make it."

Ixion snorted with disdain. "They'll lose their nerve. No earth-bound has the courage to make the jump."

Zed watched the mortal with bated breath as they approached the mountain edge. He knew it was against the rules. He knew Seth would punish him for his disobedience. But there was something about this rider. Something different. And they deserved a chance.

The sound of screeching brakes filled the valley as the earth-bound skidded to a halt just feet away from the sheer drop below. They'd lost their nerve. Disappointment washed through Zed, while Ixion smiled smugly.

"I told you. No earth-bound can ride into the eye of the storm. They're just not meant for our world."

Zed watched as the rider removed their helmet, revealing long, dark hair that billowed behind them in the wind. His eyes widened at the sight of her. The earth-bound was a *woman*.

A flash of lightning illuminated her against the darkness of the storm. A silver streak gleamed in her dark hair, as if lightning raced through her locks, while her eyes sparkled with the thrill of the race. She possessed a beauty that even the goddesses themselves would be jealous of. And she could ride. Every instinct in Zed's body drew him towards her, as if she called to him with a siren song.

Zed called to the storm that surrounded the earth-bound and felt every touch of the wind through her hair. She opened her arms to the storm, as if embracing him, until he felt every caress of the raindrops against her skin. He called on the lightning, and watched as her eyes sparkled with the burning brightness of her mortality. She was an earth-bound, of that he was certain, and yet she was one with the storm. And in all of his travels, he'd met no one like her.

Ixion revved her engine pointedly, breaking the spell the earth-bound had conjured over him.

"We should go, Zed. The storm calls us, and Seth won't be happy if we delay."

Zed nodded, feeling the tug of the storm pull him towards his next destination. But his eyes drifted back to the earth-bound who bathed in his storm. He shook his head, knowing he should resist. He'd raced through the strongest storms imaginable. He'd survived countless battles against rival gangs. And yet this woman had stopped him in his tracks. A primal instinct blazed within him, sending sparks racing along his body as he burned for the earth-bound.

It was against the rules.

Then again, he'd never been one to follow them.

The winds stirred, and Zed looked in surprise as the powerful gales faded into a gentle breeze. He watched as the storm slowed and settled over the town. In all his years, he'd never seen such a thing.

Dash looked up at the sky and scratched his head in confusion. "That's odd. We've been chasing this storm for days. Why would it just stop here?"

Ixion looked at the storm warily. "Something doesn't add up. These winds don't feel right. It's like something, or someone, is drawing the storms here."

A flicker of a smile crossed Zed's lips as he turned to the Storm-chasers.

"Change of plans. Looks like we're going to stay."

Dash and Ixion glanced at one another, their eyes wide, before shaking their heads.

"Zed, we can't. What if Seth finds out? We're supposed to deliver the storm to him."

"You said it yourself, Ixion. Something is calling the storm here." He turned back to the earth-bound, bewildered by the effect she had on him. "And I intend to find out exactly what, or who, it is. Now let's ride!"

Zed revved his engine and led his gang into the town below, the storm following them as they raced down the mountain slopes. He glanced at the woman once more, and couldn't shake the feeling that the earth-bound had done more than just stop the storm in its tracks. She had stopped *him*.

And he'd never felt so alive.

2

— · —

Tempest gasped as her bike came to a screaming halt. Her stomach lurched as gravel sprayed over the edge of the mountain, and into the deep ravine below. She drew a deep breath, and ran a trembling hand through her windswept hair. What had possessed her to do something so reckless?

She searched the stormy skies for the streak of golden lightning that had mesmerized her. But the skies emptied of their spectacle of lights, and the peals of thunder quietened. As the storm faded, so too did her adrenaline. She sighed, and watched the playful winds that raced out into the horizon beyond. She couldn't help but wonder what that would be like. To travel the world. To live a life of adventure. To be free.

The chime of the town clock rang through the valley, pulling Tempest from her daydream. She revved her engine, knowing she shouldn't risk Arthur's wrath. Reluctantly, she turned away from her daydreams of adventure, and rode towards the town below, where every day was as predictable as the last.

Tempest descended along the mountain track, until she returned to the valley. She sped past the mines, weaving through the men who spent their lives looking at the earth and never at the wonders of the sky. She raced past rows of identical clapboard houses, their manicured lawns and freshly painted picket fences looking as immaculate as ever. And she sped into the picture-perfect town, where everything, and everyone, seemed to fit in so perfectly.

Everyone, except for her.

The sound of screeching tires filled the street as Tempest came to an abrupt stop. She ignored the bewildered looks of passers-by, and raced into the library, leaving the storm, and whatever adventure it contained, behind.

"You're late. Again. And you're dripping all over the first editions."

Tempest grimaced as Arthur appeared behind a pile of books, his glasses magnifying his disapproving glare. She shook off her weather-beaten leather jacket and helped him with the precariously stacked books.

"I'm sorry, I got distracted."

"Tempest, most librarians don't ride motorcycles in storms. In fact, most librarians don't ride a motorcycle at all. Couldn't you choose four wheels like a normal person, rather than that deathtrap?"

"We've been over this..."

"And it's not just the daredevil driving. It's the noise, and the motor oil you leave everywhere. Not to mention that parking it outside scares away the patrons."

Tempest couldn't help but smile at her uncle's fretting. Her motorcycle certainly wasn't the reason the library was struggling. In a town like this, people just didn't read.

"And to ride into the middle of a raging storm! What if you'd been struck by lightning? I don't know why you insist on doing something so dangerous, when there's all the adventure you need just waiting for you in these books."

"It helps with my... condition."

Her condition. The medical mystery that no doctor could solve. The sensitivity to the storms that troubled her, just like it had plagued her mother. She'd tried everything to ease the blinding migraines, but only one thing worked. And Arthur most certainly didn't approve of it.

"Well, I can't say I care for it. Your mother should never have left you that motorcycle. Now get yourself dry before you drip over any more of our stock."

Tempest toweled herself off and took her place behind the counter. As the hours dragged by, she glanced out of the window to be greeted with the same sights she saw every day. She watched as residents followed the same routine as always, content with the comfort and safety of their lives. Day in, day out, nothing changed.

The doorbell rang, pulling Tempest from her daydream as a waft of coffee and hairspray filled the library. She glanced at the clock. Midday. The same as every other day.

"With all the inventions in the world, you'd think someone would have found a way to stop rain from ruining a fresh blow dry. The sooner this storm moves on, the better."

Despite the stormy weather, Christie entered the library like a ray of sunshine. Between her lurid pink dress and bleached hair,

Tempest didn't know whether to look directly at her for fear of going blind.

"Americano for you, decaf skinny oat milk latte for me. Morning Arthur!" Christie waved to the spectacled librarian, who grumbled from the display window. "Okay, ready for lunch?"

"Actually, I was planning on reading some of the new stock. And my head is killing me from this storm..."

"Nonsense. Books can wait, the storm will clear soon and you can take an aspirin. And besides, books bring me out in a rash."

"But..."

"No excuses. Now take a break, and leave those books behind. Last time I barely got a word out of you and you dropped pickles on my handbag."

Within moments, Tempest found herself marched out of the library, clutching onto a book that escaped Christie's attention. Christie looped her arm through hers and led her down the street, pausing occasionally to admire her own reflection in the windows.

Tempest shrank back at her own appearance next to her. While Christie's bottle blonde hair was always perfectly styled, Tempest's had a mind of its own, her dark locks streaked with a flash of silver that no hair dye could disguise. While Christie was small and petite, Tempest was too tall, too awkward, too gangly. And while Christie was popular with everyone in town, Tempest stuck out like an oddball. She often wondered how they had ever become friends. But in a town this small, even Christie had only so many options.

Tempest tuned out of Christie's relentless monologue and glanced at the sky. Another storm was brewing, and from the pressure in her head, it would be a big one.

"So, what do you think?"

Tempest looked at Christie, her mind blank. "What do you mean?"

Christie sighed and pointed across the road. "What do you think of *Mason*?"

Tempest glanced at the figure across the road. Mason swaggered through the streets with the rest of the miners, his chest inflated almost as much as his ego. He ran a hand through his blonde hair and flashed them a perfect smile.

"See, he likes you."

Tempest's cheeks burned, and she forced herself to look away. "He doesn't like me. He's barely said a word to me."

"Trust me, Dave says he can't stop talking about you." Christie waved back at him despite Tempest's protests. "You two would look good together."

"I don't know..."

"You have to choose someone, Tempest. There's only so many eligible men in this town. And Mason's a catch."

"He's a jock..."

"A *former* jock. School was years ago. Besides, he works in the mines now, and from what I hear, he's doing pretty well for himself."

Tempest glanced at the group of miners. From their confident swagger and their air of entitlement, they sure looked like jocks to her.

"I doubt we'd have much in common."

"Oh, come on. He's good looking, he's got a steady job, and he'd make a great husband too."

"*Husband*?" Tempest's eyes widened, and she clutched her book tighter.

"You need to start thinking about these things. A boyfriend. A husband. Babies. These things don't just magically happen." Christie glanced at the book in Tempest's hands. "Perhaps you need to spend a little less time in those books of yours, and a little more time here in the real world."

Heat rose to Tempest's cheeks, and she used her book to fan herself. She'd thought she was going for lunch. She hadn't expected marriage and babies to be on the menu.

"Come on Tempest, don't look like that. Surely you've thought about your future?"

"I suppose I just thought I had more time. That I'd go on adventures and explore the world before I think about settling down." Tempest glanced at the group of miners once more, and sighed. "Mason's nice enough. But how do I know he's the one, if I don't even know who I am yet?"

"Not everyone needs adventure, Tempest. Mason's a great catch, and the miners practically run this town. If you date him, the rest of your life will be taken care of."

A low rumble passed through the air, and Tempest looked to the sky. Dark clouds gathered, while the winds gathered strength.

"But what if I don't want my whole life to be planned out? What if I want something more than this?"

The rumble grew louder as Christie folded her arms. "Tempest, what else could you possibly want?"

Tempest looked at the sky longingly, and sighed. "Adventure."

The rumble grew to a deafening growl. Tempest's eyes widened as she realized it wasn't thunder she heard, but the throttle of engines. She looked in wonder as dozens of motorcycles raced past, filling the peaceful streets with their thundering growl.

Christie groaned and looked at the sight in dismay. "Oh wonderful, a perfectly nice day ruined by a biker gang."

Tempest watched the bikers as they pulled into the yard of the dive bar. Her breath faltered as she caught sight of the logos emblazoned on their jackets. A perfect circle containing a lightning bolt.

"Not just any biker gang. The *Stormchasers*."

Christie visibly paled, while Tempest's heart raced in her chest. The Stormchasers were a gang of legend. Wherever they went, chaos and destruction followed. And they hadn't set foot into this town in years.

Christie fled to the opposite side of the road, pulling Tempest along with her. She scowled at the Stormchasers as they gathered in Mary's yard, and watched as the black-garbed owner came out to greet them.

"Of course that witch would welcome them."

"She's not a witch."

"She owns a dive bar in a peaceful town, listens to death metal, and lives alone with a bunch of cats. And Dave says she once cursed him for taking a leak in her herb garden. Of course she's a witch."

Tempest watched as the bikers dismounted, filling the once-peaceful street with their brash laughter and the roar of their engines. Their leather jackets, huge motorcycles, and raucous noise were certainly at odds with the quaint town. But Mary embraced them as if they were old friends, unphased by their intimidating appearance.

"I've heard they're dangerous. Mark my words, Tempest, you should stay away from them."

Tempest knew Christie was right. But despite her fear, a rush of exhilaration swept through her. She watched the Stormchasers curiously, wondering what distant adventures they'd returned from.

"Well, let's not let a biker gang ruin a perfectly nice day." Christie ran a hand through her perfectly styled hair, and grinned slyly. "Especially not when you and Mason have a date tonight."

Tempest looked at Christie in surprise. "What? No, Christie—"

"Oh come on, Tempest. Mason keeps hanging around like a third wheel with me and Dave, and it's killing the mood. So what better than to bring you along too, and turn it into a double date..."

"Christie, no."

"I won't take no for an answer. It's about time you build yourself a life here, and Mason is perfect for you. Trust me."

"But I'm not sure I want to build a life here." Tempest glanced at her book, filled with faraway adventures and dreams of distant lands. "Don't you ever wonder if there's more out there?"

Christie shrugged. "I don't need to know what's out there. This town is perfect. Look at it, it's got everything you could possibly want."

Tempest glanced at the bikers, who cheered as a large motorcycle sped down the street. It stood a foot taller than the others, and the throaty growl of its throttle shook the very foundations of the earth. As the biker pulled into the yard, an intoxicating scent of leather and oil drifted along the breeze.

"But what if I want a different life?" Tempest gazed at the biker, wondering what it would be like to drift across the earth like the winds. "A life of adventure? Of travel? Of magic?"

"Who needs adventure when this town has everything you need?"

The biker removed his helmet, revealing a head of dark, curly hair. His back remained turned to Tempest, but her eyes were drawn to his towering figure, as if held by some magnetic force.

"But don't you want to try something new? To leap into the unknown, and see where it takes you?"

"Haven't you heard of gravity, Tempest?" Christie shook her head dismissively. "Leap into the unknown, and you'll just plummet straight back down to earth. Much better to keep your feet firmly on the ground, than get swept away by some magical dream—"

Christie shrieked as a gust of wind tore through the street, disheveling her perfectly styled hair. It plucked a loose page from Tempest's book, until it somersaulted into the sky like a leaf caught in a storm. Tempest chased it across the street, trying to seize the page from the playful currents. But her steps faltered as another hand plucked it from the air, and a towering figure loomed over her. A figure who certainly didn't belong in the town. A figure whose eyes sparkled with magic and adventure. A Stormchaser.

Tempest drew a startled breath at the sight of the Stormchaser. He radiated danger, his battle scars heightening his dark, brooding good looks. She gazed into his eyes, momentarily spellbound by the deep shades of blue and gray. They reminded her of the inky swathes of storm clouds seeping into the sky. Dark and magical, and filled with danger.

"Interesting read." The man's gravelly voice reverberated through her body, like a peal of thunder shaking the earth. His eyes flickered across the page, before he met her gaze once more. "I didn't expect to find a thrill-seeker in a town like this."

Heat rose in Tempest's cheeks, while she stood paralyzed by the terror and adrenaline that coursed through her. She glanced nervously at the thin scar that ran down his cheekbone, at the tattoos on his olive skin, at the gleaming beast of a bike that stood behind him. He was a Stormchaser. He was dangerous. But as he held her in his gaze, she didn't think she could walk away from him if she tried.

"Tempest!"

Tempest blinked as Christie's nasal voice rang through the street, breaking whatever spell had been cast on her. She delicately plucked the page from the biker's hands and drew a shaky breath.

"Thank you."

His eyes flashed with a golden glimmer, like a flicker of lightning illuminating the depths of a storm. "Don't mention it."

The stranger drew a breath, as if to speak, but Christie's disapproving voice cut through the street once more.

"Tempest, come on!"

Tempest sighed and reluctantly pulled herself away from the stranger. She returned to Christie, who sulked on the street corner, desperately trying to shield her hair from the stormy winds. But as she joined her friend, Tempest glanced at the Stormchaser once more. Their eyes met, sending sparks racing down her spine.

"What were you thinking? You can't run into the middle of a road just to save a stupid book." Christie looped her arm through Tempest's and shuddered. "And to think you came face to face with a *Stormchaser*. You poor thing, you're shaking like a leaf."

Freed from the intensity of the stranger's gaze, Tempest realized her friend was right. Her body trembled with adrenaline, while her breath grew short. She felt like the page of her book that had been swept away by the storm. And a part of her didn't want to return to the earth.

"Forget about the Stormchasers, Tempest. They'll leave as soon as the storm passes. And besides, you have bigger things to think about. Like your date with Mason tonight." Christie returned to her usual sunny smile at the prospect. "Who knows? This could be the beginning of the rest of your life."

Tempest forced a smile, and tried to calm the hammering of her heart. But as she approached the library, she glanced at the Stormchaser once again. His eyes glimmered in the darkness of the storm, with a strange power that sent sparks racing through her body. As she held his gaze, she allowed herself to dream. To imagine having a life of adventure. A life of danger. A life of freedom.

But as Christie led her back to the familiar sights of the town, Tempest shook her head. Such dreams didn't belong in a place like this. She had a life here. A future.

And she couldn't afford to be swept away by the storm.

3

— · —

The town had gone into hiding. As the streets lay deserted, the last of the shopkeepers triple-checked their locks before glancing uneasily at the motorcycles parked nearby. In a town where the biggest crime involved clashing colors in flower beds, Tempest had never seen the parade of shops so heavily guarded. With their shutters drawn, doors bolted and alarms set, it looked like they were preparing for an impending war.

An uneasy current hung in the air and, combined with the gathering storm, made Tempest's headache worse than usual. She glanced at the mountains, where dark clouds descended and covered the peaks. A roar of motorcycles echoed within them, accompanied by a peal of thunder. The Stormchasers had arrived, which could only mean one thing. A storm was coming. And something told her it would be one to remember.

The chime of the town clock rang through the empty streets, chiding Tempest for her usual tardiness. She hopped onto her bike and sped into the valleys, relishing the cool winds that raced around her. For a moment, she forgot all about the tension that hung in the air, and pushed Christie's diabolical matchmaking skills to the back of her mind. She pretended she was free. That she was one with the winds, and could drift through life without a care in the world. But as the outline of the caves came into view, apprehension settled into the pit of her stomach, and she returned to reality with a thud.

Most girls in the town would jump at the chance to be set up with Mason. But Tempest had always preferred the company of a good book to a date with a jock. Not that she couldn't appreciate Mason's good looks, but it took more than a muscled body and an impressive athletic record to impress her. The miners might practically run the town, but Tempest doubted all those years beneath the earth had sharpened Mason's intellect.

No, despite Christie's matchmaking, Tempest had never thought about Mason in that way. Truthfully, she'd never thought about dating any of the men in the town. The closer she got to the caves, the more she wished she was back at home with a good book for company.

As she approached the caverns, a hammering sound filled the air. She slowed as she neared, and saw another rider bent over their motorcycle, beating out a dent in their front fender. Her heart quickened as she recognized the Stormchaser she'd met earlier.

His muscular legs straddled his bike as he worked bare-chested, hammering the metal and filling the air with a rhythmic pounding. A flash of heat seared through Tempest as his broad, tattooed chest gleamed with sweat and oil. His huge arms delivered powerful blows as he pounded the metal, and his thighs bulged as he gripped the bike between them.

A flash of golden light sparkled in his eyes as he saw her approach, like sparks burning through the night sky.

"So, we meet again." He wiped an oil-slicked hand on his jeans, while Tempest forced her gaze away from the taut muscles that rippled before her. "It must be my lucky day."

Tempest blushed as the Stormchaser fixed her with a grin. She glanced towards the caves, knowing that Christie would have a fit if she saw her talking to a Stormchaser.

"Hey, don't go. What's your name?"

"I don't give my name to strangers." Tempest watched as a bead of sweat trickled down his chest and towards the trail of hair that snaked beneath his trousers. She drew a breath to clear her head, and tried to ignore the heat rising within her. "And definitely not to Stormchasers."

The corners of his lips flickered into a smile. "Okay, I'll go first. I'm Zed."

Tempest eyed him suspiciously as he extended a hand to her. But as his eyes glimmered once more, she sighed in defeat, and shook it warily. A spark leaped between them as their hands met, sending a tingling sensation to her very core.

"Tempest."

Zed held her gaze, while the glimmers in his eyes burned brighter. "That's an unusual name."

"Tell me about it. If I wasn't destined to stand out in this town already, my mother sealed my fate by calling me Tempest."

"Perhaps standing out in this town is no bad thing." He leaned back across his bike, his muscles rippling as he did so. "This place seems kind of stuffy. Maybe it's time to liven things up."

Tempest laughed at the mere thought. "I don't think that would be a good idea."

Zed leaned forwards, until Tempest inhaled his scent of sweat and bike oil. But there was something else that lingered in the air too, like the scent of an oncoming storm. The essence of fresh rain, and the crisp scent of lightning as it scorched the air. Her heart quickened, and her breath grew shallow as his eyes met hers.

"I've seen you ride. You're not bad, even on that old piece of junk."

Tempest folded her arms and glared at the biker. "It's not an old piece of junk. It could give you a run for your money."

"Is that so? Well, maybe you should ride with us tonight." Zed looked up at the sky before returning his gaze to her. "Looks like it's going to be a storm to remember."

Tempest felt every instinct in her body pull her towards him. But the Stormchasers were dangerous, and she didn't trust herself spending any more time with this stranger than necessary.

"Thanks, but no. I have plans."

"Are you sure? From your reading choices, I could have sworn you were looking for something more than this." Zed's eyes gleamed in the storm, while his gravelly voice reverberated through her. "That you were looking for adventure."

Tempest gulped, and forced her hammering heart to quell. She glanced at Zed, at his monstrous bike, at the storm that gathered strength on the mountain. But despite the siren song of the storm, she shook her head.

"I have all the adventure I need in the library."

"Is that so?" Zed held her gaze, as if peering into her very soul. "Perhaps it's time to stop reading about adventure, and start living it instead."

Tempest's breath faltered as she held Zed's gaze. As the revving of motorcycle engines filled the air, she wondered what it would be like to ride with him. To go on an adventure. To leave her life behind and chase the storm. For a moment, she allowed herself to get lost in his gaze, and be swept away by the storm...

"Tempest!"

Christie's nasal tones wrenched Tempest from her daydream. Christie waved impatiently from the mouth of the caves, dressed in impractical heels that wobbled on the rocky ground. Tempest sighed and glanced at Zed, the spell between them now broken.

"I don't think so. I know all about the Stormchasers. Once the storm passes, you'll leave. And I don't intend to be swept away." Tempest placed her helmet back on, and revved her engine. "See you around, Stormchaser."

Tempest sped away from him before she could get lost in his eyes again. She glanced in her side mirror and saw him beat the metal of his bike once more. With every strike of the hammer, she thought of his muscular arms, and the swell of his denim-clad thighs. She could feel the rhythmic pounding reverberate through the earth, up into her saddle, and into her. As the storm gathered power, the clouds above swelled with their pent up energy, waiting to be released. It made her restless, and she tugged at her collar as the air grew hot and close.

"I thought I told you to stay away from those bikers?" Christie scowled as Tempest approached and glanced at Zed warily. "What did he want?"

"He asked me to go for a ride."

"Absolutely not. They're dangerous." Christie shuddered and looked disapprovingly at Tempest's bike. "You should have gotten rid of that thing years ago. I know it was your mother's, but it draws the wrong kind of attention. Not to mention it ruins your hair. Now come on, we're late."

Tempest's stomach lurched as Christie looped her arm through hers, preventing any last-minute escape, and dragged her into the caves. As Christie tried and failed to tame Tempest's windswept hair, they descended deeper into the earth, until the sound of Zed's hammering grew quieter. Warm, earthy air replaced the cool breeze of the storm, and they emerged in a vast underground cavern.

Tempest looked around in wonder as the light of the mining lamps reflected off the crystallized stalactites, and filled the cavern with an ethereal glow. It was beautiful, and yet Tempest felt claustrophobic at being so deep beneath the earth. The air was too close, and she longed to see the sky.

Her stomach churned as Christie marched her towards the men, who sat drinking beer, oblivious to the beauty of the caves. Tempest flashed Mason a nervous smile as they joined, while Christie eyed Dave hungrily.

As the group shared the latest snippets of town gossip, Tempest sighed and felt her heart sink. She'd heard all the stories before. Her mind drifted back to the surface, and she recalled Zed's invitation. To join him and the Stormchasers, and to ride into the storm. For a moment, she allowed herself to dream. She imagined the feeling of riding into the center of the storm. Of being surrounded by the roar of the motorcycles and the peals of thunder. Of being swept away into a world of adventure...

Tempest shook her head, and returned her attention to her surroundings. Mason sipped his beer in silence, while Christie slipped her hand into Dave's and whispered something that made his cheeks turn a deep shade of crimson.

"Well, we'll leave you two alone to get to know each other better." Christie smiled and gave Tempest a nauseating wink. "Don't do anything I wouldn't do."

She laughed lightly and pulled Dave into the darkness of the tunnels. Tempest's face burned as Mason glanced at her awkwardly, and she tried not to dwell on what Christie was doing in the dark.

As Mason swigged his beer, Tempest distracted herself with the beauty of the rocks overhead. But as she gazed at the gleaming stalactites, Zed's hammering faintly drifted through the earth above. She thought of him once again, of his powerful muscles and sparks flying as he pounded the metal. With each strike of the hammer, she pictured his muscular arms, the sheen of sweat on his chest, the swell of his thighs as they gripped the bike...

"Is everything okay?"

Mason's voice pulled her back to reality. Tempest ran a hand through her hair, and drew a breath, as if emerging from a deep pool of water. She tried to think of something to say, of anything to fill the silence that hung between them, and mentally punched herself as her mind went blank.

Good one Tempest, what great conversation you have.

Mason glanced at her satchel, where a well-worn book poked out. He lifted it out and thumbed through it, as if deciphering a complex code. Tempest watched as his eyes squinted and couldn't help wondering if he'd ever read a book before.

"You like books, huh? You work in that library with your uncle."

Tempest sighed in relief. If there was one thing she could talk about, it was books. She smiled and nodded.

"Yeah, Arthur took me in when Mom left, so I grew up in the library. At night, I would have the whole place to myself, and read whatever I wanted."

Mason thumbed through another page. "I was never much of a reader. Too many ideas in one place for someone like me."

"You just need to find the right book. You can go on faraway adventures, explore distant lands, escape to somewhere more exciting."

Mason flicked through another page of the book, boredom scrawled across his face. "This town has all the adventure I need."

"But how do you know that, if you haven't been anywhere else?"

He shrugged. "I've never thought about going anywhere else. I always knew that this life was for me. That when I was old enough, I'd head to the mines, buy a house, find a wife, and have kids." He smiled. "Just like everyone else."

Tempest sighed. "It must be nice to know what you want in life."

"You don't?"

"I'm not sure what I want. I always figured I'd go on an adventure first, and then think about whether I want to settle down."

"Trust me, you'll want to settle down. Everyone does." Mason flashed her a smile and his hand brushed hers. "You've always been a wild one, but maybe you just need the right man to tame you."

Tempest clenched her jaw, and a flicker of anger raced through her. She didn't want to be tamed by anyone. Her anger intensified as Mason threw her book onto the floor, and the pages creased. He flashed her another smile, oblivious to her worsening mood.

"And besides, if you're bored, I know ways we can add some excitement."

Tempest tensed as Mason drew himself closer. His face was uncomfortably close to hers, and his breath warmed her skin. But despite his good looks, he did nothing for her. There was no spark. No flutter in her heart. Nothing. She looked into his eyes, and found them to be empty. It was as if he'd spent so much time looking down at the earth, he'd forgotten to look at the sky and dream. She wanted someone who shared her thirst for adventure, whose eyes glimmered with life, who sent sparks racing through her heart.

She tensed as Mason's fingers brushed hers and his body moved closer. The air became stifling, the heat from the cave too oppressive. She longed for a fresh breeze, rather than the musty air beneath the earth. A dull throbbing pounded in her skull, its pressure growing with each passing second. Great. A storm was coming. And from her pounding headache, she could tell it was going to be a big one.

"Come on, what's wrong?" Mason chuckled and moved closer towards her. "Most girls in this town would be thrilled to make out with me."

Tempest placed a hand to her forehead, and her vision blurred as her headache worsened. "Sorry, I'm just not in the mood."

Mason's jaw clenched, and she saw the mix of frustration and disappointment in his eyes. But he shrugged and backed away before taking a long sip of his warm beer. Tempest's heart sank at the sight. Mason was the one guy in town to show interest in her, and she'd blown it. If he didn't think she was an oddball before, he would now.

Tempest placed a hand to her forehead and winced as her vision blurred. Her headache was worsening by the second, and the stuffy air of the cavern was making it worse.

"I'm sorry, Mason, but I need to go. Maybe we can do this another time." She stuffed her book into her bag and turned to him apologetically. "I really am sorry."

"Look, we can take it slow, if that's what you want. Just think about it."

"But why? You're popular here. You could have anyone you want. And me, I'm…" She gestured to her oil-stained shirt, to her wild hair, to everything that made her an outcast. "I'm different. And I don't think we want the same things."

"What can I say? I've always liked the wild ones." He took a step towards her and smiled. "You'll come around, eventually. And I'll be here when you do."

Tempest's eyes widened as Mason moved in to kiss her. Instinctively, she turned her head so that his lips met her cheek. His face flushed with embarrassment as she looked at him apologetically.

"Sorry, Mason..."

Tempest tried to find something to say. She tried to think of anything that would reduce the awkwardness between them. But she knew that there was no salvaging this evening. It had been a disaster from start to finish, and she should never have let Christie talk her into it. She shot Mason one last apologetic look, and scurried away from the caves before she could embarrass herself any further.

Tempest hurried back to the entrance, her headache reduced to a dull throb as she breathed fresh air once again. Her cheeks burned with embarrassment as she thought of how much of a disaster the evening had been. Mason had offered her everything. And she'd run away.

She swore in frustration and mounted her bike as the first of the storm winds howled through the valley. This was her chance to build a life here. A *real* life. But as she looked at the storm that brewed in the distance, she couldn't help but wonder if she was ready to settle down. Whether this was really as good as life got. Whether she wanted to be *tamed*.

She needed to think, and she needed to clear her head. She revved her engine and raced towards the storm.

4

—·—

Tempest breathed in the mountain air. She relished the storm wind as it billowed through her hair, refreshing her after her evening in the caves. She rode to where the darkest clouds gathered, and pressed herself flat to her bike as she raced up the mountain tracks.

The first of the rains showered down to the earth, easing her migraine and helping her think straight once again. But with it came the realization of how much of a disaster tonight had been.

You've always been a wild one, but maybe you just need the right man to tame you.

Mason's words echoed in Tempest's mind as she raced towards the storm. A flash of anger flickered through her, and she revved her engine. She didn't want to be tamed. She wanted to be free.

The storm gathered strength as Tempest sped higher into the mountains. A flash of lightning forked through the dark skies, followed by a peal of thunder that reverberated across the plains. The pressure of the storm grew inside of her, wanting to be released, desperate to run wild. Tempest looked at where the clouds gathered and the gales blew strongest, and felt a thrill run through her. She revved her engine and raced towards it.

Tempest chased after the storm, following the steep curve of the mountain track. The storm swept her up in its chaos, lashing her with winds and rain, while lightning guided her across the treacherous tracks. She revved her engine, wanting to race faster, to soar through the skies, to leave this town, and this life, behind.

She climbed higher until she reached the peak of the mountain, where the eye of the storm pulsed with a primordial energy. It loomed before her, calling to her with its promise of adventure. Tempest sped towards it, wanting to be caught in its grip. To be swept away from this town, and taken to distant lands. She revved her bike until her engine screamed and her vision became a blur of black rain and flashing light.

A spear of golden lightning pierced through the darkness, illuminating the sharp drop that lay at the end of the track. Tempest cried out and slammed on her brakes, but the power of the storm was too strong. Her bravery turned to fear as her tires slid against the rocky track, and the storm carried her onwards, like a leaf caught in the winds. She pulled on the brakes with all of her might, fighting against the power of the storm, until she came to a screaming stop at the edge of the cliff.

Tempest gasped, and barely dared to move as she peered at the sheer drop below. As the storm raged overhead, she ran a hand through her hair and drew a deep breath. What was happening to her? She had always been affected by the storms, but never like this. It was as if the storm itself had possessed her. As if its spirit had compelled her to leap into the unknown. Just like it had to her mother.

Tempest shuddered as a boom of thunder echoed through the valley. She placed a hand to her necklace, and couldn't help but think of that night, all those years ago. The night when her mother had left in the storm, and never returned.

Tempest gripped the handlebars of her motorbike tightly. She refused to follow in her mother's footsteps. She couldn't be so reckless. She wouldn't allow herself to be swept away by the storm.

Tempest backed away from the mountain edge, all thoughts of adventure and rebellion gone. She drew a breath and sighed as she looked across the windswept town below.

Good one, Tempest. A man tries to kiss you and you try to jump off a mountain.

A flash of lightning filled the air, and she glanced at her reflection in her side mirror. She looked at her wild silver-streaked hair, her rain-soaked clothes, her old beaten-up dirt bike. Perhaps Christie was right. Maybe she needed to stop chasing dreams in the sky and start building a life here.

Tempest rode down the mountain slopes until she arrived at her favorite spot, hoping it could do something to lift her mood. She marveled as she arrived in the clearing, where nothing but an abandoned cabin interrupted the panoramic view across the valley. She watched the wind as it raced through the mountains, spiraling in graceful currents across the sky. It rushed past her with whispers of faraway adventures, while an eagle flew overhead, racing on its playful currents.

That was freedom. To follow the winds and fly to distant adventures. She sighed, knowing that the closest she would get to that life would be in the adventure section of the library.

A peal of thunder filled the valley, shaking the very foundations of the mountain. Tempest glanced at the darkening sky as golden branches of lightning darted across the valleys, and black sheets of rain fell to the earth. The storm was coming in fast, and getting stronger by the second.

Tempest cursed as the mountain track turned to mud, and the lightning increased in its ferocity. She turned her bike, looking for a safe route down, but found none. She was stranded, and as the icy rain saturated her clothing, she knew she'd need to find shelter. A flicker of lightning illuminated the deserted cabin, and she sped towards it, knowing it was her only option.

Tempest took shelter on the porch, shivering beneath her soaked clothing. The storm worsened by the second, until an icy wind howled through the valley and she jogged on the spot to keep herself warm. But as the cold settled into her bones and her teeth began to chatter, she knew her night was going from bad to worse.

Tempest peered through the layers of dust on the cabin window, into the gloom. The place had been empty for years; the family moved away and never returned. She rested a hand on the doorknob and tried it. It was unlocked. She'd never set foot inside before, had never wanted to trespass. But as the cold took hold of her body, she knew she had to risk it. No one had been here in years. And besides, it was this or catching hypothermia outside.

Tempest closed the door behind her, relieved to be out of the cold winds, and began piling wood into the fireplace. She fumbled around in the darkness and found some matches, and breathed out with relief as the fire took hold quickly. She peeled her sodden clothes off to dry and wrapped a fur throw around her trembling body. The cold had settled in her bones, but slowly, the warmth returned. She wrapped herself tighter in the furs and bathed in the glow of the fire, relishing its heat as the storm continued to rage outside.

As the trembling in her body subsided, Tempest looked at her surroundings curiously. A bookcase grabbed her attention, its shelves filled with leather-bound books that filled the cabin with a glorious smell. She opened a tome of fables detailing stories of the Greek gods, and another containing passages of ancient verses and magical scriptures. Whoever the owner was, they certainly had an interest in peculiar stories.

Tempest scanned the photographs on the walls, looking for any sign of the owner. She looked through the photos of faraway places, of strange people from distant lands. Her eyes hovered on one, a well-worn photograph of a group of powerful-looking men, with a handwritten caption scrawled underneath.

The Sons of Olympus.

Tempest raised her eyebrows at the photo. Between the muscular bodies, brooding looks and tattoos, the Sons of Olympus were either some kind of military unit, or a boy band. Each one of them oozed danger, and their eyes gleamed with a powerful yet otherworldly presence.

A flash of lightning filled the cabin, and she held the photo closer. Tempest peered at the faces of the men in the light of the storm until her breath caught in her throat.

Dark eyes gleamed at her from the center of the photo. Eyes that glimmered with golden sparks, like shooting stars in the night sky. A rumble of thunder filled the cabin, reverberating through the walls, and she held the photo closer to the light. It couldn't be, could it?

The thunder turned into a constant rumble, as if heading for the cabin, until realization dawned on Tempest. This was no thunder. It was the sound of an engine. Or more precisely, the sound of a motorcycle. And it was heading straight for the cabin.

Tempest scrambled to place the photo back on the wall, and cursed as the fur throw slipped and fell to the floor. The door opened, and Zed strode into the cabin.

5

Silence descended in the cabin. Tempest barely dared to breathe as Zed stood in the doorway. For a moment, all was still. The storm winds ceased, the lightning fizzled out, and the thunder didn't dare to speak. But then she saw the eyes that stared into her own, and became all too aware that she was very alone, and very naked, in a cabin with a stranger. No, not just a stranger. A *Stormchaser*.

Tempest tried her best to cover her modesty and look menacing at the same time, all whilst desperately trying to retrieve the fur throw from the floor. But the gleam of mirth in Zed's eyes told her that far from intimidating him, she looked more like she was doing a strange naked jig. She wrapped herself back into the furs and summoned what little courage she had left.

"You need to leave."

Zed raised an eyebrow, and he took another step forward. "Why do *I* need to leave?"

Tempest cursed. Despite her tone, he looked as though he was smirking.

"Leave now, or I'll call the police. The deputy will be here in minutes."

Zed's smirk deepened. "Then you'll have some explaining to do."

"What do you mean?"

"Well, you'll have to explain why you've broken into my cabin."

"*Your* cabin?"

Tempest glanced at the photograph of the man with eyes that glimmered with golden sparks. The same eyes that now gazed at her body. She drew a startled breath as the truth dawned on her, while her cheeks flushed with embarrassment.

"Oh, I'm so sorry!" Tempest shuffled towards her drying clothes, desperately clutching the fur throw that seemed determined to expose her once again. "I... I'll go."

Zed laughed as she tried unsuccessfully to clothe herself and ended up becoming twisted in her top. Great, now not only was she a trespasser, but she looked ridiculous too.

"It would be crazy to leave while the storm is raging outside. Stay, at least until it eases up."

He unzipped his leather jacket and removed his vest, slick with the rain. Tempest blushed as it peeled from his body, revealing his tattooed torso underneath. The sight of his muscular body sent a deep heat rising within her, until her breath faltered.

"Is something wrong?"

Tempest fumbled with the furs, positioning them around her body until she was sure they were securely in place. "No, I'm fine."

But her eyes widened as he unbuttoned his jeans and rolled them down his thighs. Her cheeks flushed with heat, and she forced herself to look away as he strode across the cabin, as if he didn't have a care in the world.

"Aren't you going to put something on?"

He turned to her from the bedroom door and broke into a grin. "You don't like what you see?"

Tempest drew a breath to respond, but her words faltered. Zed chuckled before he returned in a fur throw of his own. His hair was slicked back, and beads of rainwater glimmered on his chest as they slowly rolled down to his waist. He rummaged through the kitchen before he returned with a bottle of wine and glasses.

"It's not much, but at least my uncle left us something." He poured a glass and took a sip before he flashed Tempest a smile. "It's good. Here."

Tempest found a glass in her hand before she could object. She eyed it suspiciously. Her embarrassment at being caught in a state of undress gave way to uncertainty. Zed was a Stormchaser. He wasn't to be trusted. But he smiled reassuringly, as if reading her mind.

"You have nothing to fear, and certainly not from me." His eyes gleamed with golden sparks, glimpses of light within the inky darkness. "You can trust me."

Tempest looked into his eyes. Despite the rumors, and Christie's warnings, she knew he was telling the truth. Lurking beneath his fierce exterior was something gentler. Something that she knew she could trust.

She relaxed a little, took a sip of the wine, and felt the warmth of it flow through her. It tasted rich and indulgent, and conjured images of faraway sun-soaked lands. It certainly beat the warm beer the town had on tap. She savored the taste, but placed the glass down on the table.

"You don't like it?"

"I love it. It's not like anything we have in the town. But the storm will blow over soon. And I need a clear head for the ride back."

Zed smiled to himself. "Looks like it could be a while. The winds have a mind of their own at the moment."

He shifted in his furs, and Tempest tried to avert her gaze as they fell a little lower. The light of the fire bathed his olive skin in a golden glow, giving his muscular body a statuesque look. Tattoos covered his arms and chest, his body a beautiful work of art, while he ran his thumb along a chain tattoo on his wrist. Tempest glanced at a small rune in its center, a circle containing a beautiful lightning bolt within. In the firelight, the ink seemed to glow with a life of its own.

Zed sipped his wine and leaned back in his chair. "So, do you often perform naked burglaries, or is this a new hobby for you?"

Tempest cringed and shook her head. "I came to the mountains for some space to think. I must have lost track of the storm." She glanced outside of the window, to the sweeping view of the valleys where the winds raged. "I've never seen it come in so fast before."

Zed watched her while he took another sip of the wine. "Was something on your mind?"

Tempest glanced at him uneasily. She wasn't used to sharing her feelings with strangers. But then again, she wasn't used to having fireside conversations with semi-naked Stormchasers either. She drew a breath, and decided to take another risk.

"I've been thinking about my life here. When I was younger, all I ever wanted was some stability. To put roots down somewhere and build a home. And I have that here."

Tempest glanced at the sweeping view before them. Her eyes were drawn away from the small town, and towards the horizon.

"But lately, it's felt like something's missing. Every day is the same as the last. I've been wondering if I should try something new. To have an adventure. To take a risk."

At this, Zed smiled. "Life is always better when you take a risk. All you need to do is follow your heart, and leap into the unknown."

"That's easy for you to say. But I prefer to follow my head." Tempest sighed as she thought of the doubts that had kept her in the town for so many years. "I've built a good life here. What if I jump into the unknown, only to find it's worse?"

"But what if it's better? Surely it's worth taking a risk rather than never knowing at all? Life's too short to be safe, when you can be free." The firelight glimmered in Zed's eyes, and he ran a hand through his wet hair. "Those doubts of yours just keep you chained to the earth. But follow your heart, and you could fly."

"It's not that simple. I've tried to leave before. To jump on a plane and go somewhere exotic. To ride my bike somewhere new. But something holds me back." She placed a hand on her necklace and shook her head. "It takes strength to make a leap, but I'm too worried I'll fall."

Zed moved closer to her, until she inhaled his masculine scent. It reminded her of riding in the storm. Of fresh rain, lightning-scorched air, and motorcycle oil. He moved his hand towards hers, until a spark of static leaped between them.

"You have all the strength you need. There's a power in you, something wild and raw that burns brighter than anything I've seen before." His eyes shimmered in the light once more. "But you repress it to fit into this town, and convince yourself you're happy here."

"Hey, you don't know me..."

"Don't I?"

Tempest drew a breath, knowing he was right. All her life, she'd tried to fit in and belong in this town. But as each day passed, it became harder. Like a storm growing in power, a pressure built inside of her, waiting to burst. A spirit that yearned to leave this life behind and be free.

"If you embrace your power, you could do anything. All you need to do is stop listening to the doubts in your head, and start following your heart."

Tempest gazed into the depths of Zed's eyes and felt her self control slip. Swathes of inky black and vivid blue swirled within them, like storm clouds brewing in a twilight sky. His fingertips brushed a stray lock of Tempest's hair, and he leaned closer, until his gravelly voice sent shivers through her.

"Why don't you let yourself be free? Throw caution to the wind, and embrace your wild side?" Zed's breath brushed her skin, and their eyes connected. "Why don't you follow your heart, and take a leap into the unknown?"

Tempest felt a storm rage within her. Clouds billowed inside of her, begging to be released, while lightning sparked through her veins. She wanted to embrace it, and give herself just one reckless moment of wild freedom. To move closer to this man. To press her lips to his. To be swept away by his storm.

Tempest leaned closer, only for the cold metal of her necklace to press against her skin. She felt herself return to reality. It was a stark reminder of what happened when people let themselves get swept away by the storm. Of what they left behind. She drew a deep breath, and locked away the storm within her, before shaking her head.

"Because I'm too scared I'd come crashing back down to the earth."

She grabbed her clothes from the rack and wriggled into them underneath the blanket. The storm outside had reduced to a light drizzle, and she didn't trust herself to stay here a moment longer.

"I better go. Thanks for the hospitality."

"Surely you want to stay for a little longer?"

"Look, you're very charming, and I'm flattered. But I'm not the type of girl who's so easily swept away. I'm not just going to jump headfirst into something reckless. And besides, I know your type."

Zed leaned back, displaying his rippling muscles, and raised an eyebrow. "My *type*?"

"Yeah, the type who goes from town to town, charming women, promising them the world, until you get bored and move on. Like a storm leaving devastation in its wake."

"That's really what you think of me?"

"It's what I know about the Stormchasers. I know that you're all lone wolves, free to follow the storm wherever it takes you. That you live for the present, and never think about the trail of broken hearts you leave in your wake. That once this storm blows over, you'll move on." Tempest looked at him knowingly. "And I'm not going to be collateral damage in your storm."

Tempest turned to leave, but Zed's gaze remained fixed on her.

"Are you really going to leave in the middle of a storm?"

"I can handle myself. Besides, I've always liked storms."

He looked at her with hunger in his eyes. "But you'll get soaking wet."

Tempest turned to Zed as he watched her hungrily. She zipped up her leather jacket, and held his gaze.

"I've always liked that, too."

A smile flickered across his lips, and his eyes burned in the firelight. They were the eyes of an animal. Eyes that wanted to claim her.

"My offer still stands, Tempest. You should ride with us. We'll race here at midnight when the storm reaches its peak."

Tempest laughed at the mere thought and shook her head. If Arthur didn't kill her first, Christie most certainly would.

"I don't think so. I should get going." She gripped the door handle as Zed adjusted himself and the furs slipped lower. "The last thing I need is to be swept away by a storm."

Zed shrugged, but he smiled knowingly.

"Some storms are too powerful to resist. And something tells me I'll see you later." He flashed Tempest a grin, and his eyes glimmered in the light of the storm. "It'll be a date."

6

— · —

Tempest raced through the mountainside. The worst of the storm had eased, but the skies continued to churn overhead, threatening to unleash their power at any moment. She revved her engine and sped along the precarious roads back to town.

So much for her quiet evening. She should have stayed put in the library, where she wouldn't have gotten herself into trouble. She should never have gone along with Christie's disastrous matchmaking, and should never have embarrassed herself in front of Mason. And she certainly shouldn't have had fireside wine with a naked biker hunk.

The thought of Zed sent a primal instinct through her body. She fought the urge to turn back to the cabin, and pressed onwards to the town. That man was no good for her. He was a player. He knew what he was doing, with his delicious wine, his promises of adventure and his inability to cover himself with a fur. And she refused to get swept up in his storm.

She had to think with her head, not with her heart. He probably did this in every town, promising the world to women, before moving on without a second thought. That's what the Stormchasers did. In their endless pursuit of adventure, they didn't care what damage they caused or who they left behind. Exactly like her mother.

Tempest placed a hand to her necklace as she thought of her mother. A free spirit, who drifted from town to town like the currents of the wind. Someone who saw magic in the everyday, who lived more in her fantasies than in the real world. Someone who recklessly sought adventure in life. Just as she had the night she disappeared.

Tempest felt the jagged edges of the broken heart on her necklace and recalled that fateful night. The town had been plagued by storms for weeks, causing her mother's condition to deteriorate. Until one night, she couldn't take it anymore. She'd leaped onto her motorcycle, and raced into the middle of the storm, never to be seen again. She left everyone behind to pursue her own adventure, without looking back at the destruction she'd caused. Just like the Stormchasers.

From that moment, Tempest had sworn she would never follow in her mother's footsteps. She'd stayed in the town, and sought a life of safety over recklessness. She'd been content to read about adventure, rather than pursue it herself. She'd followed her head, and stopped listening to her heart.

But recently, she'd felt her mother's rebellious spirit stir within her. She dreamed of excitement, of magic, of faraway adventure. A power bloomed inside of her heart. A wild, reckless spirit that she feared. And she knew that if she let it free, she would never contain it again.

Tempest shook her head. This town was enough. This life was enough. Zed might have tempted her with his talk of adventure and excitement, but that would be the last of it. From now on, she'd stick to the safe life that she knew.

No more talking to mysterious bikers.

No more wine in romantic cabins.

And certainly no motorcycle races in the middle of a storm.

Tempest pulled into the library and made her way to her attic room, cursing as she left a trail of wet footprints behind her. She peeled off her sodden clothes and headed straight for the bathroom, knowing a hot shower would be the perfect thing to take her mind off of him.

The storm rumbled overhead as Tempest stepped into the water. Thunder reverberated through her body, while the static in the air made her skin tingle. The scent of the storm drifted through the window, and conjured memories of Zed. She pictured him as the droplets of water caressed every inch of her skin. Another peal of thunder echoed in the sky, and she wondered what it would be like to ride with him. She imagined her body pressed against his as they raced through the howling winds, caught up in the ferocity of the storm...

Tempest grasped the shower and turned the temperature down until a torrent of cold water poured over her, as if she was caught in the storm outside. A flicker of lightning streaked past the window, bathing her in its golden glow, while the thunder continued to shake the very foundations of the earth. As the water saturated her skin, she thought of Zed's eyes. Eyes that radiated with the essence of the storm. She imagined his weight pressed against her, their bodies slick with rain. Of being swept away by the storm, with only each other to hold on to...

The sound of a car alarm outside snapped Tempest to attention. Slowly and reluctantly, she returned to reality. She sighed and ran a hand through her hair. So much for sticking to her rules. She had to do better. She couldn't risk being swept away by his storm.

Tempest wrapped herself in a towel and headed for her bedroom, trying her best not to think of Zed. She tried to read, tried to sleep, tried to stare blankly at her bedroom ceiling. But the rain continued to tap against the windows, as if reveling in torturing her. Her mind spun, and she felt the onset of a headache from the storm outside. She groaned and moved to the window seat, hoping some fresh air might clear her head.

The storm was in full flow, reaching its peak above the mountains. Tempest looked at the cabin, where silhouettes of bikers gathered. She glanced at her clock. 11:45pm. Soon, the storm would be at its strongest. Already some of the Stormchasers raced within it, their bikes gleaming like bolts of lightning darting across the mountain slopes.

It was reckless.

Dangerous.

And every part of her wanted to join.

Tempest cursed and pulled the curtains closed to block out the storm. She returned to bed, but tossed and turned as the rain relentlessly tapped at the windows. She pulled her duvet higher, trying to block out the storm's siren song, as it called to her with its promises of adventure.

But with each passing moment, the storm grew inside of her. It raced through her body, filling her with an electric charge that needed to be released. And as the sound of revving engines echoed through the sky, Tempest knew that resistance was futile.

She threw off the bed sheets before looking at the cabin once more. A shiver ran down her spine as she saw Zed's silhouette against the light of the storm, as if he waited for her. With a groan of defeat, she grabbed her keys and pulled on her leather jacket.

It was time to ride with the storm.

7

— · —

"You should move on, earth-bound. The roads aren't safe."

Tempest glanced nervously at the woman before her. Her bright purple Mohawk gleamed menacingly in the storm's light, its edges razor-sharp like a weapon. A man peered behind her, his eyes hidden behind his shoulder-length turquoise hair that billowed in the wind. Tempest's courage fled as the two Stormchasers blocked her path to the cabin. Suddenly, riding into a storm at midnight with a dangerous biker gang didn't seem like such a good idea.

"Well, what are you waiting for? Why don't you turn around, and return that bike to whatever scrapheap you found it in?"

The rest of the Stormchasers snickered, and Tempest felt what little courage she had left desert her. Next to them, she looked ridiculous. Their giant motorcycles towered over her Mom's beaten-up dirt bike, while their tattoos, piercings and shocking haircuts made her feel as though she'd stumbled into a rock concert. She turned back to the mountain slopes in defeat, until a gravelly voice cut through the howling winds.

"I invited her to ride with us." Tempest turned to see Zed stride out of the cabin, dressed in leather and denim, his eyes gleaming in the darkness. "Unless you have a problem with that, Ixion?"

The purple-haired woman scowled and glared at Tempest.

"But she's an outsider."

"She might not belong to our gang, but she could outride you any day."

Laughter filled the clearing, and the woman's cheeks burned with embarrassment. Her scowl deepened as she looked disapprovingly at Tempest's bike.

"On that piece of junk? Not likely."

Tempest drew a breath to argue, but the sound of Zed's revving engine cut through the air.

"She rides in the front, with me."

Another murmur ran through the Stormchasers. The turquoise-haired man turned to Zed worriedly.

"What if Seth catches us?"

"You worry too much, Dash. Seth won't find out."

"But she's an *earth-bound*. If Seth hears about this, there'll be hell to pay."

Tempest looked at the blue-haired man in surprise. She'd heard her fair share of biker gang insults from passing by Mary's bar, but this one was new. But if she was an earth-bound, what did that make the Stormchasers? Before she could ask, Zed turned to the young biker and spoke in a low growl.

"Seth won't find out about this." Zed cast a warning glance towards the gang, while his growl deepened. "Got it?"

Dash groaned in defeat, before he scampered to Ixion's side. Every Stormchaser watched Tempest suspiciously, while Dash and Ixion spoke in hurried whispers as they glanced in her direction. Great. She was an outsider in her hometown, and now she was an outsider with this bunch of misfits, too. But Zed grinned at her, seemingly oblivious to it all.

"Looks like we'll get our first date after all."

Tempest rolled her eyes. "Let's get one thing clear. I came for the storm, not for a date. Okay?"

He laughed and his eyes gleamed in the light. "If you say so." He started his engine with a thunderous roar and turned to the Stormchasers. "We ride!"

At once, the air filled with the throttle of dozens of motorcycle engines. Tempest marveled at the cacophony of noise that enveloped her. It was as if the engines contained the raw power of thunder itself, and she'd found herself in the center of a storm. Her own bike burst to life, dwarfed by the more powerful motorcycles, and she couldn't help but return Zed's smile.

"Get ready for the ride of your life."

With a roar of his engine, he set off. He rode hard and fast, taking corners at exceptional speed. But Tempest kept up with him at every turn, her knowledge of the tracks giving her an edge he lacked. Her heart pounded in her chest as she raced faster than she ever had before, and the deafening growl of the biker gang surrounded her. If Christie could see her, she would have a fit. The thought filled her with glee, and she revved her engine to go faster.

"You're a natural!"

Tempest pressed herself against her motorcycle and sped ahead, feeling more alive with every turn. She emerged through the woods and onto a scree slope that took them to the peak of the mountains. The storm clouds billowed above, and she marveled at the lightning that pulsed within them. Dark winds howled across the peak, carrying sheets of rain that spiraled like a solid wall before them.

"We're heading straight for the storm?"

"You bet."

"Isn't that dangerous?"

"Exactly!"

Zed revved his engine and let out a thunderous roar. Tempest followed him and felt the power of the winds as they pulled her closer. She drew a deep breath as she neared the wall of rain, revved her engine, and entered the storm.

The storm captured Tempest in its powerful grasp. Her bike raced along the track as if it had a mind of its own, reaching speeds she'd only dreamed of. The winds tore at her with a power she'd never known, while spectacular colors of lightning filled the air, like fireworks exploding in a night sky. She watched the lightning as it raced across the sky, and peals of thunder reverberated in the heavens above. It was magical. And she'd never felt more alive.

She laughed with wonder as the Stormchasers raced each other across the mountaintop. She watched Ixion ride up a rocky slope, her purple Mohawk gleaming as she leaped off the makeshift ramp, while Dash zoomed beneath her, his blue-hair billowing behind him. They wove in-between each other, becoming a blur of violet and turquoise hues as they sped across the mountain.

Together, they rode deeper into the storm until they reached a swirling vortex in its center. It pulsed with a dark energy and drew vast sheets of rain and wind into it. Blinding strobes of lightning flickered within it, while peals of thunder growled in the darkness. Tempest had seen nothing like it. It was deadly, yet beautiful. And every part of her wanted to ride into it.

"What is that?"

Zed turned and grinned. "The eye of the storm."

They rode towards it together, drawn in by its powerful currents. The air became alive with electric sparks that made her skin tingle. Tempest glanced at Zed, his bike gleaming with a golden color as he sped across the track. Her laughter filled the air as they raced across the mountain, and wove in-between each other's drifts. She relished the feeling of the wind as it tousled her hair and marveled as strands of lightning streaked through the sky alongside them.

Tempest looked at Zed once more. His eyes burned in the darkness, gleaming with the thrill of the ride. And she knew that despite what she had said, she hadn't just come here for the storm. She had come here for *him*. He'd unleashed something inside of her, and shown her a world she hadn't known existed. And she was having the ride of her life.

A boom of thunder erupted overhead, and the sparkling streaks of lightning darted away. Tempest sensed the air shift around her, as the playful winds were overcome by a ferocious gale, and the rain turned into a violent hailstorm. A blast of red-hued lightning struck the ground beside her, causing her to veer sharply away from the eye of the storm. Zed called to her, but his words were drowned out by the strength of the winds.

Tempest cursed as she lost sight of him in the dark torrent of winds. She veered once more as the lightning blasts followed her, striking the ground and sending a shower of rocks and debris into the sky. Another red-hued flash of lightning struck the ground, larger than before, filling her vision with a blinding, violent light. Tempest narrowed her eyes as something emerged before her, and felt her blood turn cold.

Another rider raced towards her. Tempest slammed on her brakes as the roar of their engine filled the air, and their bike drew closer. Her tires screamed as they struggled to maintain their grip on the rocky slope, and she used all of her strength to keep herself from flying off her saddle.

Tempest gasped as her bike came to a screaming stop just inches from the stranger before her. She lurched in her seat, and her body trembled, her knuckles white from gripping her handlebars so tightly. She looked up at the man before her and balked at his appearance.

Shadows clung to the angular features of his face, while his fiery red hair was styled into short spikes that shone fiercely in the light. He was beautiful, yet terrifying. A red gleam shot through the darkness of his eyes, like a hellish bolt of lightning in the darkest of skies. Despite his fearsome appearance, anger flickered through Tempest. He'd appeared out of nowhere, and his recklessness could have killed them both.

"Watch where you're going! You nearly crashed into me."

His cold laughter boomed across the mountain, and he sneered as two other bikers joined him.

"Did you hear that, boys? We should watch where we're going." They laughed in return, and his eyes narrowed at her. "No one gives us orders. Especially not an earth-bound."

Tempest drew a breath to retort, but heard Zed call her from across the storm. He raced through the winds until he stood beside her, closely followed by Dash and Ixion. She looked at his eyes and, for the first time, saw his bravado replaced with something else. Fear.

"Tempest, are you okay?"

"I'm fine. I just nearly crashed into this idiot here."

The stranger's eyes blazed with anger, while Dash's face turned so pale he looked as though he might pass out. The biker leaned forward on his motorcycle, anger radiating from his body. As he drew himself closer, the scent of burned metal clung to Tempest's nostrils, like air that had been scorched by a violent thunderstorm.

"She's rather mouthy for an earth-bound."

Tempest glanced at the newcomer uneasily. From the smirk on his face, being called an earth-bound certainly wasn't a compliment. She turned to Zed questioningly, only to see something stir within his eyes. Fear.

Zed's jaw clenched, while he spoke in a deep growl. "I thought you were on the East Coast, Seth."

Seth? So this was the Stormchaser they had spoken of. From his fearsome demeanor and lack of manners, Tempest could see why everyone seemed so terrified of him.

"When I heard the storm took an unexpected detour, I decided to see for myself what made my second-in-command decide he could take a vacation in this town." Seth narrowed his eyes at Tempest. "And now I see why."

"It was just one ride, Seth. I'll take her back to the town now."

"What's the rush? Me and the boys have just arrived. And we're dying for some entertainment."

Seth smiled while the bikers closest to him cackled and leered at her. Tempest shuddered and felt her skin crawl. Who were these creeps?

"You know the rules, Zed. No earth-bounds." Seth glanced at the scar on Zed's cheekbone. "Or do I need to teach you another lesson?"

"She saw nothing. We didn't reach the eye of the storm. Just let her go." Zed's voice was low and gravelly, practically a growl. "There doesn't need to be trouble."

Trouble? Whatever bravery Tempest had possessed fled before her. She glanced at Zed and saw the tension crackle in the air. Even Dash's face was tense, his eyes never leaving the other bikers, his hands clenched into fists. It felt as though a fight might break out at any moment. And she was in the center of it all.

Seth dismounted from his bike and paced towards Zed. "I'm the alpha. You obey my rules. I'll take the woman as a welcome gift and excuse your disobedience."

Zed squared up to Seth, his muscles tensed and eyes flashing with anger.

"Do whatever you want with me, but let her go."

Seth smirked at him. "Or you'll do what, exactly?"

With inhuman speed, Zed grabbed Seth by the collar of his leather jacket. Tempest gasped as his eyes burned with an intensity she'd never seen before, and sparks burst angrily between the two men. But Seth laughed and seized Zed by the throat, lifting him into the air as if he weighed nothing. Zed might be fast, but this man was strong. Inhumanly strong.

Red sparks flew in the air, and Tempest's eyes widened as a pulsing light crackled in Seth's hands. It was impossible. The light danced and flickered, as if he held electricity, or lightning, in his palms. It raced through his fingers and into Zed, crackling across his body and causing him to roar out in pain.

Tempest gasped and staggered backwards. It was impossible. It couldn't be real. But as another surge of lightning shot into Zed's body, she knew she had to do something. Before she could think twice, she jumped off her bike and struck Seth, her blows glancing uselessly off his muscular body.

"Stop it! Stop it, both of you. Let him go!"

Seth turned to her, his eyes burning through the darkness with a red hue. He released Zed, who fell to the ground, and laughed once again, a sound devoid of warmth or humor.

"You're reckless for an earth-bound. I like that in a woman." He flashed a smile at the men gathered. "Boys, change of plans. Let's stick around for a while and see what makes the women in this town so fiery."

With a sneer, Seth mounted his motorcycle and revved his engine, descending into the town with his thugs following close behind. As they raced away, the howling winds and violent lightning faded into a gentle breeze. Tempest turned to Zed, her mind spinning at what she'd just seen.

"Zed, are you okay? We need to get you to a hospital."

He staggered to his feet and looked at Dash and Ixion. "Follow him. Make sure he doesn't do anything reckless."

They nodded and climbed onto their bikes. Dash glanced worriedly at Tempest, while Ixion glared at Zed, before they revved their engines and raced down the mountain.

"Zed, what just happened?"

"I'm fine. Just forget about it."

"Forget about it? I just saw a bolt of lightning shoot out of a man's arm and into you. And you're walking around as if it's nothing." She took a shaky breath. "How did Seth do that? It's impossible, it's…"

"Whatever you think you might have seen, you need to leave it."

Tempest crossed her arms and looked at him defiantly. "What are the Stormchasers hiding?"

Zed shook his head as a cold wind swept through the valley. "You've had a fright. Whatever you think you saw, you need to let it go."

Tempest shivered as the wind howled around her. "Just tell me what's going on."

Zed drew a breath and met her gaze, his beautiful eyes searching her own. But the golden sparks in his eyes faded, and he mounted his bike.

"You should forget this ever happened, Tempest. Go back to your life and let the storm pass. The best thing you can do is forget about the Stormchasers, and forget about me."

Before Tempest could say anything, he rode away, back towards the eye of the storm, and disappeared into the wall of rain and wind. Tempest watched the flashes of lightning warily as the storm continued to rage. Despite Zed's warning, she knew what she had seen.

The Stormchasers were hiding a big secret. And she intended to find out exactly what it was.

8

"Has something in there caught your eye?"

Arthur looked suspiciously over the pile of books stacked next to Tempest. Storm clouds and thunderbolts sat on every cover.

"What's this? Do you have a sudden interest in meteorology?"

"Actually, I was hoping to find something about the Stormchasers. With a reputation like theirs, you'd think there'd be more written about them." Tempest groaned and tossed the book onto the pile. "But there's nothing. Nothing in the press. Nothing in the books. Nothing more than gossip and hearsay."

"And quite right, too. You don't need to pay them any attention. I don't want you getting mixed up with those unsavory types." He cursed as the street filled with the sound of revving engines as more bikers arrived in Mary's yard. "And I, for one, will appreciate peace and quiet again once they're gone."

"But don't you think it's strange? There's so much secrecy around them. No one really knows who they are, or why they follow the storms. What if they're hiding something?" She closed another book in defeat. "Did Mom ever say anything about them?"

Arthur laughed uneasily and busied himself by tidying the bookshelves. "No, Tempest, I don't recall your mother paying any interest in them."

"But they were here, the night she..."

"The best thing you can do is to forget about the Stormchasers. In a few days, the storm will blow over and you'll never have to think about them again."

Tempest narrowed her eyes as Arthur moved to the window display. She knew he was hiding something. But what it was, she couldn't be sure. She thought about last night's events, about the bolt of electricity that had raced through Seth's hands. It was impossible. It was the stuff of fairytales. And yet, she'd seen it with her own eyes...

Tempest was pulled from her thoughts as the doorbell rang, and the smell of caffeine and hairspray wafted into the library. With everything that had happened last night, she'd completely forgotten about her disastrous date with Mason. She looked up from her book and gulped as a pair of perfectly mascaraed eyes narrowed at her.

"Tempest, why is it I hear that you ran out on Mason last night?"

Tempest groaned. "I didn't run out on him. He was just so full-on, and I wanted to think about things..."

"What's there to think about? He's single, you're single. He's interested, you've been on the market for years. He's hot, you're... well, you're nice enough looking if you would just comb your hair and wear a bit of makeup for once."

Tempest rolled her eyes. "When you put it like that, how could I possibly say no?"

"Save the sarcasm. The miners practically run this town, and if we play our cards right, our lives will be taken care of. I won't let you ruin this... for *either* of us." Christie's eyes narrowed in warning. "I've arranged another double date for tonight."

"Wait, no, Christie. I can't, I..."

"Don't tell me you're planning on spending the night reading your books. I won't hear of it. And besides, I need you. When you bailed last night, Mason spent the whole evening with Dave, and I was the third wheel. It was quite the buzzkill, and not what I had planned at all." Her nostrils flared, and she placed a hand on her hips. "You're coming. And this time, you're staying for the whole evening. Just where did you go, anyway?"

Tempest gulped, and couldn't help but glance at the Storm-chasers gathered in Mary's yard. "Oh, I just went for a ride..."

"A *ride*? Tempest, why on earth would you waste your time on that beaten-up dirt bike when you could have the man of your dreams? Would you just try to be a little more normal tonight, please?" Christie fixed Tempest with a stern glare, broken only by the chime of the clocks. "Well, I must be off to my appointment. After last night, I want to make sure Dave can't be distracted by anyone else, least of all by his buddy. See ya, Tempest."

Tempest sighed with relief as Christie left the library and made a beeline for the nail salon. Arthur watched her from the window display and chuckled.

"What warranted that scolding?"

"Christie's decided to play matchmaker. And I'm her victim."

"The course of true love never runs smooth." He sighed and glanced at Mary's dive bar. "Take it from me."

Tempest followed his eyeline towards Mary and smiled knowingly.

"You should tell her how you feel."

"Tell *who* how I feel?" But Arthur sighed as Tempest raised her eyebrow. "Oh, blast! Is it really that obvious?"

He glanced longingly at Mary as she collected glasses from outside of her bar. She couldn't be more different from him. She was an aging rocker with wild unkempt hair, a mischievous gleam in her eyes, and, if rumors were true, a talent for witchcraft. Next to the bespectacled library owner who was never seen out of his tweed suits, they looked like complete contrasts.

"What's stopping you from telling her, Arthur? It's been so many years."

He smiled sadly. "Precisely. After all these years, I think I'd rather live with the fantasy of what could be rather than risk her turning me down. What if I make the leap only to find out it's worse?"

"But what if it's better? Surely it's worth taking a risk rather than never knowing at all."

Tempest's eyes widened as Zed's words flowed out of her. She hated to admit it, but he had a point. Maybe some change in the town would be a good thing.

The doorbell jingled, and Arthur busied himself with the rare sight of a visitor, leaving Tempest to her thoughts. She glanced at Mary's yard once more, where the bikers gathered. She scanned

the crowd, searching for Zed, disappointment rising within her as
he remained nowhere in sight.

He was hiding from her, she was sure of it. It was typical. He'd
thought nothing of inviting her for a midnight race in a dangerous
storm, but now he wanted to play it safe. But as a bolt of bright
blue and violet raced through the crowd, she realized Zed wasn't
the only one who had answers. She glanced at Arthur, and seeing
him occupied, crossed the road to Mary's bar.

Tempest's stomach churned as every eye turned to her as she
approached. The crowd parted before her, as if she was some kind
of leper, while silence filled the yard. Dash's eyes widened as she
approached, and he whispered to Ixion, who fixed Tempest with
a scowl.

"I thought Zed was clear last night. You're not welcome here."

A flicker of frustration ran through Tempest as they turned
their backs and ignored her. She watched them as they fixed their
bikes, and saw they had the same chain tattoos on their wrist,
held together by the lightning bolt in a circle. Like Zed's, they
shimmered on their wrist, as if glowing with a life of their own.

Ixion sighed loudly as she continued to busy herself with the
bike. "Why are you still here, earth-bound? Zed said you're not
welcome. What part of that is unclear?"

"Perhaps he can tell me that himself, rather than avoid me."

Dash blew his long turquoise fringe from his face and shook his
head. "He's not avoiding you. He's just preparing for the storm
tonight."

Dash's face paled as the words tumbled out of his mouth, while Ixion fixed him with a deathly glare. But Tempest grinned and glanced at the mountains in the distance.

"Is that so? Maybe I'll pay him a visit."

Ixion stepped forward, her eyes blazing in warning. "Whatever you think you saw last night, just forget about it and move on." She sighed, and her eyes softened slightly. "It's for your own good."

Dash nodded. "Trust us, you want to stay out of Seth's way. He has a mean streak and tends to hold a grudge." He looked around the yard warily, as the Stormchasers watched them in silence. "You really should go, before people start talking."

Dash whimpered as a booming sound filled the street and a dozen more bikers pulled into Mary's. The crowd moved swiftly to make space for them, their faces wary at the new arrivals. Tempest turned to see Seth lead the pack, his appearance even more terrifying in the daylight. His dark eyes met hers, and pulsed with red sparks of light.

"There's nothing I dislike more than an earth-bound ruining a perfectly good ride." Seth's eyes narrowed into an angry glare. "Except, perhaps, for an earth-bound librarian who pokes her nose where it doesn't belong."

"She was just leaving."

"Well, it better be for good this time." He turned and narrowed his eyes at Tempest. "So long, earth-bound."

Tempest returned his glare with one of her own. "I can't say it's been a pleasure."

A deadly silence fell across the yard, while Dash looked as though he might pass out at any moment. Seth sneered and stepped closer.

"You're bold for an earth-bound. But perhaps you should stick to reading about adventure, rather than step into a world where you don't belong."

"I'm not scared of you."

"You should be. I could show you storms so terrible you would lose yourself in them for eternity. With winds so powerful they'd blow you to the edges of the earth. With lightning that blinds and kills, and thunder so loud it would burst your eardrums. I can show you the true power of the storm. A storm that could turn this town to ashes."

The air crackled as Seth glared at her. Tempest stepped backwards as something flickered in his eyes, like small bolts of lightning within the darkness of his gaze. Thick storm clouds gathered in the sky above and coated them in a dark gloom, while the winds gathered strength and howled through the street. Tempest shivered as Seth's eyes gleamed with power. This man was anything but ordinary. And she knew that every second she spent with him put her in danger.

"The storm calls, Seth. We should ride."

A flash of violet filled the air as Ixion stepped in between them. Seth drew a breath and slowly lowered his gaze, until Tempest felt she could breathe again. Whoever this man was, he was dangerous. And from the fear in Ixion's eyes, Tempest could see she wasn't the only one at risk. Seth studied the skies where the storm clouds gathered, and nodded.

"See you around, earth-bound. I'll be watching."

The air filled with the rumble of engines. Seth led the charge as he raced towards the billowing storm clouds, the Stormchasers following him like a pack. Tempest drew a shaky breath as the yard emptied, and turned to see Dash and Ixion reluctantly mount their bikes.

"Consider that your last warning. Next time, you might not be so lucky." Ixion scowled at Tempest, and started her engine. "Ride well earth-bound. Just do yourself a favor and stay away from the storms."

With a rev of their engines, the last of the Stormchasers raced to the mountains. Tempest's heart sank as they sped towards its peak, where the eye of the storm gathered power. She was still no closer to finding any answers. And something told her she'd just made an enemy in Seth.

"Few people in this town would be foolish enough to ride in the storm. And even fewer would be foolish enough to ride with the Stormchasers."

Tempest turned in surprise to see Mary standing before her. Charms jangled from the array of bracelets that gleamed on her wrists, while the scent of wild flowers and herbs filled the air. She broke into a smile, her crow's feet wrinkling around her dazzling green eyes.

"You... saw me?"

"You were magnificent, dear. I can see you take after your mother in more ways than one." But Mary's smile faded as she looked at the mountain, where Seth led his pack of Stormchasers. "But you need to be careful, Tempest. Seth is dangerous. You don't want to get lost in the storm with him around."

Tempest crossed her arms. "He doesn't scare me."

"Oh, but he should. Seth has powers you wouldn't believe. And he has a particular dislike for earth-bounds."

"What does everyone keep calling me that? What does it even mean?"

"It means people who walk on the ground, dear. Mere mortals." Mary smiled as if it was perfectly obvious. "And Seth views the earth-bound as nothing more than the Stormchaser's playthings."

Tempest scoffed. "Well, if I'm just a mere mortal, what does that make him?"

Mary turned to her, her green eyes sparkling in the light. "They Stormchasers aren't mortals like us, Tempest. They're gods."

9

— · —

Tempest looked in wonder at the illustration before her. A half-human, half elemental spirit that could harness the power of the storms. Demigods whose beauty was surpassed only by the danger they posed. Beings who could be calm and gentle one moment, but cruel and destructive the next. And if Mary's books were anything to be believed, they were the Stormchasers.

Tempest ran a hand through her hair. It was impossible. A few days ago, she would never have believed in such a thing. But that was before she saw a man shoot electricity from his fingers. The storm raged beyond, coating the sky in thick, turbulent clouds. But for once, Tempest was happy to stay inside and read on.

The descendents of Zeus and the lesser storm gods, the Storm-chasers spend their lives following the storms, never resting in one place. They travel the earth in packs, enslaved to their alpha by the chains that bind them, and bring fear and terror wherever they go.

Tempest thought of the tattoo the Stormchasers shared. The chain that encircled their wrists, that shimmered with a life of its own. So far, they fit the bill.

Despite their human appearance, the Stormchasers can never hide their true form. Their eyes burn with the essence of the storm. Those brave enough to look into them will see a glimpse of the power within.

Tempest thought of Zed. Of how his dark eyes shone with glimmers of light, like sparks of golden electricity within inky storm clouds. Okay, two out of three.

They take their true form in the eye of the storm. It is their play-ground, and while mortals quake in their homes, the Stormchasers race across the skies.

Well, that was harder to prove. Thanks to Seth's arrival, the eye of the storm, and whatever it contained, remained a mystery. Tempest turned from the book and looked out of the window. The storm raged outside, and flashes of lightning flickered on the mountaintop. Something strange was taking place up there, that was for sure.

Beware of the Stormchasers. Whilst they might appear human, they are the descendents of the gods. Elemental beings of raw and savage power. And, like a storm, they are powerful, ferocious and destructive.

Tempest thought of what she'd seen. The description fit Seth, for sure. But there was something different about Zed. He could be all of those things, she supposed, but there was something else underneath. Something gentler, like glorious beams of sunlight that emerged after the ferocity of the storm.

She closed the book and sighed. A few days ago, she wouldn't have ridden into a storm with a biker gang, and she certainly wouldn't have entertained the idea that they were the descendents of Greek gods. This was the land of fairytales and make-believe, not logic and reason. But after what she'd seen, she couldn't help but wonder if there was more to them than met the eye.

She glanced at the page again. Descendants of Zeus? That would certainly explain Zed's god-like body, charm and womanizing ways. But she needed more proof.

Tempest looked out to the mountains. She watched as the Stormchasers raced towards the eye of the storm. They sped across the mountain in a blur, until they approached the dark vortex of the eye of the storm. Tempest watched them with bated breath, wondering what lay in the center of the storm. But as the Stormchasers crossed its threshold, the sky filled with a great flash of lightning, and the town was plunged into darkness.

Tempest gasped as every light in the town faded to darkness. The power cut swept through the streets until only the light of the storm remained. She pressed herself to the windowpane and looked at the mountain peak in disbelief. The Stormchasers were gone. It was as if they'd vanished into the eye of the storm itself. She drew a shaky breath, and glanced at Mary's book once more.

They take their true form in the eye of the storm. It is their playground, and while mortals quake in their homes, the Stormchasers race across the skies.

Tempest looked back at the eye of the storm. She knew the Stormchasers were hiding something. Something that lurked in the center of the storm. But there was only one way to find out for sure.

Tempest checked the time, torn with indecision. She was supposed to meet Christie in an hour. But despite her promise, her eyes were drawn back to the storm. If she was quick, she could still make it in time. After all, the Stormchasers might be terrifying, but they were nothing compared to Christie's tantrums.

Tempest grabbed her leather jacket and leaped on to her dirt bike before she could think twice. As she sped towards the mountains, she glanced at the eye of the storm. Colorful forks of lightning flashed inside, while the growl of hundreds of motorcycles rumbled within the vortex. Something was happening in there. Something that drew the Stormchasers in like a magnet. And she was determined to find out what it was. She revved her engine and began the ascent into the mountains.

The winds picked up speed as she raced through the woods and onto the rocky slopes of the mountain. The storm gathered power as she neared, until she found herself caught in its dark embrace. Despite the powerful rumble of thunder and violent flashes of lightning, she pressed onwards towards the eye of the storm. It was time to get answers.

A trio of Stormchasers raced further ahead and disappeared behind thick sheets of black rain. Tempest revved her engine and followed them, until she neared the threshold of the eye of the storm. She drew a deep breath as she approached the wall of rain, and sensed the savage power held within.

This was it. She would find answers, whether or not Zed wanted to hide them. It was time to see what lay within the eye of the storm.

Tempest sped through the sheets of rain and gasped as blinding flashes of lightning filled the sky. She gripped her handlebars tightly as the wind tore ferociously across the mountain, while black rain struck her from the heavens. Colorful flashes of lightning streaked overhead, while the sound of booming motorcycle engines filled the air. It was disorienting. It was overwhelming. And yet, Tempest smiled as the rumble of hundreds of motorcycle engines reverberated across the mountain. It was wonderful.

But as Tempest surveyed her surroundings, she realized something was amiss. While the sounds of racing motorcycles filled the sky, the Stormchasers were nowhere to be seen. Tempest searched through the dark winds, and peered across the gloomy mountain top. Despite the cacophony of noise that surrounded her, she was the only one on the mountain.

Tempest looked around in confusion. The trio of Stormchasers had been right in front of her. They had to be here somewhere. As she searched for them, she glanced at the sky, where technicolor lightning bolts raced through the air. She watched as violet and turquoise bolts of lightning chased each other playfully, while others collided and ricocheted away from the storm.

Two bolts of lightning raced overhead, glowing brighter than any other. One was a deep shade of red, and sent a deep peal of thunder echoing through the sky. The other was a beautiful shade of gold, and sent a trail of sparks behind it as it sped through the sky like a shooting star.

A blinding light filled the sky as the red bolt of lightning collided with another. The impact sent a streak of lightning spiraling through the air, until it struck the ground in an explosion of sparks. Tempest blinked in surprise as something emerged from the smoking pile of rubble. The silhouette of a bike appeared, its engine still running as it lay sprawled on its side. She narrowed her eyes in confusion. Bikes didn't just fall out of the sky, did they?

A blast of lightning struck the ground nearby, forcing her attention back to the road. She yelped as another struck the track before her, sending a plume of rock dust into her path. Tempest glanced nervously at her surroundings as the beauty of the storm turned into something savage and destructive.

Her eyes widened as the red lightning bolt descended towards her. She tried to veer away, but it darted across the sky towards her, sending forks of lightning in her path. She weaved in between the blasts, trying to escape as the road exploded into a shower of debris and sparks. But as the bolt of lightning pursued her, something told her the storm had no intention of letting her go.

Tempest gasped as she glanced at the lightning. Within its pulsing, red glow, a silhouette of a biker emerged. She blinked in disbelief, but the figure grew closer, until her blood froze as she recognized the rider. Their fiery hair gleamed in the light, while a pair of dark eyes glared at her with a destructive rage. It was Seth.

Tempest lurched in her seat and cursed as she veered from the track. She pulled sharply on her brakes, her panic rising as the bike slipped against the loose stones. The ground beneath her turned to rubble, and she cried out in fear as she approached the mountain edge.

She'd driven too fast. She'd been too distracted. She'd been too reckless. Her screams echoed across the sky as her bike soared off the edge of the mountain, and a deep ravine opened up beneath her.

Tempest cried out as her motorcycle fell before her, clattering down the mountaintop in an explosion of shrapnel. Her screams filled the sky as she tumbled through the air, and plummeted towards the ground below. She drew a breath, and braced herself for the impact.

A flash of golden lightning tore through the sky. It raced towards Tempest at breakneck speed, filling the air with a thunderous roar. The golden light enveloped her, and she gasped as a pair of hands reached for her own. She clutched onto them for dear life and looked up into a familiar pair of eyes that shone with golden sparks. It was Zed.

"Hold on!"

Tempest clambered onto the seat of his bike as Zed pulled her towards him. She wrapped her arms around him and braced herself as they fell through the sky. They hit the ground hard and fast, ricocheting off the rubble before landing with another thud. Before she could draw a breath, Zed revved his engine once more and took off along the track.

Tempest turned to see the eye of the storm rage on the mountain peaks. She shuddered as the red-tinged lightning filled the sky with a furious display of power, and clung tighter to Zed.

The storm might be the playground for the gods. But it was clearly no place for a mortal.

10

— · —

$\mathbf{B}$ lack rain poured from the heavens. Tempest shivered, while her heart pounded in her chest. A flash of red lightning filled the sky, its forks branching through the darkness like tendrils, as if searching for her. She shuddered at the thought, and drew herself closer to Zed.

They take their true form in the eye of the storm.

Her body trembled as she held on to Zed. Could it really be true? She glanced at Zed in the side mirror of his bike. He looked human. He felt human. But she couldn't help but wonder if something entirely different lurked within him.

Her stomach lurched as Zed revved his engine and took another corner at breathtaking speed.

"Hey, can you slow down?"

Tempest's words died in the wind. They continued to ride in silence, the anger radiating from Zed's body. Another sharp corner, and she felt herself slip from the saddle.

"Hey, I said slow down!"

Zed slammed on the brakes and they came to a screeching halt outside of his cabin. He leaped from his bike and shot her a furious glare. The gentle golden sparks of light in his eyes were replaced with an anger that burned ferociously through the darkness.

"I told you to forget about me. I told you not to come. You could have been killed!"

Tempest drew a startled breath. His body shook with fury, like a thunderstorm that raged with a primal destruction. But she folded her arms, and scowled at him in return.

"Well, maybe if you hadn't spent the day avoiding me, I wouldn't have had to follow you."

Zed blinked, as if regaining his senses. The sparks in his eyes dissolved, and his anger faded into remorse.

"This is my fault."

His hands balled into fists as the power of his rage turned inwards. But Tempest stepped closer and cautiously placed her hands to his. She looked into the darkness that rippled within his eyes and shook her head.

"It's not your fault. But I want you to be honest with me. Tell me what's in the eye of the storm."

Zed's eyes met hers, and he drew a breath. But a boom of thunder filled the sky, and his eyes clouded over once more.

"I can't."

"Fine, suit yourself. Don't tell me." Tempest's frustration and fear boiled inside of her. "I've had it with you, and your secrets. The sooner you and the Stormchasers leave this town, the better."

She turned to leave, anger flowing through her, but gasped as pain shot through her ankle. She stumbled, but Zed caught her before she fell, his movements lightning-fast.

"You're hurt." Tempest followed his gaze and saw the cuts and bruises from her fall on the mountain. "Let me help."

Before she could protest, he draped his coat around her and carried her in his arms. He ignored her cries of indignation and strode into the cabin, before laying her down near the hearth.

She clenched her jaw as he lit the fire, her anger still bubbling inside of her. "You can't hold me hostage here."

"You have no bike and a twisted ankle. How exactly do you plan on getting home? Walking in the storm?"

Another flash of red-hued lightning filled the air, and she shuddered at the thought. Zed's eyes softened, and he spoke once more.

"Just let me help you. I'll see to your ankle, and I'll take you back to the town. Please, just don't go into the storm by yourself. It's not safe."

Tempest's body trembled as she met his gaze. Now that she was out of the storm, cold fear coursed through her. Someone, or *something*, had attacked her. And if it hadn't been for Zed, she would have fallen to her death. An icy terror spread through her, and a numbness seeped into her bones. Zed wasted no time and wrapped her in the furs, trying to get the warmth back into her body.

"Let me help you, please."

She nodded reluctantly and winced as she removed her jacket. Her hands and wrists were scraped and bloodied, while a deep bruise bloomed on her ankle. Zed returned with a first aid kit and gently cleaned the wounds, before he bandaged her ankle. As he did so, Tempest saw the anger in his eyes fade, the golden sparks disappearing into the inky darkness.

"This is my fault. I should never have invited you to ride with us."

His words stung more than the antiseptic. "Hey, I was more than capable of keeping up with you."

"I didn't mean it like that. It's just, if something had happened to you... I could never forgive myself."

Fear crept through her once more. "And what would happen to me, Zed? What happens in the eye of the storm?"

Zed remained silent as he bandaged her ankle. "Whatever you think you might have seen, forget about it."

"Forget about it? I just saw a bolt of lightning chase me and try to kill me. And you... you appeared from thin air. It was as if... as if you appeared from lightning." A peal of thunder echoed in the mountains, while winds howled through the valley. "Zed, we both know that storm isn't normal. Tell me who the Stormchasers really are. Tell me *what* you really are."

He remained silent, but Tempest watched as golden sparks shimmered within the darkness of his eyes.

Their eyes burn with the essence of the storm. Those brave enough to look into them will see a glimpse of the power within.

Tempest's stomach churned. She might not have the proof she wanted, but even she couldn't deny what was right in front of her. This man, this stranger, was from a world completely different to her own. A world of gods and magic.

The sky flashed with red-hued lightning, and thunder shook the foundations of the earth. Zed turned to the door and his body tensed, as if expecting someone to appear at any moment. It was as if, Tempest thought with a shudder, he expected someone to drop out of the sky.

Tempest glanced at the storm that raged above the mountain. She thought of what she had seen, of Seth's silhouette following her in the lightning. And she looked back at the tattoo that snaked around Zed's wrist, her eyes widening in understanding.

They travel the earth in packs, enslaved to their alpha by the chains that bind them.

"You're bound to him, aren't you?"

Zed remained stony and silent. But the look in his eyes gave Tempest all the confirmation she needed. He drew a breath, as if unsure of where to even begin.

"Seth has rules. Rules that forbid us from riding with those who aren't our own kind. Rules that forbid us from sharing anything about who we really are." He looked at Tempest pointedly, acknowledging the unspoken truth that hung between them. "If he knew you were here, we'd both be in danger."

"Well, he sounds like a jerk. Maybe you need a change in leadership."

"I tried that once before, and it didn't work out so well." He pointed to the thin scar on his cheekbone, and shook his head. "The Stormchasers follow power, and Seth's the most powerful of us all. And so we're forced to serve him. And every year, his storms get more and more violent."

"Then why be a Stormchaser at all?"

"Because we weren't always like this. We weren't always so... destructive. I suppose I hope that one day we'll return to a peaceful way of living. That we can focus on the beauty of the storm rather than its destruction."

Silence descended once more. Tempest looked at the pain in his eyes, and felt a million questions form in her mind. But Zed sighed, and his eyes shone with regret.

"I know you have questions, Tempest. But the less you know, the better." He looked into her eyes mournfully. "The best thing you can do is to forget about everything. Forget about the Stormchasers, forget about tonight, and forget about me."

Tempest knew he was right. If tonight had shown her anything, it was that the Stormchasers were from a world filled with danger. A world of magic. A world in which she didn't belong.

This man had brought nothing but trouble since he'd arrived in the town. And yet, he'd saved her. He'd sped through the sky like a beacon of light. He'd introduced her to a world of magic and excitement. And despite the doubts in her head, Tempest couldn't help but listen to her heart.

Tempest moved her hand closer to his, until a small spark danced between them. She looked into Zed's golden eyes, and felt her heart flutter in her chest.

"What if I don't want to forget about you?"

Golden sparks shimmered within his eyes, like fireworks in the night sky. Slowly, she placed her hand in his, and traced her finger in the palm of his hands, marveling as sparks burst from his skin. She knew it was reckless. She knew she should return to the safety of her life. But Zed was right. Some storms were too powerful to resist. And she wanted to be swept away.

Zed gazed at her with a longing that burned through him. His breath brushed Tempest's skin as she drew herself closer. Sparks flickered between their bodies, and a flash of heat pulsed through her as she gazed into his eyes. For so long, the doubts in her head had stopped her from making a leap into the unknown. But now she was ready to follow her heart. She parted her lips, and leaned closer...

A blinding flash streaked across the sky, and a peal of thunder boomed overhead, shaking the cabin with its ferocity. At once, Zed tensed and pulled away from her, the spell between them broken. Tempest's cheeks burned as she looked at him uncertainly.

"Zed? What's wrong?"

His breath grew short, and he backed away from her. He looked at her with a mixture of fear and rage. Of all the reactions she'd expected, this certainly hadn't been it. She ran a hand through her hair self-consciously. Had she misread the signs?

"You should go, Tempest."

Tempest felt the burning in her cheeks deepen. "What? You've got to be kidding."

But as the golden sparks in his eyes faded, so too did his warmth. He clenched his jaw and fixed her with a cold glare.

"I'll give you a ride back to town." Zed drew a deep breath, and his eyes darkened until all traces of light were gone. "This was a mistake, Tempest. After tonight, you'll never see me, or the Stormchasers, again."

11

— · —

They rode in silence. Even the deafening roar of the motorcycle and the peals of thunder weren't enough to disguise the awkwardness that settled over them. The silence enveloped them like a thick storm cloud, until it was all Tempest could notice.

As each second passed, Tempest's anger grew. Zed had been the one to flirt with her first. He'd been the one to ask her to ride with the Stormchasers. And he'd been the one to charm her with his wine, with his sense of adventure, with his inability to keep a fur throw in place. And now? Now the thought of kissing her made him dive to the other side of the room.

She thought she'd seen all the signs. He'd thrown himself into danger for her. He'd looked at her with a burning desire in his eyes. Sparks had literally flown from his touch, for goodness' sake. But she'd been wrong. He wasn't interested in her. He didn't want to be anywhere near her.

She felt his body beneath her hands as they rode. It felt different. Colder. As if he couldn't stand her touch.

Tempest's frustration bubbled to the surface as lightning flashed overhead. She'd known the risks of getting mixed up with someone like him. She knew that the Stormchasers left a trail of destruction in every town they visited. And yet she'd allowed herself to get swept up in his storm. She scolded herself for being so foolish. She'd been nothing but a fool to believe that someone like her could have a moment of adventure.

Well, from now on she'd play it safe. No more dreaming of adventure. No more looking for excitement. And certainly no more taking leaps into the unknown. Christie was right. She needed to stop chasing dreams in the sky and keep her feet planted firmly on the ground.

Zed barely came to a stop before she dismounted from his bike. If he wanted to play games and keep secrets, then she didn't want to be anywhere near him. He tried to help her as she dismounted, but she pulled away from his touch.

"I'm just trying to help you. You're hurt."

"I'll be fine." She narrowed her eyes at him. "I wouldn't want you to touch me, given it upsets you so much."

Pain flickered through his eyes. Good. She hoped her words hurt.

"I didn't mean to hurt you." He drew a breath as the sparks in his eyes faded. "I didn't mean for any of this..."

"You can push me away, but I know what I saw in the storm. And I won't just let it go."

"Whatever it is you think you saw, you need to leave it." The clouds rumbled overhead, while Zed's eyes flashed in the darkness. "These storms are too dangerous for your kind."

"Is that a threat?"

Lightning flashed overhead and thunder echoed through the sky. Zed's eyes hardened, and he spoke in a growl.

"It's a warning."

"Is this what you do, Zed? Do you go from town to town, and sweep women away with your stories of adventure and fantasy? Am I just the latest in a long line of gullible fools for you to string along?"

Zed held her gaze as the storm gathered strength and the wind howled through the streets behind him.

"Don't you get it? I'm not trying to hurt you. I'm trying to protect you."

"The only person I need protecting from is you." Tempest's anger coursed through her, while lightning raged in the skies above. "I guess everything about the Stormchasers is true. You descend into towns, cause chaos wherever you go, and leave destruction in your wake. And the sooner you're gone, the better."

A noise from across the street drew Tempest's attention. Christie called to her, her voice tinged with fury at being stood-up once again, while Mason and Dave loitered nearby. With a final glare at Zed, Tempest turned to leave, but gasped as pain shot through her ankle. Zed moved inhumanly quickly, and gathered her in his arms before she fell to the ground.

Tempest cursed and pushed him away. "Let go of me Zed. Just leave me alone."

The sound of racing footsteps filled the air. Tempest turned to see Christie gasp at the sight of her.

"Tempest! You're hurt!" Christie's eyes widened at her bandaged hands, her drenched clothes, and her wild hair. A flicker of fear raced through her as she caught sight of Zed. "Get away from her this instant!"

Tempest stumbled to her feet and shook her head. "No, Christie, it's not like that—"

"Somebody help us!"

"Christie, no!"

Before Tempest could say anything else, a figure raced through the darkness. Footsteps pounded across the wet pavement, sending water spraying into the air as another figure emerged. Tempest gasped as Mason roared in anger, fueled by a rage more powerful than the storm above. His hands curled into fists, until he charged at Zed, ready to strike.

12

Lightning flashed in the sky, illuminating the two men who brawled in the raging storm. They grappled with one another, their shirts slick with rain as they fought in a battle of strength and testosterone. The air grew thick with their hot-blooded fury, their rage more savage than the dark winds that howled through the streets.

Tempest cursed as she found herself caught in the center of another type of storm entirely. She ran towards the brawling pair, desperate to break up the fight, but Christie dragged her back to the sidewalk. Mason roared in fury as he struck Zed, until they tumbled to the ground and wrestled each other on the wet road.

"Stop it! Both of you, stop it!"

Tempest's words died in the wind that tore through the street. Deafening peals of thunder shook the earth as the two men continued to fight. Mason fell to his knees and hurled rainwater at Zed's eyes, blinding him, before he lunged towards him. He struck him over and over again in a violent rage, his eyes ablaze with the thrill of the fight. Tempest staggered forwards and tried desperately to pull him away.

"Let him go! He's done nothing wrong!"

Tempest cried out as Mason pushed her away, sending her sprawling to the asphalt. As she hit the ground, Zed roared with fury, and grabbed Mason by the throat. His eyes burned with a terrifying intensity, like violent lightning within the darkest of storm clouds.

"You'll pay for that earth-bound."

Zed's voice boomed across the street like a peal of thunder. The air crackled around him, and sparks flew from his fingers. Tempest gasped as a golden light bloomed within his hand, and a ball of lightning emerged in his palm. He'd lost himself to the savagery of the storm. And unless she did something, she knew that its power would consume the humanity within him.

She shook herself free of Christie and ran towards him, splashing through the puddles until she reached them.

"Stop it! Both of you, just stop!"

She gasped as Zed turned to her. His eyes blazed with a deadly light, while shadows draped across his face, giving him a darkness she'd never seen before. He reminded her of a violent storm, intent on destroying everything in its path. He reminded her of Seth.

Like a storm, they are powerful, ferocious and destructive.

Tempest's heart pounded in her chest as she looked at Zed. Every instinct told her to run. To flee to safety, until the storm had passed. And yet she knew his humanity was buried within the darkness. He was just lost in the savagery of the storm. She forced herself to step forwards and placed a hand on his arm.

"Zed, please. Let him go. You're scaring me."

He blinked, and the intensity of his eyes faded as he regained control of himself. The darkness waned from his face, replaced with a look of remorse. He released Mason at once, who fell to the ground with a thud.

"Tempest, I'm sorry, I..."

Mason scrambled to his feet and forced himself between them. He glared at Zed, his face flushed with anger and embarrassment.

"So, is this what the Stormchasers do? Attack helpless women?"

"He didn't hurt me, Mason. He... he saved me."

"Yeah, right."

"It's true. I lost control of my bike and fell. If it hadn't been for Zed, I don't know what would have happened."

"Well, who gave you the idea to ride in the storm in the first place?" Mason nodded triumphantly as Tempest faltered, and he turned to Zed. "So what was the plan? Lure her in with the promise of adventure? Try to impress her before making your move?" He shook his head and sneered in disdain. "Tempest would never go for someone like you."

Zed clenched his jaw, and he spoke in a low growl. "Maybe some adventure in her life wouldn't be such a bad thing."

"She doesn't need adventure. She doesn't know what she wants. And she doesn't need people like you spurring her on."

Tempest narrowed her eyes at Mason, stung by his words. Since when did he decide what she wanted?

Zed fixed Mason with a glare. "I think Tempest can speak for herself."

Tempest's cheeks burned as both men turned to her expectantly. Right now, she didn't know what she wanted. She looked from Mason to Zed, caught between a life of safety and a life of danger. She heard footsteps behind her, and for once, felt relief at Christie's intrusion.

"Come on Tempest, let's get you home. You're soaked, and the sooner you're out of this storm, the better."

She took Tempest's hand and led her away. Tempest glanced at Zed, who looked at her longingly through the pouring rain. He lowered his eyes in defeat, and turned to his motorcycle.

Mason's goading voice cut through the street as he continued to taunt Zed. "I don't like strangers in this town, and I sure as hell don't like Stormchasers. This town isn't meant for people like you."

"Don't worry, we won't be staying." Zed started his engine as lightning crackled in the sky. "We'll be leaving tomorrow."

Tempest spun to face him, her eyes wide with surprise. "You're leaving?"

Zed refused to meet her gaze, but spoke once more. "The storm can never stay in one place for long."

Mason sneered and an arrogant smile creeped across his face. "Well, good riddance."

Before Tempest could argue, Christie steered her towards the library and away from Zed. A numbness spread through her as she was led away. She thought she had more time. She turned to Zed once more, her mind still full of unanswered questions and unresolved feelings, as he rode off into the night.

"You poor thing, you must be terrified. You're shaking like a leaf."

Christie was right, Tempest was shaking. But it wasn't because she feared Zed. It was because she was scared of losing him. The realization hit her like a bolt of lightning, and her breath faltered.

"The best thing you can do is put this behind you. By to-morrow, the storm will be gone, and so will the Stormchasers." Christie turned to her with a smile. "And then you can get back to your normal life."

Tempest forced herself to nod. But she wasn't sure if she wanted life to go back to normal. She wasn't sure if she wanted the storm to leave town at all. What she wanted was more time.

But as the sounds of Zed's motorcycle grew distant, she knew that time was running out.

13

— · —

Tempest studied the picture of the storm spirit before her. She could practically feel the lightning crackle across the page. She gazed into the eyes that burned with an irrepressible rage and a destructive power. A power fueled by the fury of the storm itself.

Like a storm, they are powerful, ferocious and destructive.

She thought of the darkness in Zed's eyes as he'd attacked Mason. A savage power resided within him, a darkness that had taken over. And she realized that perhaps she'd been wrong. Perhaps he was no different from Seth.

Tempest shook her head and closed the book. If last night had taught her anything, it was that someone like her didn't belong in the world of the gods. Perhaps Christie was right. Maybe it was better to stay here, where it was safe, rather than chase adventure. Because next time, she might not be so lucky.

"With a frown like that, you'll scare the patrons away."

Tempest glanced at the empty library pointedly. "We don't have any patrons."

Arthur sighed and shook his head. "Well, someone woke up on the wrong side of the bed today. What's on your mind?"

"I was just thinking about my life here. That perhaps it's time for me to put down some roots. That maybe I need to get my head out of the clouds and focus on the real world."

"I'd be happy for you if you didn't look so miserable about it."

Tempest forced a smile. "I'll be fine, Arthur. Besides, it's like you always said. Why bother with adventure when there's plenty to be found in a book?"

Arthur's mustache quivered, and he lowered his spectacles thoughtfully. "When I became your guardian, I thought my role was to keep you safe. That if I filled your imagination with books, I could give you all the adventure you needed, without any danger."

"And you did. You gave me everything I needed, and more."

Arthur smiled sadly, deepening his frown lines. "Perhaps. But you take after your mother, Tempest. I can see her spirit inside of you. The wild, untameable force of nature that always hungered for adventure. And I can't help but wonder if we both have an important lesson to learn from her."

Tempest looked at him uncertainly. "Like what?"

"That sometimes it's important to take a risk and leap into the unknown. Even if it feels scary." Arthur adjusted his tie and glanced at a bouquet of flowers that sat behind the counter. "I've been thinking about my life, Tempest. I've spent so many years living in safety that I've nearly missed my chance to take a leap of my own. And I think it's time to change that." He looked out at Mary's bar and sighed. "Although I wish it didn't leave me feeling quite so nauseous. I've been trying to pluck up the courage to visit her all day."

Tempest broke into a smile. "What's stopping you?"

"I'm not sure I have the strength. What if Mary doesn't feel the same way?" Arthur dabbed his forehead with a handkerchief, and the flowers seemed to droop. "Perhaps it's better like this. To be separated, but to see each other from afar. Like a modern-day Pyramus and Thisbee, doomed to never be united."

Tempest looked at the way Arthur gazed longingly across the road. And she realized that perhaps Zed was right. Perhaps some things needed to change in this town. She placed the flowers in Arthur's hands, before looping her arm through his.

"What are you doing?"

"It's time to take the leap, Arthur."

Arthur's eyes widened in fright. "But what if she says no?"

"But what if she says yes?" Tempest thought of Zed and fixed Arthur with a meaningful look. "Surely it's worth taking a risk rather than never knowing at all?"

Arthur's mustache quivered, and he glanced nervously at Mary's bar. Before he could back out, Tempest marched him out of the library and across the street. Arthur muttered protests under his breath with every step, while the bouquet trembled in his hands. His steps faltered as they approached the bar, where a group of Stormchasers glared at him.

"This was a bad idea, Tempest. A very bad idea indeed. We should head back…"

A flash of violet and blue emerged from the group as Dash and Ixion appeared. Arthur trembled as Ixion folded her arms and frowned at the bouquet.

"Are those for Mary?"

Arthur gulped, and tried to hide behind the wilting flowers. "No, no, no. They're for no one..."

Ixion shrugged, but her frown deepened. "Well, if they are for Mary, you should put some peonies in them. They're her favorites."

Tempest's eyes widened, and she broke into a smile. With her ever-present scowl and intimidating Mohawk, Ixion was the last person she'd expected to give floristry advice. Arthur let out a laugh of relief and nodded.

"Peonies! Of course, why didn't I think of that?"

He excitedly ran to the florist, before reappearing with a peony-laden bouquet. He extended his hand to Ixion and shook it eagerly.

"Thank you. You're my purple-haired savior."

Tempest smiled as Arthur approached the bar. He stood at the doorway, adjusted his tie, and watched Mary as she moved about the bar in a flurry of her robes. He'd been waiting for this moment for all of his life.

Nerves raced through Tempest as Arthur drew a deep breath and stepped into the bar. But something told her he would be okay. She smiled and turned to Ixion and Dash.

"Thank you."

"Don't mention it." Ixion glanced around the yard and her usual scowl returned. "Seriously. Mingling with an earth-bound has been ruinous for my social status."

"I hear you'll be on your way soon enough."

Ixion shrugged and looked at the sky. "The storm never stays in one place for long."

"Well, I learned last night that the storm isn't to be messed with." Tempest shook her head, recalling the events of the evening. The violent lightning, her terror as she rode off the mountain edge, the sight of her dirt bike tumbling down the ravine. "At least not for people like me."

Dash swept a lock of turquoise hair from his face. "Are you kidding me? You're one of the best riders we've seen. Ixion could barely shut up about how impressive you were."

"Is that so?" Tempest grinned as Ixion's scowl deepened. But she sighed and shook her head. "Well, I think my riding days are over for now, anyway. The last I saw of my bike, it was somewhere at the bottom of a ravine."

"I wouldn't be so sure about that."

Dash rubbed his hands in glee and sprinted away, before he wheeled a bike towards them. Tempest gasped as she looked at the gleaming bike beneath his hands. It was her dirt bike.

"How did you..."

"Zed made it clear that there'd be hell to pay if we didn't get it back into tip-top shape." Dash looked proudly at the bike and grinned. "Consider it a gift from the Stormchasers."

Tempest ran her hand over the handlebars in disbelief. It was even better than she remembered. She started the engine and almost jumped out of her skin as a powerful rumble blasted from it.

Ixion nodded approvingly at the deep growl of the engine. "It might still be a piece of junk, but at least it sounds the part now."

"I hope you don't mind, but I made a few adjustments." Dash lowered his voice and a mischievous gleam sparkled in his eyes.

"Press the blue button underneath the throttle when you really want a thrill."

Tempest looked at the bike in amazement. It called to her with promises of adventure and excitement. But something held her back. The fear from last night remained, filling her mind with doubts. She had made the leap, but she'd fallen to the earth.

As if sensing her worry, Ixion stepped forwards. "Even the hardiest of Stormchasers fall. It's what you do afterwards that really matters. You just need to pick yourself up, dust yourself down, and get back into the saddle."

Tempest sighed. "It's not that simple. Zed's made it clear he doesn't want me anywhere near him, or the storm."

Dash shook his head. "He's just saying that to protect you. He can barely keep himself away from you. To think, the great Zed has an earth-bound for a fated mate, hah!"

"His fated what...?"

Ixion fixed Dash with a murderous glare, and a boom of angry thunder filled the town.

"The storm calls. See you around, earth-bound." Ixion mounted her bike, and her scowl softened into a smile. "You ride well... for an earth-bound."

Without another word, Ixion rode into the distance, followed by dozens of Stormchasers. With her departure, the skies began to clear as the storm prepared to drift away. Tempest turned to Dash as his engine roared to life.

"What was that you said? About me being Zed's whatever-you-called-it...?"

Dash glanced around sheepishly, as if checking for Ixion's disapproving scowl. As the yard emptied, he turned back to Tempest and lowered his voice to a whisper.

"His fated mate. The yin to his yang. The sun to his moon. The—"

"Okay, I get it. But you're wrong. Zed doesn't feel that way." Tempest thought back to the humiliation of when she'd tried to kiss him. "Trust me."

"Oh yeah? I've been riding with Zed for years, and I've never seen him like this. He was a lone wolf, riding from town to town without a care in the world. He never stopped to think about anything but the storm. But you stopped him in his tracks." Dash grinned and ran a hand through his windblown hair. "The only reason he's pushing you away is to protect you. Seth isn't overly keen on earth-bound..."

Tempest shuddered as a peal of thunder echoed in the distance. She thought of the flash of red lightning that had followed her last night, of the silhouette within it, of the eyes that burned with a savage power.

"Even if you're right, it doesn't matter. Zed and I... we're from different worlds." Tempest folded her arms and shivered in the winds. "And last night showed me I'm no Stormchaser."

"You might be an earth-bound, but you ride like one of us. All it would take is a leap of faith." Dash smiled, until turquoise sparks danced in his eyes. "It's not too late to catch the storm before it leaves, Tempest."

Tempest looked at the storm as it drifted further away from the town. She wanted to follow it. To race into the depths of the storm, and stop Zed from leaving. But despite the pull of her heart, the doubts in her mind kept her chained to the earth.

"I think Zed was right. Maybe it's better if I stay on the ground, where I belong."

The sparks in Dash's eyes dimmed, and he sighed. "Stay here if you wish, earth-bound. But some things in life are worth taking a risk for. And I bet that if you made the leap, you'd fly."

Without a sad smile, Dash revved his engine and rode off towards the storm. Tempest watched him race into the distance, until the sound of his engine faded, and the skies began to clear.

The storm, and the Stormchasers, were gone.

14

—·—

Tempest looked at her reflection in the mirror. She barely recognized the woman who stared back at her. Thick make-up caked her face while her stubborn hair lay in a sleek ponytail after a merciless assault from Christie's hair straighteners. She looked like a doll, and nothing like herself. Then again, perhaps that was the point.

Her eyes wandered from the mirror and towards the window, where patches of clear sky bloomed. The worst of the storm had lifted, and the thick clouds drifted from the mountains and into the world beyond. By the end of the night, the storm would be gone.

A handful of Stormchasers loitered by Zed's cabin, readying themselves for the journey ahead. Tempest sighed as she thought back to the evening she'd spent there. When Zed had first swept her away into a world of magic and adventure...

Tempest yelped as a sharp yank to her head brought her back to attention. But Christie smiled, oblivious to Tempest's protests, as she put the finishing touches to her hair.

"There, that's perfect. Look at you. You're stunning!" Christie beamed in the mirror. "I must say, I'm quite proud of my handiwork."

"I barely look like myself."

"Oh, nonsense, you look beautiful. And Mason will love it. This is the kind of look men like. Sleek and pretty, not wild and tomboyish."

Tempest sighed and glanced at her reflection once more. Was this really all that mattered to men? This painted face and clothes so tight she could barely breathe? A sadness flowed through her as she thought of Zed. He had liked her for who she really was. Her wild hair, her leather jacket, her oil-stained jeans. He'd embraced the wild spirit inside of her. He hadn't wanted to tame her.

Christie's arm looped through hers, pulling her out of her thoughts and down into the library below. The sound of humming filled her ears, and she raised an eyebrow as Arthur merrily twirled around the library, dancing with an invisible partner.

"Arthur, are you okay?"

"Okay? I'm more than okay, my dear. I've just had the best afternoon of my life."

Tempest grinned as Arthur's joy pulled her from her gloom. "Did things go well with Mary?"

"Oh, it was just wonderful. We talked for hours, like we were a pair of loved up teens. To be so close to her, to no longer be separated by these infernal windows, was simply terrific." He stepped towards Tempest, his eyes sparkling. "And I have you to thank, my girl. If you hadn't encouraged me to take the leap, I'd have regretted it for the rest of my life. Thank you, my dear, thank you!"

Tempest laughed as Arthur danced around the library once again. She'd never seen him so happy. Bewilderment spread across Christie's face as Arthur began waltzing with an umbrella.

"Come on, Tempest. We don't want to be late."

Arthur smiled as he continued his dance across the library. "Oh, are you off to spend more time with those Stormchaser gentlemen again?"

"Stormchasers?" Christie snorted with disdain. "Absolutely not. Didn't you hear? Mason saved Tempest from one of those terrifying bikers last night. He raced to her defense, like a knight in shining armor saving his damsel in distress. It was so romantic."

Arthur's mustache quivered. "Tempest doesn't strike me as a damsel who needs saving..."

"Well, we better be off." Christie waved goodbye to Arthur with a flick of her hand. "Just think, Tempest, tonight could be the start of the rest of your life. Play your cards right, and soon we'll hear the sound of wedding bells."

Arthur's eyes widened, while Tempest's stomach churned. Before she could protest, she was marched out of the library and forced to follow Christie towards the caves. She glanced at the mountains as a peal of thunder echoed through the sky, sounding more distant than ever. Christie followed her eyeline to Zed's cabin, where the Stormchasers readied their bikes to leave.

"Let's hope they never come back." She held Tempest closer and looked fearfully at the Stormchasers. "Thank goodness Mason was there last night. It was so brave of him to fight that awful biker. What a gentleman."

"Well, I wish he hadn't. Zed had done nothing wrong."

"Oh, that's nonsense. That biker knew exactly what he was doing. Preying on a poor girl like you." Christie sighed and shook her head. "They always go for the inexperienced ones. The ones who don't know any better. It's probably why he didn't go for me. He knew I wouldn't fall for his act."

Tempest felt a spark of anger flicker within her, but forced herself to bite her tongue. She'd made the right decision. She had to let the storm pass. She belonged here, in this town, not racing through storms with demigods.

They entered the caves, where Mason and Dave already worked their way through a pack of beers. Tempest grimaced as Christie paraded her around like a doll, while Mason's eyes widened as he caught sight of her.

"Tempest, you look... wow."

Christie beamed proudly. "Didn't I do a great job?"

Mason nodded, while even Dave's eyes rolled over her approvingly.

"You look incredible."

"Boys, save some compliments for me, please." Christie giggled and placed her hand in Dave's, before flashing Tempest a grin. "We'll give you two some time alone. I'm sure you'll want to thank your knight in shining armor."

Christie shot Tempest a knowing smile, before dragging Dave into the darkness of the caves. Tempest's heart sank as she found herself alone with Mason once more. An awkward silence descended, and she glanced at his bruises from his fight with Zed.

"I'm sorry about your face."

He shrugged. "That guy is just lucky you stepped in when you did. I'd have made him pay." He laughed bitterly and shook his head. "So much for being a tough biker. He was saved by a girl."

Another spark of anger raced through Tempest, and she forced herself to take a breath. "I don't think that has anything to do with it..."

"I knew those bikers were bad news. Did you see that woman with the purple Mohawk? As if she's going to find a husband looking like that."

"I thought it suited her. And besides, I doubt Ixion's worried about finding a husband."

"Call me old fashioned, but I like my women looking more... normal. Like you."

Normal? Tempest shuddered at the thought. Zed would never have called her normal. And besides, what was normal about the inches of makeup Christie had caked on her face?

"You know the real problem isn't the bikers." Mason took another swig of his beer as he continued. "It's that awful dive bar and the witch who runs it. If she didn't welcome them, they wouldn't come here at all."

"Mary? She's not a witch—"

"She's an oddball, and she doesn't belong in this town. At her age, she should rest at home with her feet up, not listen to rock music and run a dive bar. It's indecent."

"Just because she's different doesn't mean there's anything wrong with her."

"It sets a bad example to the other women." Mason took another gulp of his beer, and his eyes narrowed. "Maybe that uncle of yours can talk some sense into her. Tame her a little."

Tempest felt her spark of anger take hold. Mason wanted women to be tame, to be meek. She thought of Zed, of how he had encouraged her to embrace her inner power. He would never have wanted to tame her. He only wanted to set her free.

"Anyway, let's not let the Stormchasers ruin our evening." Mason put his hand in hers and grinned. "Not when we have the entire place to ourselves."

Mason drew himself closer, until she could feel his breath on her skin. His closeness made her feel claustrophobic, and she struggled to breathe. She cursed as a pounding headache settled within her skull, and black spots bloomed in her vision.

"I think I need to get some fresh air."

"Don't tell me you're going to run out on me again." Mason flashed her a smile and moved in closer. "We can take it slow, if that's what you like?"

Tempest tried to swallow, but her throat was too dry. She tried to step back, to move away from Mason, but his grip remained firm. Her migraine throbbed in her skull, growing in power like the darkest clouds of a thunderstorm.

"Come on, Tempest. I can give you everything you've always wanted. All you need to do is take the leap."

Tempest looked into Mason's eyes as he moved in closer. Eyes that were ordinary. Eyes that failed to stir her heart. Eyes that had grown dull from a lifetime of looking at the ground, and never at the sky. She thought of Zed. Of how his eyes had glimmered with the promise of adventure. They were eyes that sparkled with magic. Eyes that sent sparks racing through her heart. Her stomach lurched, and she drew a breath as the truth dawned on her.

She had made a terrible mistake.

The realization struck her like a bolt of lightning. She didn't know about fated mates, but she knew that Zed had brought more magic into her life than a lifetime in this town could. She needed to make a leap, just like Arthur had done. She needed to throw caution to the wind, and follow her heart. Despite the danger, despite the doubts in her mind, she couldn't let Zed leave.

Tempest pulled her hand from Mason's, and shifted backwards as he moved in for a kiss. His cheeks reddened in embarrassment, and a flicker of annoyance ran across his face.

"Playing hard to get won't work on me. Come on, I can give you the life you always wanted."

He took a step forward, but Tempest took two backwards.

"I've realized something, Mason. I don't think I want that life. I don't want safety. I don't want to spend the rest of my life in this town. And I certainly don't want to be *tamed*."

A cool wind blew into the cave, refreshing her with the scent of the storm outside. Tempest inhaled its invigorating scent and felt its call to adventure flow through her. She turned to leave, but gasped as Mason grabbed her hand.

"Why would you turn me down, Tempest? I'm offering you everything you could want. Is there someone else?" His eyes widened as realization struck him. "You're going to choose *him*?"

For a moment, pure rage flickered across his face. And Tempest knew that whilst she had nothing to fear from Zed, she had plenty to fear from a small-minded man with wounded pride. Christie raced into the cavern, her face pale as Mason's voice echoed around the walls.

"What's going on here?"

Mason turned to her, his eyes narrowed with fury. "Why don't you ask Tempest? She's the one turning me down."

"Tempest? What is this? What's going on?"

Tempest glanced between Mason and Christie. They both wanted to change her into someone ordinary. Someone lifeless and dull, just like them. And she realized that she was anything but ordinary.

"I'm sorry, Christie, but I don't want this any more. I don't want this life. I want adventure. I want excitement. I want magic.
"

"Where are you going?" Christie's eyes widened as Tempest took another step towards the mouth of the cave. "Tempest, if you dare leave again, that's it. We're finished. You'll have nothing, you hear me, nothing!"

Tempest looked at her supposed friend, and at the man she'd been set up with. People who didn't love her for who she was, but what they could turn her into. She shook her head and marched to the surface.

"Tempest! Where do you think you're going?"

At this, she smiled.

"I'm going to ride with the storm."

15

—·—

Tempest revved her engine, knowing she had no time to waste. She pressed herself flat to her bike and took hairpin corners at breathtaking speed as she raced up the mountain tracks. She glanced at the sky, where the storm drifted into the distance. There was little time. But she still had a chance.

Tempest pushed the throttle to the max and raced up the rocky tracks. The road became a blur as she sped across the mountain. She had to stop him from leaving. She had to find him in time.

She came to a screeching halt and braced herself as gravel sprayed in the air. Tempest turned to the cabin, to see it swathed in darkness. The Stormchasers were gone, and Zed's bike was missing. She cursed and slammed her fist on her handlebars. She was too late.

A gust of wind howled through the valley, carrying the distant sound of thunder. But Tempest's breath grew short as she heard another sound within it. Motorcycle engines. Her eyes widened, and she looked at the mountain peaks. A flickering, pulsing light radiated on the mountaintop as the last of the storm raged above. Which meant she still had a chance.

She revved her engine once again and raced to the peaks. The light faded as she climbed, the gentle winds replaced with a howling storm. Lightning angrily forked through the sky while gale force winds struck her with a savage power. The storm raged across the mountain, trying to disorient her and scare her away. But she was stronger this time. She wouldn't allow herself to become lost in the storm. She wanted to be part of it.

Tempest sped across the mountain, following the storm to where it raged strongest. But her heart sank as the eye of the storm drifted further away, towards its next destination. She revved her engine to the max, but the storm was faster, and grew more distant by the minute.

She looked down as something gleamed on her handlebars. A blue button that shone in the storm's light. The 'thrill' that Dash had promised her. With one last glance at the retreating storm, Tempest drew a deep breath, and pressed the button.

Her eyes widened as a sonic boom blasted behind her, and she soared across the mountain. She clutched onto her handlebars and glanced at the speedometer as it shot upwards, barely able to keep up with her. A blue flame blasted from her exhaust pipe, propelling her along the rocky track. Of course Dash would think it was a good idea to fit a rocket launcher onto her bike. What could possibly go wrong with that?

The world became a blur as Tempest's bike reached impossible speeds. Her knuckles turned white as she gripped onto her handlebars and raced past boulders and steep drops, the eye-watering speed making the journey even more perilous than usual.

It was dangerous. It was reckless. There were a million reasons she should turn back. And yet, as Tempest raced into the center of the storm, she realized it was the ride of her life.

Tempest looked at the skies above as the flashes of lightning intensified and sped overhead like shooting stars. She searched for the golden-hued lightning, but felt her heart sink as it was nowhere in sight. Anxiously, she raced deeper into the storm to search for him.

"Zed!"

She called his name with all of her might. But the winds continued to howl and peals of thunder boomed overhead, drowning out her call.

"Zed, come back! Please!"

Tempest called out his name again and again. But her call went unanswered. The blue flames sputtered out from her exhaust, until her bike slowed and the storm drifted into the distance.

"No, no! Please, come back. I want to take the leap. I'm ready! Please, don't leave me here."

Tempest's heart sank as the storm drifted into the valley beyond. Her bike came to a stop at the precipice of the mountain, reaching the end of the track. Zed had gone.

"Zed!"

Her call echoed across the valley and into the distance beyond. She freed herself of the doubts in her mind, and called his name with the power of her heart. But as the clouds lifted, revealing patches of clear sky, she knew she was too late.

The Stormchasers were gone.

Tempest's spirits sank as she gazed at the clear skies above. Zed had offered her a life of magic and adventure, but she'd been too scared to take the risk. And now she was stuck here, in this small-town, with her equally small-minded friends. And she would never see him again.

Tears of frustration stung Tempest's eyes. Perhaps people like her didn't get to experience magic and adventure. Perhaps she'd been wrong about this whole thing.

Her breath faltered as something stirred in the air. She looked around in wonder as the currents of the wind changed direction, and the surrounding breeze grew stronger. The sky darkened once again and thick clouds billowed overhead. Tempest drew a shaky breath, and a small flicker of hope ignited within her.

"Zed?"

The clouds darkened, and the wind gathered strength until it howled around her. Golden lightning flashed in the sky and struck the rocks nearby. Peals of thunder blasted in the heavens like war drums, and shook the ground beneath her. Wind and rain spiraled around her, until she was caught in the center of a dark swirling storm.

The flashes of golden lightning grew stronger, like shooting stars in the night sky. But despite the strength of the storm, Tempest knew she had nothing to fear. She watched the golden lightning, and instinctively knew it was him, and him alone. With a deep breath, she closed her eyes and spread her arms to embrace the storm.

The storm raged around her. The rain removed the thick layers of makeup Christie had forced her to wear, while the wind returned her hair to its natural wild state. She let the rain drench her clothes until they clung to her skin, let the wind caress her body, let the rumble of the thunder vibrate through her. Tempest reached out to the storm and pulled its caressing touch closer. She felt it solidify, and drew her body against it. She felt his breath in the wind and inhaled his scent of leather and motorcycle oil.

It was him. Zed had returned. And she would never let him go again.

A flash of lightning filled the air as the wind solidified, until Zed emerged from the storm, his golden eyes gleaming in the darkness. Tempest drew him to her and pressed her lips to his. He embraced her with a passion that burned through his being, until she lost herself in the kiss. Sparks leaped from their lips, sending waves of pleasure rippling through her body and down to the base of her spine. It was a kiss that swept her away. A kiss that held the primal power of the storm. A kiss that told her life would never be the same again.

Tempest gasped as Zed's hands roamed her body. The winds caressed her, guided by his masterful touch as he removed her clothing, until their rain-slicked bodies met. Like the storm clouds above, a pressure grew within her, and begged to be released. She held Zed to her, this man, this god, in her desire to be swept away by his storm.

She sank backwards onto the ground below. The pair roamed each other's bodies, exploring with their hands, their lips, their tongues. She savored the taste of his skin, the fresh rain of the storm mixed with the salty taste of his sweat, and gasped as small sparks raced across their bodies. She pressed herself closer to him as his hands explored her, teasing her, building her up into the crescendo of the storm, until she could take no more.

Tempest mounted him, kissing him fiercely as she opened herself up to the storm. For the first time, she threw away the shackles of fear that had kept her chained for so many years, and unleashed the wild spirit inside of her. She let herself become one with the storm. She let herself be free.

Tempest looked into Zed's eyes, and marveled at the golden sparks of lightning held within them. She pressed her lips to his as the pressure of the storm grew within her, like giant clouds ready to burst with rainfall. She was ready.

Tempest gasped as she lowered herself onto him, and saw his eyes burn with the intensity of his pleasure. She moved slowly at first, savoring every feeling, every sensation, until she lost herself to the power of the storm. His hands grasped hers and they clung to one another, as if they were the last two souls left in the world.

Zed raised himself and laid her backwards as he explored her with his body, roaming deeper and deeper. She gasped as his hands teased her, and sent shimmering sparks cascading across her skin. His mouth found hers again, and she clung to him as their love-making became more frenzied. Rain poured over her skin like a thousand kisses, each droplet charged with electricity that sent tingling sensations rippling through her body.

Tempest held Zed's gaze as the storm raged around them. The golden sparks radiated in the storm's light, burning brighter with each second. She looked deep into those magical eyes as the pressure inside of her built, until she reached the point of no return.

She cried out as waves of pleasure exploded through her body. Lightning filled the sky as Zed arched his back and roared out, his golden eyes ablaze in the storm. The winds tore around them, carrying their cries of passion into the valley below, the sounds of their love-making echoing through the mountain like peals of thunder.

Tempest clung to his body, gasping for breath. A gentle rain fell from the sky, until their skin glistened like marble in the storm's light. Her lips found his, and she lost herself in a deep kiss once more. The storm had consumed her, raged within her, had set her free. And as she looked into Zed's eyes, she knew that life would never be the same again.

Zed laced his fingers through hers, and he kissed her neck tenderly. Tempest gasped with pleasure as electricity flickered from his lips and he hardened once more. The winds gathered speed around them, and his eyes burned with passion as he drew himself to her.

She was part of the storm now. And she was ready to be blown away again.

16

―・―

Tempest gazed into the golden eyes before her. They glowed serenely, like the sky after a storm. She reached up and drew Zed to her, her heart fluttering at the thrill of his lips on her own. She breathed him in, reliving every moment of their evening together. The sensation of his skin on hers, as they'd succumbed to their passion on the mountaintop. The sparks that had flown between them as they'd ridden back to his cabin. The peaceful hours they'd spent together, in calm and blissful serenity as the worst of the storm passed. She sighed as their lips parted, and he rolled out of the bed.

"Come with me."

Tempest pulled his leather jacket over her bare shoulders and followed Zed into the living room of the cabin, where a pile of fur throws, candles and wine awaited. He handed her a glass, and she savored the rich taste of wine on her lips. Together, they sat by the window and gazed at the glorious sight before them. Now that the worst of the storm had passed, they had a clear view over the valley and into the great vista that lay beyond the town.

"This is my favorite part of the storm. Once the darkness clears, and the light returns."

"It's beautiful."

"People always see the destruction in storms, but never the beauty that comes afterwards." Zed sipped his wine as he gazed at the view before them. "After the darkness of a storm always comes light. A light that brings change, hope, new beginnings."

"I've never thought of it that way." Tempest watched as the storm cleared, and inhaled the scent of fresh rain. "I've always loved storms. Being in them, seeing them take hold and grow in power. They always reminded me of Mom." She closed her eyes, and placed her hand to her necklace. "Sometimes, I can still sense her in the storm. I can smell her perfume in its breeze."

"She sounds like an interesting woman."

"She was a free spirit. Someone who played by her own rules and refused to be tamed. But one night, she left, and never returned." Tempest glanced at the heart-shaped locket on her necklace, forever missing its other half. "After she disappeared, I fought against every similarity I had to her. I vowed I would stay here and make a life for myself. But it's been holding me back. The fear of leaping into the unknown almost stopped me from being with you."

Zed placed his hand to hers. His fingers brushed her skin, and golden sparks raced between them. Tempest marveled as the sparks crackled around her, bathing her skin in golden light. She turned to him, a million questions forming on the tip of her tongue.

"Who are you, Zed? *What* are you?"

Zed turned and pulled a photo from the wall, the one Tempest had seen before. She studied the group of men in the photograph, their eyes radiating with an otherworldly power.

"They call us the Sons of Olympus. Descendents of the Greek gods, who walk the earth with the gifts of our ancestors. These men are like brothers to me, each of us descended from different gods. Every one of us is blessed, and cursed, by the powers of our forefathers."

"And the Stormchasers... they're all descended from gods too?"

Zed nodded. "There were many gods who claimed the storm as their own. Aeolus, Astrape, Bronte. They had many children. And those children became the Stormchasers."

"And you? Who are you descended from?"

At this Zed smiled. "I'm descended from the man himself. Zeus."

Tempest drew a bewildered breath. She might not have the longest dating history in the world, but she was pretty certain that spending the night with Zeus' great-grandson wasn't an everyday occurrence for most people.

"The storm gods blessed us with their greatest powers. The ability to control storms. To ride across the skies, and race across the world in pursuit of adventure." Zed looked at the chain tattoo on his wrist. "But we've inherited their curse, too."

"What curse?"

"As the number of Stormchasers grew, so did the in-fighting. The heavens themselves nearly fell from those who sought to claim Zeus' throne for themselves. And so he cursed the Storm-chasers, forcing us to ride in packs, to work together rather than against one another. He hoped it would force us to build a better world for ourselves, and for a while, it did. But there were always those who used the curse for their own gain."

He ran a finger along the tattoo and the sparks in his eyes faded. "Every gang of Stormchasers is ruled by an alpha. We're bound to them, forced to submit to their will, and lend them our strength. The most respected alphas have used their position to bring peace, to build vast cities in the sky, to unite us. But there are others who grow corrupted by the power. Those who use it for their own destructive means. And we have no choice but to follow them."

"And Seth is your alpha."

"It should have been me. As a descendent of Zeus, I was next in line to be alpha. But my father... he had an unexpected fall when out on a ride. I was too young to take the position, and Seth claimed the power for himself. And ever since, he's undone everything my father stood for." Zed's eyes hardened, while dark shadows bloomed within. "His hatred of earth-bounds means he wants us to return to the old ways. Every year, he grows more powerful, and the storms get more destructive. And this scar is proof that there's nothing I can do to stop him."

"What happened?"

"With the power he drew from the gang, I was no match for him. He left me with this scar as a warning to anyone who dared to challenge him again. And I was one of the lucky ones." Zed ran a finger along the thin scar on his cheekbone and sighed. "There have been others who have contested his leadership. And when they failed, he imprisoned them within the deepest recesses of the earth, so they would never see the sky again."

A peal of thunder echoed in the distance. Zed looked mournfully across the valley, before he continued.

"It's the worst kind of death imaginable for a Stormchaser. Every moment we're separated from the sky is agony. The pain makes Stormchasers go mad, until our powers and bodies fail."

Tempest placed a hand on his. "I'm so sorry, Zed."

"Since then, I've been forced to follow Seth's orders. For all my talk of freedom, I'd resigned myself to living a life serving him. I abandoned my humanity and gave into my savage nature, until I became lost in the storm's darkness. But all that changed when I met you." Zed's eyes glimmered with hope as he turned to her. "You were the earth-bound who stopped the storm."

But despite the warm glow in Zed's eyes, Tempest could see the shadows remain.

"What's wrong?"

"Seth has rules for the Stormchasers, and this breaks all of them." Zed sighed, and he gazed at the skies glumly. "He insists we live as lone wolves, to strengthen ourselves by avoiding attachments. And his hatred of earth-bounds puts us in even more danger. If he knew about us, there's no telling what he'd do."

"Then he won't find out. It can be our secret."

"There's only so long I can fight against his will. Even now, I can feel his hold over me, calling me to return to the storm." Zed watched the wind as it raced across the valley, as if summoning him into the horizon beyond. "I can hold the storm here for a while. Long enough to buy us some time. But with every minute that passes, I'll grow weaker, and Seth will get more suspicious. And sooner or later, he'll find out."

"I can take care of myself." But a warning look from Zed told Tempest she'd be no match for a superpowered demigod. "What if I became a Stormchaser?"

"Only those descended from the gods can become Storm-chasers. And even then, such a feat is highly dangerous." Remorse lingered in Zed's eyes as he turned to her. "You and I are from two different worlds. Worlds that aren't supposed to collide."

Tempest's heart sank as she thought about Dash's belief in fated mates. Only the gods would pair up a Stormchaser and an earth-bound who could never be together. Already, she'd had quite enough of the gods and their twisted sense of humor.

"Well, the gods haven't met someone like me before. We'll find a way for this to work." She turned to Zed and smiled. "We just need to follow our hearts, remember?"

"It's dangerous, and reckless, and breaks all the rules." A flicker of light glimmered in Zed's eyes and he drew himself closer. "But maybe together, we can make the leap."

Zed pressed his lips to hers, until she lost herself in the feeling of his touch and the richness of the wine on his lips. Tempest inhaled his intoxicating scent and bit her lip in anticipation as his hands reached for her under the furs.

She might not know much about fated mates, but she'd never felt this way about anyone before. This man had brought magic and adventure into her life, and she would find a way to be with him.

But as his hands roamed her body, she lost track of all thoughts. She pulled her god to her, ready to live in the moment and leave her troubles for another day.

17

Tempest beamed as she tidied the library. She felt giddy, as if she was walking on air, while sunshine radiated out of every pore. She danced around as she placed books on the shelves and waved in greeting to Arthur as he emerged from the stockroom.

"Tempest! You're early." Arthur cleaned his spectacles, before looking at her with disbelief. "You're never early. And you certainly have a spring in your step."

It was true. Everything felt different this morning. Tempest felt as though she'd gained a clarity she'd never had before. She even looked different. For the first time, she'd embraced her wild hair rather than battle against it, and used what little makeup she owned to create a dark and smokey eye. Dressed in her mother's leather jacket, she looked daring, she looked dangerous, and she finally felt like she was herself.

Tempest smiled at Arthur and looked across the road, where a bouquet of flowers stood proudly displayed in the window of Mary's bar.

"I could say the same to you."

Arthur beamed. "We're going on another date tonight. I suppose it's silly at my age, but I feel like a love-struck teen all over again. I just wish I hadn't waited so long. But now we have the rest of our lives to spend together."

Tempest smiled, but a stab of heartache flowed through her. Despite her happiness, she knew her time with Zed grew shorter by the day. She returned to the counter and studied the pile of books before her, knowing she had no time to waste.

"More mythology for you again, Tempest?"

"I borrowed them from Mary. I was hoping for something, anything..." She cursed and shook her head. "But they're no help at all."

"Well, what are you looking for?"

Tempest drew a deep breath, unsure of how much to tell Arthur. He'd never been one to approve of biker gangs, and certainly not those of the supernatural kind.

"It doesn't matter."

Arthur looked at the books, then at Tempest, and his mustache quivered suspiciously.

"I've seen that look before. It's the same look your mother had all those years ago." Arthur held her gaze, as if deciding what to say, before he sighed. "I know about the Stormchasers, Tempest. About who they really are."

Tempest's eyes widened in surprise. "Why didn't you say anything?"

"Because I knew the moment I did, your curiosity would get the better of you, and you'd throw yourself into danger to find out more." Arthur's mustache quivered, and he shook his head. "I'll tell you the same thing that I told your mother back then. People like us don't belong in their world. You've read enough mythology to know that things never turn out well for mortals who interfere with the gods."

"But what if there was a way for me to join them? What if I could become a Stormchaser?"

Arthur's eyes widened, and he adjusted his glasses. "Tempest..."

"Mythology is filled with love stories between mortals and gods. I know it's risky, but I'm sure I'm not the first to want to try." Tempest sighed and closed the book before her. "But there's nothing in these books that helps. Nothing at all. It's hopeless."

"Perhaps that's for the best. I know you and Zed are happy, but are you really ready to become a Stormchaser?" Arthur sighed sadly and shook his head. "It's one thing to want adventure, but quite another to spend your life chasing after the storm. To never rest in one place. To be at the mercy of their leader your entire life. It's not a decision to take lightly."

"Hey, you're the one who encouraged me to take the leap."

"This is different, Tempest. If you became one of them, you'd be forced to follow that awful alpha of theirs. No, if Zed truly cares for you, then he wouldn't want that life for you. He'd want you to be free."

"Zed doesn't think it's even possible. He thinks only those descended from the gods can become Stormchasers."

Arthur visibly relaxed and nodded. "Quite right too."

He turned to leave, but Tempest kept her eyes fixed on him.

"You said Mom knew about the Stormchasers, too." Arthur froze on the spot and avoided her gaze as she spoke. "Did she ever find out anything? Anything that might help?"

Arthur cleared his throat and busied himself with rearranging the first editions.

"I'm sorry, Tempest. There are some adventures that mortals aren't meant to go on. Perhaps it's best to stay here, where it's safe." He forced a weak smile. "Maybe Zed can visit."

Tempest sighed as Arthur left to tidy the window display. She'd been certain she would find a way for her and Zed to be together. That she would find some clue, some magical loophole, some way to break Seth's hold over him. But there was nothing. She felt like a ball and chain, tying Zed to the earth when he should be free to roam the skies. What she needed right now was a miracle.

She looked at Arthur once more as he busied himself with the display. He glanced at her uneasily, and his mustache quivered uncontrollably. Perhaps she was imagining things, but she couldn't help but get the feeling he was hiding something...

The doorbell rang, pulling Tempest from her thoughts. Her eyes widened as Mason strolled in, leaving a trail of dusty footprints behind him. He flashed her an apologetic smile and held out a bouquet of flowers like a peace offering. Arthur looked from him to Tempest and sighed knowingly.

"I'll be in the back. I'm sure there's some stock somewhere that needs checking." Arthur frowned at the handprint smear Mason had left on the door. "Call me if you need anything. And keep the first editions away from those sooty hands."

Tempest's stomach churned as Mason stepped closer. He handed her the flowers, and smiled apologetically. The sickly smell of the bouquet cloyed in her nostrils, and a feeling of nausea swept through her.

"I'm sorry for how I behaved last night. I was a jerk."

Tempest's eyes narrowed. "Yeah, you were."

"Why don't you let me take you out for dinner to make up for it? A real date, away from the others. We can take it as slow as you like."

Tempest shook her head. "I meant what I said. We're not right for one another. We're too different."

"Too different? Tempest, we're perfect for one another."

"No, we're not. I want to travel, to see new things, to have adventure. And you want to stay here."

"That's nonsense. This is just a phase. You'll change your mind, sooner or later."

"No, Mason. This is who I am. I'm not someone who wants to be... tamed."

Mason's jaw clenched. "Look, most girls in this town wouldn't turn me down."

"Then maybe you should take them out on a date."

"But I chose you. I can give you everything you want. Stability, marriage, kids. It's what every woman wants."

Tempest drew a deep breath as a spark of anger raced through her body. She wasn't sure if she wanted any of those things. But she was sure of one thing. She certainly didn't want them with Mason.

The doorbell rang again, until the smell of hairspray and coffee wafted into the library.

"There you are. Would it kill you to answer my calls, Tempest?" Christie glanced between Tempest and Mason and smiled with relief. "Thank goodness. Have you two put an end to this silly fight?"

But Mason's scowl deepened. "It turns out Tempest meant what she said last night. She's not interested in me at all."

Christie glanced at Tempest in bewilderment. "What? Tempest, don't be ridiculous. Think about this."

"I have thought about it. If you want to find Mason a girlfriend so badly, perhaps you should date him."

Christie's cheeks blushed. "What's gotten into you? You're acting strange. You're not at all yourself."

"Maybe I'm exactly who I should be. Maybe, for the first time, I'm following my heart, rather than listening to the doubts in my head."

Christie took another step closer, her perfectly painted face narrowing into a formidable glare. "Tempest, listen to me. You can't just walk away from everything. You have a life here."

"But it's not the life I want. Perhaps I'd rather take a risk and leap into the unknown."

"We've been over this. You should keep your feet firmly on the ground, not get swept away by some dream." Christie placed her hands on her hips in exasperation. "Just what is this magical adventure you're so willing to throw everything away for?"

Tempest's breath faltered as the doorbell cheerfully announced another visitor. Her stomach lurched as Zed entered the library, his smile fading as the others turned to him. Christie spluttered on her morning coffee, whilst Mason's face turned a shade of purple.

"*Him*? You've chosen him instead of me?"

Mason drew in a shaky breath, while Christie's face paled.

"Oh Tempest, tell me this isn't true."

Zed loitered in the doorway awkwardly. "Maybe I should leave."

"No." Mason shot Tempest a look of rage. "I'll leave, since I'm not wanted."

Mason shouldered past Zed as he stormed out of the library, while Christie chased after him, calling out to him as he marched down the street.

Tempest buried her face in her hands, while Zed wrapped his arms around her.

"I'm an awful person."

"Hey, you're not an awful person. You should be free to live the life you want."

"I just wish I didn't have to hurt people in the process."

Zed sighed and gazed at her with his beautiful eyes. "Sometimes things get broken in the storm. But after the darkness of a storm always comes light. Everything will be okay."

He kissed Tempest's head and drew her closer to him. Maybe he was right. Perhaps this was all just part of the storm. But right now, all Tempest could see was the destruction she was causing.

And as she felt Zed's arms around her, she couldn't help but wonder. What would be left once the storm blew over?

18

— • —

"**O**pen your eyes."

Tempest looked in surprise as Zed's motorcycle stood before her. It gleamed in the daylight, a powerful monster of a machine, and as large as a small horse. Zed broke into a smile and patted the bike affectionately.

"I thought you could come for a ride with us. Seth's out of town, and I figured it would take your mind off things."

Tempest glanced at the giant bike uneasily. "Why can't I ride my bike?"

"We're going for a special kind of ride. One that only Storm-chasers can go on."

Tempest's breath faltered as Zed's eyes sparkled. She could barely dream of what adventures awaited. She ran her hand over the bike, and marveled as it hummed with energy and life. It was as if it was as excited about the ride as she was.

"Are you sure about this, Zed?" Ixion scowled as she approached, while Dash peered out from behind her. "We wouldn't want an earth-bound tarnishing the Stormchaser name by screaming around every corner we take."

Tempest folded her arms, and flashed Ixion a defiant grin. "Oh, I'm up to it."

Ixion nodded and a flicker of a smile crossed her lips. "Good. I was hoping you'd get over your fall. And this is the best way to do it. Dash, ready the bikes."

Dash let out a sharp whistle. A rev of an engine filled the street as two bikes raced towards him, driving themselves through the streets as if by magic.

Zed raised an eyebrow at the sight. "Another new modification, Dash?"

Dash shrugged and patted his bike affectionately, as if it was a noble steed. "I figured it saved on parking."

As the Stormchasers readied themselves, Tempest glanced at Zed's bike uneasily. It was so big, she wasn't even sure she'd be able to climb onto it, let alone steer it. She placed a hand on the bike, and sprang backwards as it roared to life.

"Do you really expect me to ride this thing?"

Zed roared with laughter and jumped into the saddle. "No one rides this bike but me. Now hop on the back. We've got a storm to catch."

The Stormchasers mounted their bikes, and revved the engines in anticipation. As the gang readied themselves, they glanced at Tempest with a mixture of curiosity, of wariness, of intrigue. But none of them looked at her with Seth's resentment. She was safe in their company, and could enjoy the ride.

She grinned and clambered onto the back of the saddle, while Zed revved the engine. "Let's ride!"

The air filled with a cacophony of noise as dozens of engines roared to life. It was louder than Tempest had ever experienced, as if she were caught in the midst of a thunderstorm. She looked around in wonder and saw Mary give her a friendly wave of support. Before she could wave back, Zed revved the engine, and they took off at full speed.

Tempest gasped as the wind struck her, taking her breath away. They were going fast. Really fast. But fear soon gave way to excitement as they sped through the streets.

They rode as a pack, the noise of the engines making Tempest feel as though she were shepherding the storm itself. She held onto Zed and eased into the ride, allowing the wind to tousle her hair. She caught her reflection in the shop windows as they sped past. She looked dangerous. She looked alive. She looked free.

They swerved around a corner, and Tempest screamed out with delight at their speed. Two of Christie's friends gawked at her from the sidewalk, and she couldn't help but burst into laughter at the terror on their faces. She gave them a cheery wave before Zed sped out of the town and into the plains.

Tempest marveled as they raced further out of the town than she'd ever been before, until the plains rose into the mountains. The winds grew stronger and the clear skies gave way to thick thunderclouds that flashed ominously overhead. Tempest held on tightly to Zed as they climbed higher and higher, until the storm thickened and the plains below disappeared out of sight.

"Okay, get ready for the jump!"

"Jump?"

Tempest looked ahead, and her eyes widened. They were heading straight for the mountain edge. It curved upwards into a makeshift ramp, ending with a sharp drop into a deep ravine below. She thought back to her fall and shook her head as fear flooded through her body.

"Are you kidding? There's nowhere to land. We'll be killed!"

"Don't you see it?"

Zed pointed to the sky, where the eye of the storm raged. Blinding flashes of lightning raced within the dark vortex, while powerful winds howled across the sky. Tempest's stomach lurched. If they didn't get electrocuted first, they'd fall to their deaths below.

As they approached the mountain edge, Dash hollered with excitement, while Ixion's eyes gleamed with anticipation. Something was up there. And as Tempest's nerves gave way to curiosity, she realized she was about to discover the secrets of the storm for herself.

"Do you trust me?"

Tempest glanced at the sheer drop to the abyss below. Her heart pounded in her chest, and she broke out into a cold sweat at the mere thought of the daredevil stunt. But she knew that this was her chance for adventure. Her chance to see another world. She just needed to make the leap. She nodded and Zed revved his engine.

Panic and fear flooded through her as they raced up the ramp. This was a mistake. There was nowhere for them to land. They would plummet into the ravine below. But despite Tempest's panic, Zed pulled on the throttle until the engine screamed with power. As the motorcycle left the slope, she knew it was too late to turn back.

Her screams echoed through the mountains as they soared in the air. The mountain track fell behind them, and the ravine below opened up like a gaping jaw ready to devour them. But as they neared the center of the storm, Tempest saw something else. Strong currents of wind spiraled within the eye of the storm, leading into its center like magical highways. Her eyes widened as the bike thudded onto a current of wind, as if landing on solid ground.

It was impossible. Tempest looked down and gasped as the motorcycle tires sat on the current of air, as if it were a solid road. They were suspended in the sky, held afloat by nothing more than the power of the wind. She glanced through the transparent road and her stomach lurched at the drop below.

"How is this possible?"

"The jetstreams are the highways of the gods." Zed's eyes gleamed in the storm's light. "There's no better way to travel."

Tempest looked in wonder at the makeshift road. She glanced ahead to see dozens of jetstreams form a path to the glowing center of the storm. It had more curves, hairpin bends and loops than any road she'd seen before. It was terrifying. And yet, a smile crossed her lips. She finally understood why this was the Stormchaser's playground. It was the perfect racetrack.

"Is this what you do in the eye of the storm? Race each other?"

Zed nodded and broke into a grin. "There's nothing else like it. It's a battle of strength and speed. Of courage and endurance. The storms are the best racetracks in the entire world."

"It's also deadly." Ixion pulled up next to them, the violet streaks on her motorcycle gleaming in the storm's light. "Don't let its beauty fool you, earth-bound. I've seen more than my fair share of Stormchasers take a corner too fast and fall."

A flash of turquoise burst into the sky as Dash appeared on the jetstream. "Don't listen to her, Tempest. She's just trying to spook you. Although watch out for the lightning. And for the torrential rain. And for the winds that can knock you off course..." Dash paused and turned to Zed. "On second thoughts, are you sure this is a good idea?"

"Enough!" Zed revved his engine. "We race to the finish line."

Tempest followed Zed's eyeline to the center of the storm, where the jetstreams led. Within it, lightning gathered into a pulsing orb that bathed the track in an ethereal light. It was as if it contained the very essence of the storm, and gleamed with its raw power. Tempest could feel its siren song echo through the winds, calling those brave enough to prove themselves on its tracks.

Ixion revved her engine, while violet sparks shot out of her Mohawk. "This time I'm going to win."

Dash grinned, and his eyes blazed with turquoise electricity. "Not if I beat you first!"

He revved his engine and zoomed past them, his bike blurring into a turquoise bolt of lightning that sped across the track.

"That's so typical of you, Dash! You're such a cheater!"

Ixion raced after him, her body transforming into a bolt of violet-hued lightning. Tempest watched as the bolts of lightning chased after one another, painting the sky in a beautiful blur. Zed turned to Tempest, and a smile flickered across his face.

"What do you say? Feel like giving them a real match?"

Tempest returned his grin as more Stormchasers joined the race. She marveled at the sights and sounds before her, as the sky filled with bolts of lightning of every color imaginable. She wrapped her arms around Zed and nodded.

"Let's do this!"

At once, Zed revved his engine, and they soared forwards, the track propelling them with a mind of its own. A golden light surrounded them, infusing Zed and his bike with its magnificent glow, and they raced ahead with a speed that took Tempest's breath away. Her heart pounded in her chest as they took hairpin bends with the speed of a fighter jet. She braced herself as they took another corner, and a flash of violet and turquoise appeared nearby.

"Nice of you to catch up with us, Zed," laughed Dash.

"I'm surprised the earth-bound hasn't insisted you return to the ground yet."

Tempest fixed Ixion with a glare. "The earth-bound intends on showing you both how this is done. Come on, Zed!"

Zed roared with laughter, and the four of them sped along the jetstream. The road ahead split into three branches, each veering off into its own daredevil course. Ixion revved her bike and took the track to the left, while Dash let out a cry of excitement and veered to the right. With a roar of his engine, Zed headed straight for the center, before he called to Tempest over the howling winds.

"Whatever you do Tempest, don't let go! And don't panic!"

"Why would I panic?"

Tempest's eyes widened as she saw the answer to her own question. The track before them curved upwards into the sky, until it curled in a giant loop. Her jaw dropped at the sight, and her stomach churned as she glanced at the drop below.

"Please tell me gravity doesn't apply to Stormchasers."

Zed revved his engine. "You're about to find out!"

They raced towards the loop, gathering speed as they soared upwards. Tempest cried out as they hit its peak, and felt the world lurch as they raced upside down in the sky. But as they began their descent, her screams of terror turned into cries of delight.

They soared forwards at an impossible speed, until they leaped from the track and towards the glowing center of the storm. Zed turned to her and grinned as the bike soared through the finish line, his skin bathed in the ethereal light that surrounded them. His eyes shone brighter than ever before, while lightning danced across his skin. As they sped through the light, Tempest saw him in his true form. He was a god.

Zed roared out with victory as they sailed across the finish line, before he took the jetstream down to the mountain top. He pulled sharply on the brakes, sending dust billowing behind them, until they spun to a stop, Ixion and Dash following close behind.

Silence fell across the mountain as, one by one, the Stormchasers descended from the sky, and cut their engines. The surrounding air grew still as the winds died down and the storm faded. The bikers turned to Tempest expectantly, and she felt a wild grin form on her face.

"That was incredible!"

The air filled with roars of joy and revelry as the Stormchasers shared her victory. Zed lifted Tempest into his arms and spun her in the air, before pressing his lips to hers. Tempest laughed with a carefree abandon she'd never felt before, and looked at the faces of the Stormchasers who cheered for her. Men and women she had once feared. And she realized that she'd never felt more at home.

Zed lowered her to the ground, and she ran a hand self-consciously through her windswept hair. "I must look like such a mess."

He ran his fingers through a stray silver lock of her hair and grinned. "No, Tempest. You look like a goddess."

Tempest returned his smile, and turned as Ixion approached, her usual scowl replaced with a grin of approval.

"Not bad for an earth-bound."

Dash glanced at Ixion incredulously. "Are you kidding? No earth-bound could do that. She has Stormchaser blood in her for sure. Maybe even enough to do the Trials."

Tempest felt the air change around her. An icy stillness descended, as both Ixion and Zed glared at the blue-haired Stormchaser.

"What are the Trials?"

Dash's cheeks turned crimson as he glanced warily at the menacing looks cast in his direction. He shook his long fringe over his eyes and avoided Tempest's gaze.

"Nothing. No, I must be mistaken. Very mistaken." His voice trembled, and he cowered under Ixion's furious scowl. "Is it me, or is it hot up here?"

Ixion rolled her eyes and mounted her bike once more. "The storm calls, Dash." She glanced at Tempest and revved her engine. "Ride well, earth-bound."

The two sped away in a blur of turquoise and violet light. Tempest watched the turquoise bolt of lightning race away, and wondered just what she'd stumbled across. She turned to Zed questioningly, but he revved his engine expectantly.

"Come on Tempest, we'll miss it if you don't hurry."

"Miss what?"

At this, Zed broke into a smile. "A chance to see real magic."

They sped across the mountain once more, before they jumped onto another jetstream and raced across the sky. They followed it higher and higher, beyond the storm, until the earth below faded away.

Tempest marveled as the air grew cooler, and a thick white mist surrounded them. She drew herself closer to Zed as they raced through it, and inhaled their combined scent of leather, of electricity, of adventure. Onwards they climbed, until the mist lifted, and the jetstream flattened into a wide plateau.

"Where are we?"

"We're at one of my favorite places in the world." Zed turned to her with a grin. "And we're just in time."

"For what?"

Tempest's eyes widened as the view cleared around her. The sky filled with a glorious sunset, painted with vivid hues of burned orange and gold, while the surrounding clouds turned to pink wisps of cotton candy. Tempest gasped at the beauty of it. They were higher than she'd ever been before, perched above the clouds with an uninterrupted panorama of the view below. It was as though they were on top of the world.

"It's beautiful."

As she marveled at the beauty of it all, she couldn't help but think about her mother. She wondered what she would have made of this. This was the magic she had always dreamed of. The adventure she had searched for. As a distant storm rolled in, Tempest inhaled a faint scent of her mother's perfume, still carried on the winds even after all this time.

She looked at the race-course below in wonder, as Stormchasers soared along the jetstreams. Tempest smiled as violet and turquoise bolts of lightning raced each other across the track, playfully weaving in and out of each other's path. It was beautiful.

"Dash and Ixion. They're together, aren't they?" Zed nodded, while Tempest thought of what Dash had once said. "Are they fated mates, too?"

At this, Zed smiled. "If you'd have asked me that before I met you, I'd have told you that Dash was nothing more than a hopeless romantic. But now I'm not so sure." Zed ran a finger along Tempest's hand, sending sparks dancing across her skin. "Legends say that every Stormchaser has a fated mate. Someone they're born to race through the skies with. When they're united, a bonded pair are stronger, faster, more powerful. No matter how dark the storm, they can always find each other. And that's exactly why Seth tries to keep us alone."

"He's trying to keep you weak on purpose?"

Zed nodded. "He lives in constant fear of being overthrown as alpha. And so he makes us live our lives in loneliness, to stop us from finding our fated mate. He spreads lies that love chains us down and makes us weak. But he's wrong."

As Tempest watched the violet and turquoise lightning race together, a feeling of melancholy swept through her. How could she and Zed be fated mates, when they were from worlds that didn't belong together?

Zed smiled sadly, as if reading her mind. "Close your eyes."

Tempest did so, and felt the surrounding air crackle with power. Zed's hand grew warm, and a pressure built in the air, until a peal of thunder echoed through the mountains below. Its power reverberated through her body, stirring something deep within her.

It was him. It was his call. And it was the most beautiful thing she'd ever heard.

"That's the sound of my thunder call. Every Stormchaser's is unique. If you follow it, you'll be able to find me, no matter how dark the storm." Zed looked deep into her eyes and smiled. "Only true fated mates can use it to find one another."

Her heart fluttered as the thunder call echoed through the sky once more. They might be from different worlds, but with this, she could always find him.

Tempest pressed her lips to his and kissed him with the passion that burned inside of her. She eased herself backwards against the leather seat of the motorcycle and smiled as she unzipped her jacket.

"You know, there's no one else around for miles. It's just the two of us here, on top of the world."

Zed watched her hungrily, and unbuttoned his jeans before she drew him to her. She kissed him once more, her body alive with carefree abandon as they lost their clothes and inhibitions.

The sky burned with the magical hues of the sunset, while the surrounding air flickered with the sparks that flew between them. Tempest held Zed's gaze, knowing that this moment was everything she had wanted. She pulled him to her and vowed she would never let him go.

19

—‎ · ‎—

Tempest looked across the bar in wonder. Oddities and trinkets lined every wall, while the air was filled with raucous laughter and the sound of clashing guitars. After all these years of seeing Mary's dive bar from the outside, she was finally here.

The bikers cheered as Zed returned with a tray of beers. Ixion slurped thirstily from one, before she wiped away the foam from her lips and turned to Tempest.

"It takes great strength to ride with the storm. I've seen many Stormchasers lose their nerve and fall. But you showed us that it doesn't matter if you're born an earth-bound or a Stormchaser. What matters is your spirit." Ixion broke into a rare smile. "You might be an earth-bound, but you have the heart of a Stormchaser."

Cheers erupted from the bikers. Tempest drank the foamy beer, savoring the taste as her newfound friends celebrated the ride. Zed wrapped his arms around her and swept her into a kiss.

"You were magnificent today, Tempest."

"It was incredible. To feel such speed, such power. I've never experienced anything like it." Her heart raced as she recalled the exhilaration of the ride. "I just wish I could have ridden it myself."

"It's one thing to experience it as a passenger. But it's quite another to ride it." Ixion shook her head at the mere thought. "I've seen some earth-bounds foolish enough to try. And they all end the same way."

Tempest turned as Mary and Arthur approached, grinning like a pair of love-struck teens. She repressed a giggle as Arthur glanced around the bar nervously. Between his tweed suit and his bookish looks, he couldn't look more out of place if he tried.

"Does the music have to be quite so loud in this place?"

Mary sighed and shook her head. "It's a metal bar. Of course it has to be loud!"

Arthur sighed and stuffed a pair of earplugs into his ears, before Mary marched him to the dancefloor. Zed took Tempest's hand into his own and grinned as he pulled her in the same direction.

"Come on earth-bound, let's see what you can do."

Tempest found herself swept up in a dance with Zed as the music blasted through the bar. They danced wildly, and moved across the dancefloor in a blur of sparks. The bikers danced around them, beer sloshing everywhere, while Arthur and Mary joined in, moving in their own unusual jig. Tempest marveled at the chaotic energy, at the cacophony of drums and guitars, at the joy that filled the air. It was as though she was caught in the center of a storm.

Tempest laughed with joy as she moved across the dancefloor, and watched friends old and new dance with each other. She drew herself closer to Zed, and gazed into his eyes as the revelry unfolded around them.

"I used to dream of adventure. Of excitement. Of magic. And because of you, I've found it." Tempest placed a hand to Zed's face, feeling the roughness of his stubble beneath. "You gave me the strength I needed to make the leap."

Zed smiled, but shook his head. "You were the earth-bound who stopped the storm. The mortal brave enough to ride with us. And you already had all the strength you needed. You just needed to learn to embrace it."

"I just wish it was enough. That I could join you in the skies." Tempest sighed, and glanced at the outline of his tattoo as it shimmered with light. "I wish that I was strong enough to become a Stormchaser, too."

"Tempest, you have more strength than any Stormchaser I've met." Zed held her gaze, and ran a hand through a silver lock of her hair. "I was lost before you, aimlessly drifting like a storm with no purpose. But you changed everything. You gave me purpose. You gave me strength. And I'll find a way for us to be together. Because my heart belongs to you."

Sparks raced across her skin as Zed pressed his lips to hers, sending a wonderful tingling feeling down to the base of her spine. But their kiss ended abruptly, and the golden sparks in his eyes flashed with warning.

"What's wrong?"

A gust of wind tore through the town, carrying with it a distant peal of thunder. Zed staggered backwards and placed a hand to his head, while his tattoo burned with a fiery glow, as if branding his skin. As the winds stilled once more, he drew a deep breath and forced a weak smile.

"It's nothing."

Tempest looked at the other Stormchasers and saw they suffered from the same pain. She listened to the distant thunder and recognized its fury with a cold fear.

"It's Seth, isn't it? He's calling you."

"It's fine. I can handle it."

"But for how long?" Tempest's heart sank as the sparks in Zed's eyes faded. "I wish Seth didn't have this hold over you. I wish we had more time."

"Hey, I'm still here right now, aren't I? And I'm stronger than the average Stormchaser. I can defy Seth for longer."

"And what happens when he finds out? What will he do to you then?"

"He can't do anything worse to me than leaving you."

"But Zed..."

Zed pressed his lips to hers and kissed her with a power that told her everything would be okay. That he would fight for her, and would find a way for them to be together. He wrapped his arms around her, telling her he would never let her go. It wasn't a kiss. It was a promise.

"Trust me. I'm not going anywhere."

Tempest placed a hand to her lips, savoring the kiss. But her doubts remained. Despite what Zed might say, he couldn't defy Seth forever. And she knew that once Seth discovered his betrayal, there would be hell to pay.

Tempest turned as a flash of blue raced across the bar. She saw Dash stand alone, separate from the revelry that unfolded around him. He glanced at her and retreated further into the shadows, as if hiding. But why?

As Zed headed to the bar for another round, Tempest spotted Dash's turquoise hair drifting further away into the crowd. She squeezed through the crowded dance floor and followed him as he retreated into a booth. His eyes widened as she approached, before he lowered his gaze to the floor.

"I'm under strict orders from Ixion not to talk to you." Dash sighed and his long blue fringe flopped over his eyes. "I suppose even this is against the rules."

"Why would Ixion forbid you from talking to me?" Tempest looked around to check they were alone, and lowered her voice to a whisper. "Is it because of what you said earlier? About the Trials?"

He peered from underneath his fringe and met her gaze. Tempest knew he was hiding something. Something big. She placed her hand on his arm and looked into his eyes.

"Please, Dash. If you know anything that might help, you have to tell me."

His eyes flashed with turquoise sparks. As he held Tempest's gaze, he let out a theatrical sigh and groaned in defeat.

"It's no use. I'm terrible at keeping secrets. They should never have trusted me with this."

"Then tell me, Dash. What are the Trials?"

He glanced at Ixion uneasily and lowered his voice. "You're not the first earth-bound to want to become a Stormchaser. Some want to be with us, some want to be us. And the Trials are there to determine whether they're worthy."

"You mean an earth-bound can become a Stormchaser?" Tempest looked at Dash in surprise. "So, there is a way?"

"Most of it's myth and fable, and I can't say I've heard of anyone succeeding. But if the rumors are true, some earth-bound are born with Stormchaser blood. Supposedly, if they race in the eye of the storm and cross the finish line, they'll complete the Trials." He paused and held her gaze. "And they would become a Stormchaser."

Tempest's eyes widened in shock. "But why wouldn't Zed tell me this?"

"Because we don't know if it's true. Even the gods think this is nothing more than a myth. There must be hundreds of earth-bound who have attempted the Trials, but I've never heard of a single one succeeding." Dash sighed, and his hair seemed to droop in defeat. "Zed didn't tell you because he wouldn't want his new girlfriend to go splat over nothing more than a rumor."

Tempest thought about their race along the jetstreams. Of the steep plummet down to the earth below. The thought of riding it by herself made her feel queasy enough, let alone riding it on nothing more than blind faith.

"But surely it's worth a try..."

"Tempest, you're more of a Stormchaser than half the gang put together. But there are some leaps that are too risky to make. And until we have proof that an earth-bound can complete the Trials, you need to stay on the ground." Dash paled as Ixion's purple Mohawk bobbed along the crowd, searching for him. "Look, I better go. Best to put this out of your mind, and not to mention this to Zed, okay?"

Without another word, Dash disappeared into the crowd. Tempest cursed as she watched him leave. What use was a myth

157

that not even the gods believed in? What she needed was proof. Something, anything, that told her she had a chance. She looked at the sky worriedly as another distant peal of thunder echoed through the town, and knew time was running out.

"You've fallen for him, haven't you?"

Tempest turned to see Mary watch her with her deep emerald eyes, her crow's feet wrinkling as she smiled warmly.

"It's no use, Mary. Sooner or later, Zed will have to return to the storm." Tempest sighed sadly, and felt her heart sink. "Stormchasers and earth-bounds aren't supposed to be together. It's impossible."

"My dear, nothing is impossible. And I believe you stand a better chance than most at keeping up with the Stormchasers."

"And why's that?"

Mary smiled as she turned to Tempest. "Because, my dear, your mother was one."

20

—·—

T empest looked at the photograph of her mother. Her eyes sparkled, bursting with life as she sat astride her motorcycle. She was a woman who had spent her life drifting from town to town, never settling in one place. A woman who suffered from a debilitating condition every time she ignored the call of the storm. A woman who was no woman at all, but a Stormchaser.

"How could you tell her, Mary? I specifically asked you not to discuss her mother."

"Tempest has a right to know. It's not right to keep this from her, Arthur."

"But you know what this means. You know what could happen. And I'll never forgive you if she falls."

"But what if she flies? This is a part of who she is, whether you like it or not."

"This could end in disaster, Mary. You should never have gotten involved!"

"Enough!"

Tempest's cry cut through the library. All eyes turned to her in surprise as she fixed Arthur with a steely glare.

"You lied to me. You told me my mother ran away. And you…" she turned to Zed, who stood brooding by the window. "You told me there was no way to become a Stormchaser." Tempest folded her arms and glared at both of them. "I want answers. Now."

Arthur's mustache trembled, and he shook his head. "I never meant to lie to you, Tempest. Everything I've done, I've done to protect you. To keep you safe."

"No more lies, Arthur. Tell me the truth about Mom. Tell me who she really was."

He sighed and removed his spectacles, using his tie to clean them. "Your mother was a mortal, just like me. But she always had a sensitivity to storms. There were the migraines, of course, but other symptoms too. She could see things in the storms, and hear things in the winds, as if they spoke to her. She spent her life searching for the secret of the storms, until she learned of the Stormchasers and the Trials. She thought it was the opportunity she'd been waiting for. That finally, she could leave the earth behind and join the sky, where she belonged."

Arthur gazed out of the windows mournfully, and looked at the mountain peaks in the distance.

"We fought terribly the night she left. When I learned what she had planned, I raced to stop her. I begged her to turn back. I pleaded with her to stay and make this town her home. But she wouldn't listen." He shook his head, while his eyes glimmered with pain. "And so I did the best thing I could. I realized I couldn't stop her, but I could keep you safe. I kept you here, while your mother rode off into the storm. And I never saw her again."

"So she became a Stormchaser?"

"I don't know, Tempest. I saw her race from the mountain top and into the sky. I saw a brilliant flash of lightning. And then... nothing." Arthur sighed, and he moved away from the window. "For a while, I wanted to believe her. I prayed that she was riding in the skies, rather than face the dreadful alternative. But don't you think that if she'd succeeded, that if she'd become a Stormchaser, she'd have returned?"

Tempest's breath faltered, and she felt her hope fade. She turned to Zed, who brooded among the first editions.

"Well? Do you know what happened to her?"

"There are thousands of Stormchasers, Tempest. Hundreds of gangs scattered across the world. We can ask around, but it will take time." Zed's eyes filled with regret as he met her gaze. "Even if your mother had Stormchaser blood, the likelihood of her completing the Trials is slim."

"But it's possible."

"Tempest, we're talking about something that even the gods don't believe in. Until recently, I thought the Trials were nothing more than a myth. And I've certainly never heard of anyone completing them."

"Tell me about the Trials."

Zed clenched his jaw, but sighed in defeat. "The Trials are a test to determine those worthy of joining the Stormchasers. The myths say that those who want to become a Stormchaser must leap into the eye of a storm, race the track and be the first to cross the finish line."

"But that sounds simple. We did that today."

"Not just any storm will do. The storm we rode in today was a light breeze compared to those used for the Trials. I'm talking hurricane winds and clouds so thick you lose all sense of direction. Black rain that makes your tires slip at the slightest turn and lightning so intense it will blind you if it doesn't incinerate you first." Zed looked to the skies, then shook his head. "It's too dangerous, Tempest. I've seen too many earth-bounds perish in the attempt. And I won't let the same happen to you."

Mary looked out of the window, her emerald eyes reflecting in the glass. "Tempest's mother might have been born on the earth, but she belonged in the sky. I have no doubt she succeeded in the Trials. Sometimes, I can sense her in the winds, as if she's trying to find her way back here." She looked at Tempest and smiled. "You all underestimate Tempest's mother. And you underestimate Tempest too."

Tempest nodded in agreement. "Neither of you should have kept this from me. I can take care of myself, and I can make my own decisions." She turned to Arthur and felt her anger brew like a violent storm cloud. "I always thought Mom had abandoned me. That she'd left me here to pursue her own adventures. But this is different. She left to become the person she was supposed to be. And maybe I'm supposed to do the same."

"For all we know, your mother died trying." Arthur's mustache quivered with anger of his own. "This is why I never told you. Because I knew the call to adventure would be too great."

"But I can do it. I can make the leap. I can complete the Trials."

"No, Tempest. There's no proof your mother survived. You'd be making the leap on nothing but blind faith." Lightning flashed

162

in the sky beyond, and thunder rumbled through the library. "It's far too dangerous. I forbid you from entering the Trials, and I forbid you from seeing the Stormchasers again."

Tempest's anger flared in retaliation. "You don't get to decide what I do anymore. You can't keep me locked away in this library forever. I need real adventure. Real excitement. A real life. And this is my chance. What if I fly, Arthur?"

Thunder boomed across the town as he fixed her with a stern glare. "And what if you fall?"

Without another word, he stormed out of the library. Tempest trembled as Mary chased after him, and drew a shaky breath. She'd never argued with Arthur before, and had never seen him so angry. Hot tears stung her eyes as she vowed she would prove him wrong. She would make the leap, just like her mother had.

Zed approached her cautiously, and the sparks in his eyes faded to a soft glow. "I'm sorry, but Arthur is right. It's too great a risk. And even if you succeed, you'll have to follow Seth as your alpha. He'll never accept an earth-bound as one of his own."

"But it would mean we could be together. Don't you want that?"

"Of course I want that. I want it more than anything in the world. And I would do anything for it. I would put myself through any trial, throw myself into danger, fight for it with my last breath." Zed took her hand in his and met her gaze. "But I won't let you put yourself in danger."

Tempest snatched her hand away and fixed him with a scowl that even Ixion would approve of.

"I'm not some Princess who needs saving. I can make up my own mind, and fight for my own future." She drew a deep breath, until her anger faded. "And I want to do this. Not just for us, but for me. I want a life of magic, of adventure. I want to make the leap."

"Tempest, there's a million different ways this could go wrong. You need to be careful, you need to think..."

"If there's one thing I've learned from the Stormchasers, it's that I need to stop listening to the doubts in my head, and start following my heart." She stepped closer and looked deep into Zed's eyes. "Life is about making a leap into the unknown, and having the faith that you'll make it. You said that to me, once, remember? Let me do this, Zed. You just need to believe in me."

Golden sparks flickered in his eyes. When he spoke, his voice was barely a whisper.

"I'm scared of losing you, Tempest."

Tempest ran a hand through his hair as the storm raged outside. "Well, that makes two of us."

She placed her hand on her necklace and felt the edges of the heart-shaped pendant. It had served as a caution against leaping into the unknown for so many years. But now she realized it was a gift. A symbol of the importance of believing in herself, and taking a risk. She turned to Zed, and broke into a smile.

"I've made my decision. I want to do the Trials. I want to become a Stormchaser."

21

—*—

Tempest's heart raced as a peal of thunder echoed in the distance. She tried to distract herself by stacking the bookshelves, but clutched her stomach as it somersaulted nervously. She glanced at Arthur, who continued to sulk near the window display, and sighed. The air was heavy with an oppressive humidity that made her skin itch, while gray clouds hung moodily above the town. She looked at Arthur once more, who tried his best to avoid her gaze.

"Oh, come on, Arthur. You can't ignore me all day. Just say something. Anything."

"I don't have to say anything at all. You know what I think of your decision."

Tempest looked across the road to the dive bar, where Mary readied her yard, her emerald eyes unusually dimmed.

"It doesn't mean you should take it out on Mary."

Arthur snorted. "She should never have given you those books to start with. They gave you all sorts of ideas."

"But I thought that's why you opened this library. To give people ideas, and show them other worlds."

"That's different..."

"You told me it was time I made a leap. That I should pursue adventure. Real adventure."

"Well, I didn't mean this. There's adventure and then there's suicide." Arthur grumbled and shook his head. "Now, if you'll excuse me, I'm needed in the stockroom."

Tempest sighed and slumped by the counter. She should be excited. She'd made the biggest decision of her life. But as she ran her fingers along the edges of her necklace, she knew Arthur had a point. She had no idea if her mother had completed the Trials. She was staking everything on a leap of faith. And if she was wrong, she'd have a long way to fall.

A flash of blue and violet filled the street, followed by a blur of gold. Tempest smiled nervously as the Stormchasers waved to her. Behind their bravado, she could see that they were more on edge than usual, while the air around them crackled with tension. It was time.

Tempest grabbed her leather jacket and moved to the stockroom, where Arthur sulked amongst a pile of first editions.

"Arthur, it's time. Please, I don't think I can leave without your blessing."

Arthur shook his head. "I'm a man of logic, Tempest. A man of fact. What you're about to do... I can't give you my blessing. You're making the same mistake your mother did. You're following your heart, and not listening to your head."

"Arthur, please."

"You and Zed belong in different worlds. You've read enough books to know how relationships between mortals and gods end.

Sooner or later, the gods move on, and the mortals are left with nothing. I'm afraid nothing good will come of this."

"That's different. Zed's not like that."

Arthur laughed sadly. "Oh really? Look at him, Tempest. He's a Stormchaser, a being driven by his emotions, with impulses as changeable as the winds. A god who lives for the present and leaves a trail of destruction in his wake. Are you really so sure his feelings for you are nothing more than an impulse? Nothing more than a fleeting fancy? Are you really so willing to bet your future on it?"

Tempest recoiled and shook her head. Arthur was wrong. Zed had changed. She was sure of it.

"I've made my decision, whether you like it or not."

"This is what the Stormchasers do. They descend into towns and sweep people into their storm. But mortals don't belong in the world of the gods. I know you've always had big ideas and dreams of adventure, but one of these days, you're going to come crashing down to earth."

Arthur turned to leave, leaving Tempest alone in the library. Tears formed in her eyes and a flash of anger raced through her at his words. He was wrong. He was just like everyone else in this town, too scared to take a leap of his own. She stormed out of the library and slammed the door behind her, ready to leave this life behind.

Zed's eyes flashed with concern as she approached.

"Tempest, are you okay?"

"I'm fine." Thunder rumbled overhead, as if sensing her mood. "And I'm ready to be as far away from this town as possible."

Zed wrapped his arms around her and drew her into him.

"After the darkness of a storm always comes light. Arthur will come around eventually."

Dash stepped forward, and cleared his throat pointedly. "Sorry to break up you two love-birds, but can we give Tempest her present yet?"

Zed chuckled and nodded. "Okay, okay. You need to whistle, Tempest."

Tempest glanced uncertainly at the trio of Stormchasers, who all nodded eagerly. She shrugged, and placed a finger to her lips before letting out a sharp blast of a whistle.

The air filled with the sound of a revving engine as a bike raced towards them. It wove through the streets with a mind of its own, and came to a screeching halt before her. It was long and lean, like a dagger that sliced through the air, and revved excitedly with a life of its own. Tempest ran a hand along it and gasped as it hummed to life beneath her, as if begging to be ridden. It was beautiful and dangerous, and just looking at it sent a shiver down her spine.

"It's beautiful."

"It's yours."

Tempest turned to Zed, her eyes wide with disbelief. "You can't be serious."

He smiled and nodded. "We got some of the finest metals and parts sent from Olympus, and we worked on it all night. This bike is swifter than lightning, lighter than the winds, and handles as surely as Zeus' thunderbolts. And it's yours."

Tempest gasped as she sat on the leather seat. She ran her hands across the handlebars and marveled as it hummed to life. It was a bike fit for a Stormchaser. And it was hers.

Dash wasted no time explaining the basics to her. How it handled, how it moved, how to make it soar through the skies. Tempest admired its beauty and glanced at her mother's old dirt bike, parked outside the library. There was no comparison. This was the motorcycle of a real Stormchaser. With this bike, anything was possible.

She turned to the three Stormchasers, their eyes sparkling as they admired their handiwork. "Thank you, all of you. This is the most wonderful gift I've ever been given."

Ixion's usual scowl softened into a smile. "Well, we couldn't have you tarnishing the Stormchaser name riding that piece of junk, could we?"

Dash glanced at the sky, while sparks crackled out of his fingertips nervously. "We better leave now, while the storm is in place. We brought in a good one for you, but it will only stay here for so long."

Tempest nodded and glanced at the library, where Arthur watched her from the window display. She wanted to go to him, to set aside their differences, to make everything right. But he turned away from her and shook his head with disappointment.

One of these days, you're going to come crashing down to earth.

"Tempest, are you sure you're okay?"

Her hands clenched into fists and she revved her bike, until the throttle of her engine echoed down the street. She'd prove him wrong. She'd prove she belonged in the world of the gods. She'd prove that she could make the leap.

"Let's ride."

Tempest took off at once, leaving the familiarity of the town behind, and raced towards the mountains. She eased into the saddle and pushed her thoughts about Arthur to one side. If she wanted to pass the Trials, she had to focus.

Tempest marveled at the bike as it took corners with ease, as if sensing them before she did. Like everything else about the Stormchasers, it was magical. They rode upwards to the top of the mountain, where thick clouds drifted through the sky.

"Take that slope over there to make the jump." Zed pointed to a rocky outcrop that jutted out into the heavens. "You'll have to wait until the eye of the storm is dead center. Don't go too early or late, or you'll fly straight through it. Timing is everything. Got it?"

Tempest nodded, but a flicker of fear raced through her as the winds gathered strength. If she misjudged the jump by a few seconds, she risked missing the jetstreams and falling straight through the sky. She watched the speed of the winds carefully, her body tense with anticipation.

"Wait for it!"

The winds picked up speed, and the eye of the storm grew closer. Tempest looked at the flashes of lightning inside, at the pulsing lights where the storm raged strongest. She visualized crossing the finish line, and tightened her grip on her handlebars.

"Wait!"

A boom of thunder erupted from the eye of the storm, like a cannon fired through the sky. Tempest's eyes widened as it neared. It was unlike anything she had seen before. Its power emanated through the air, filling it with a wild and savage spirit. And she knew that once she made the leap, she would need to be prepared for the ride of her life.

"Now, Tempest!"

She wasted no time and revved her engine, picking up speed as she raced across the mountaintop. The storm sailed towards the slope until it aligned with its center.

"Quickly!"

Tempest hit the ramp at breakneck speed, knowing that there was no backing down now. She drew a deep breath as her heart hammered in her chest. She could do this. She could ride the storm. She could make the leap of faith.

Tempest screamed out as her motorcycle left the slope and she soared through the air. Her stomach lurched as a ravine opened below her and gravity pulled her downwards. But as the eye of the storm drifted in front of her, her screams turned into a cry of jubilation. Her wheels struck solid ground, until she skidded across the jetstream of wind. She had done it. She had leaped into the storm.

Tempest drew a startled breath and looked ahead at the track before her. It was full of hairpin bends and sharp twists and turns, made even more lethal by the powerful winds that tore through the sky. But she looked beyond the danger that surrounded her and gazed at the pulsing light of the finish line. Just one race around the track, and it would grant her the power she sought. Before she could think twice, she revved the engine, and took off.

The jetstream pulled her motorcycle along at breakneck speed. Tempest braced herself as she turned a corner too wide, and used all of her strength to stay on the road. Her arms throbbed and ached, and beads of sweat formed from the exertion. She was already exhausted, and the Trials had barely even begun.

A flash of golden lightning filled the air, and Zed appeared on a jetstream alongside her.

"That's it, Tempest," he roared over the winds. "Just keep going. Ixion and Dash are scouting ahead, and I'll be beside you all the way. We'll do this together."

Tempest nodded and pressed herself flat to the bike. The wind tore at her as she made a sharp turn, and she dug her thighs into her bike to avoid being thrown off. As she journeyed deeper into the storm, the air grew bitterly cold, numbing her hands. She cursed as they slipped on her handlebars, and her movements became sluggish. She took another sharp corner and gasped as she struggled to make the turn. This wasn't a race. It was a battle.

A flash of violet erupted nearby as Ixion sped towards them, her scowl even deeper than usual.

"The jetstream ahead is broken. You'll need to ride across to the next track."

Tempest's stomach lurched as she looked ahead. A blast of lightning struck the jetstream, destroying part of the road, leaving an empty stretch of sky where it had once been. Ixion revved her engine and sped towards it, racing along its curve upwards, before jumping off and landing smoothly onto an adjacent jetstream. Tempest glanced at Zed, fear clawing at her insides.

"Please don't tell me I have to do that."

"Just think of it as a normal jump. You can do it."

But it wasn't a normal jump. They were thousands of feet in the sky, on a track that was nothing more than a narrow sliver of air, with gale force winds that threatened to throw her to the earth. Doubts raced through her mind, and nerves settled in the pit of her stomach.

"I believe in you, Tempest. Just watch how I do it."

Zed revved his engine and sped across the jetstream. He soared majestically through the air before landing on the other side. Tempest felt the palms of her hands grow sweaty as he landed, knowing it was her turn next.

"You can do it." His eyes blazed with golden sparks, shining in the darkness. "Commit to the leap, and you'll fly."

Tempest nodded, knowing it was too late to back down now. She revved her engine and raced to the slope ahead. She glanced at the glimmer of Zed's golden eyes, guiding her through the depths of the storm. But as she ascended, her stomach lurched at the sheer drop that opened up before her.

Mortals don't belong in the world of the gods.

Arthur's words echoed in the recesses of her mind. She cried out in fear as winds tore at her, nearly knocking her from the track. He was right. She was a mortal, lost in the playground of the gods. And sooner or later, she would fall.

This is what the Stormchasers do. They descend into towns and sweep people into their storm.

Tempest's mind raced as she sped across the jetstream. The storm pulled her further along, catching her in its powerful currents, dragging her towards danger, and further away from the life in the town below. She glanced at Zed, and couldn't help but think of Arthur's warning. She was lost in his storm, caught in its grip, powerless to fight against it. Was she really so willing to throw away her life for a leap of faith?

One of these days, you're going to come crashing down to earth.

Tempest cried out in fear as she became all too aware of her surroundings. She was too high, the jetstream was too narrow, the winds too strong. She felt her heart pound in her chest and her breath catch in her throat as she approached the edge of the track.

"You can do it, Tempest!"

Tempest glanced at the golden sparks within Zed's eyes. Eyes that had swept her away with their promise of adventure. Eyes that had encouraged her to take a leap into the unknown. Eyes from a world in which she didn't belong.

Fear took hold of her as she neared the jump. It coursed through her veins until she froze with terror. It told her she was a mortal in the land of the gods. It told her she wasn't ready to make the leap. It told her to listen to her head, and not to her heart.

Tempest cried out and slammed on the brakes. At once, her motorcycle slid across the jetstream. She pulled on her brakes with all her strength, desperate to come to a stop before she reached the end of the track. The scream of her tires and the smell of burning rubber filled the air, but she knew it was too late.

Zed's eyes widened in horror as Tempest flew from the jetstream. Their eyes connected, and she watched as his golden sparks flashed in fear, before they dissolved into the darkness. She committed every detail of those beautiful eyes to her memory, and held it close to her heart.

Because she knew they would be the last thing she saw before she plummeted to the earth below.

22

The wind howled around Tempest, filling her ears with its merciless roar. Like a rag doll thrown from the heavens, she hurtled towards the earth, her screams echoing across the skies.

A blast of golden lightning raced towards her as Zed dived from the jetstream, his bike and body infused with a golden gleam. He jumped from his seat, soaring through the sky like a powerful diver, and wrapped her in his arms.

"I've got you. Hold on."

With a piercing whistle, Zed called his bike towards them. He grabbed onto the handlebars, and revved the engine as he tried to correct their fall. Tempest clung on to the saddle as he tried to direct them upwards, back to the sky.

"Come on, come on!"

The engine roared to life and strained as it tried to race back to the sky. But they were falling too fast. And as the ground approached, Tempest knew they had run out of luck. She braced herself as the bike struck the earth and crashed into a pile of boulders. A plume of rock dust exploded around them, until she was thrown from the saddle.

Tempest hit the earth with a force that knocked the wind out of her. She gasped out in shock and a sharp pain exploded through her arm. She coughed from the rock dust that billowed around her and blinked to clear her vision.

Overhead, dark storm clouds bloomed, gathering power the likes she'd never seen before. A terrible icy wind blasted through the plains, while raindrops pummeled her from the skies above. Tears of defeat stung her eyes as she glanced at the eye of the storm. She hadn't had the strength to make the leap. The doubts in her mind had chained her to the earth. She had failed.

Tempest staggered to her feet and called out for Zed, searching for him in the piles of rubble and rock. A figure emerged in the distance, enveloped within a plume of dust. Dark rain fell from the sky as she limped towards him, mixing with her tears.

"Zed, I'm sorry. I..."

She glanced at the rubble that surrounded him, and gasped.

"Tempest, don't..."

But Tempest looked in horror at the debris that littered the ground. Broken and bent scraps of metal lay scattered on the ground. A torn wing mirror, a smashed tail light, an exhaust pipe that still crackled with electricity. And in the center lay a mangled heap of a bike, smoke rising from its twisted corpse.

"Your bike!"

"Just leave it."

Zed's expression was grave, while shadows bloomed in his eyes. But Tempest shook her head.

"No, no, we can't leave it." She staggered over to the bike as sparks flew from the remains of its engine. "Maybe we can fix it. If we take it to Mary's, we could try..."

"No, Tempest."

"But Dash can do something. He can fix this, can't he? He can fix anything."

"I said just leave it!"

Zed's words became a peal of thunder that echoed across the valley. Lightning blasted through the sky, while rain poured from the heavens above, drenching them in its terrible downpour.

"None of this would have happened if it wasn't for me. Your bike... I'm so sorry." Tempest shivered as she looked at the storm that raged above them. "I don't know what happened."

"I saw the look in your eyes. I know that look." Zed clenched his jaw and shook his head. "You weren't ready to make the leap."

Tears welled in Tempest's eyes, and she took his hands into hers. "I'm sorry. I froze. I panicked."

"You weren't ready to leave this life behind."

"This has all just happened so quickly." Tempest drew a shaky breath as Arthur's warning continued to echo in her mind. "I just need some more time."

"I can't wait forever."

Silence descended, and an icy wind blew through the valley.

"What are you saying?"

Droplets of rainwater fell from his hair as he turned to her. "I thought that our feelings for one another would be enough. But now..." Zed looked at the sky, where the eye of the storm raged, and shook his head. "This was my fault, Tempest. If it wasn't for me, you'd never have put yourself in such danger."

Tempest stepped forwards and a cold dread swept through her body. "What are you saying, Zed?"

"I'm saying..." He drew a breath as the storm gathered power. "I'm saying that I should never have put you in such danger. I was wrong to think you should join my world."

A flash of lightning filled the sky behind him, and a boom of thunder shook Tempest to her core. Arthur's warning rippled in her mind once more.

"Zed, you don't mean that. I can do better next time."

"Next time?" His voice rose with disbelief. "There won't be a next time. You nearly died, Tempest. I won't let that happen again."

Another roar of thunder ricocheted across the valley. The wind swept around her, its cold breeze whispering to her with doubts.

"So you're just going to leave? Chase the storm to another town? Move on elsewhere and forget about me?" A flicker of anger raced through her as she thought of Arthur's warning. "That's what the Stormchasers do, isn't it? Follow the storm and never think twice about the trail of devastation they leave in their wake."

Pain flickered in Zed's eyes. "Tempest, no, I..."

"Well, I'm not going to just give up. I'll prove you wrong. I'll do the Trials myself."

But Zed simply shook his head. The golden sparks in his eyes faded into inky darkness.

"You don't have a bike, Tempest. And now, neither do I."

He picked up the broken wreck of his motorcycle before he wheeled it back towards the town. Tempest watched him as he began the journey, his head bowed low, the sparks in his eyes dimmed to darkness. Slowly, she followed him, picking up the pieces of his bike along the way.

One of these days, you're going to come crashing down to earth.

Arthur was right. She had reached for the heavens and fallen to the earth. She thought of how much had been lost to the storm. Her friendship with Christie. Her relationship with Arthur. And now she could feel herself losing Zed.

An uneasy feeling spread through Tempest as Zed wheeled the bike in silence. She was the reason he was staying. She was the reason he grew weaker each day. She was the reason he risked Seth's wrath. And she realized Seth was right. Zed was supposed to be free to follow the storm. But she kept him chained to the earth.

She looked at Zed's reflection in a broken side mirror that hung from the bike. In the cracks of the mirror, Tempest saw the emptiness of his eyes. A grayness that reminded her of a storm drifting aimlessly.

The storm worsened as they arrived at Mary's, the skies churning with thick black clouds that rumbled with a savage power. A flash of purple and turquoise raced through the sky as Dash and Ixion appeared before them, their eyes wide with fear.

"We have a problem. A big problem."

A flash of lightning filled the air. Tempest gasped as it struck the mountains in the distance. It filled the sky with an angry red hue, and the roar of dozens of motorcycles echoed through the valley. Seth had returned.

Zed looked at Tempest, his eyes burning in the darkness. "Tempest, listen to me. You have to leave. If Seth knows we betrayed him, there's no telling what he'll do." He turned to Dash and Ixion. "Take her with you. Ride as far as you can and don't stop until you're far away from here."

Tempest shook her head and fixed them all with a defiant glare. "I'm not going anywhere. This is my fault. Whatever Seth wants, we can face it together."

A flash of lightning caused them all to turn. It struck the road, filling it with a violent burst of light and sparks. A Stormchaser appeared within it, his engine revving like a war cry. Another emerged by the entrance to Mary's bar, and another in the yard. One by one, the street became filled with Stormchasers, until the bar was surrounded.

"They're Seth's men. We don't have much time."

Another burst of lightning struck the ground, larger than the others. The smell of burning asphalt and smoke filled the air as Seth emerged from the lightning. Red electricity ran along his bike and his body, and his dark eyes pulsed with a demonic energy. He was even more terrifying than Tempest remembered.

"You disobeyed me. Again."

Zed clenched his hands into fists. Tempest stepped forwards, but Ixion and Dash stood in her way, shielding her from Seth. His eyes flickered towards her, and the air filled with his laughter.

"Of course. The earth-bound. I should have known." Seth narrowed his eyes at Zed. "You know the rules. We're lone wolves. We live for the storm and nothing else. Attachments to others make us weak."

"No Seth, you're wrong. Our bond doesn't make me weak. It makes me stronger."

"Is that so?" Seth sneered and glanced at Zed's beaten-up bike pointedly. Sparks flew from his feet as he took a menacing step closer. "I'll give you a choice. You can return to the storm, and forget all about the earth-bound. Or you stay with your earth-bound pet, and face the consequences."

The air grew still as silence descended across the yard. Zed clenched his jaw and his eyes burned in the darkness. But a cruel smile flickered across Seth's lips, and he stepped closer.

"Come on, Zed. We both know that this won't last." A flash of anger raced through Tempest, but Ixion and Dash continued to block her path. "You don't belong down here, chained to the earth. You belong in the skies, free to follow the storm."

The air crackled with sparks as Seth stepped closer. His eyes gleamed with a violent red glow, while the tattoo on Zed's wrist burned into his skin. And Tempest knew Arthur was right. Whatever Zed might feel for her, they were fighting a losing battle. He could only fight against his true nature for so long.

Seth smiled menacingly, and red electricity raced through his skin. "You need to make a choice. A choice between chaining yourself to this earth-bound, or returning to the skies where you belong."

Despair flooded through Tempest as she glanced at Zed. She could see the longing in his eyes as he looked at the skies. He gazed at the storm above, as it called to him with its siren song. A song that was impossible for him to resist.

Zed drew a breath, and his lips flickered into a smile as he met Seth's gaze.

"This was the easiest choice I've had to make."

Despair flooded through Tempest as Zed turned to her. His eyes burned with a savage power, just like Seth's. Was he really so ready to just throw her away? To return to the skies and forget about her?

But Tempest's breath faltered as the sparks in Zed's eyes softened and flashed with warmth. She looked at him uncertainly as light gathered in his hands, and a golden bolt of lightning emerged.

"I used to think there was nothing more powerful than the storm. That nothing else in the world could bring such excitement, such adventure, could make me feel so alive. But that was before I met you." Zed smiled, and his eyes shimmered with golden sparks. "I was wrong to think you should join my world. Because I should join yours instead. I'll relinquish the storms, and live on the earth with you."

Tempest drew a startled breath. The golden sparks in his eyes gleamed against the darkness. Zed wasn't leaving her. He was willing to give up everything to be with her.

"I choose you, Tempest."

Seth's face contorted with rage. "You bring shame to the Stormchasers. You let this earth-bound chain you, and take your freedom."

"The only person who chains us is you, Seth. And that ends now."

At once, Zed sent a stream of golden lightning racing towards Seth. Seth roared in fury and attacked in return, sending a blast of red lightning streaming from his hands. The lightning bolts collided and exploded into a blinding light that sent sparks flying through the air.

"You won't win, Zed." Seth's lips curled into a cruel smile. "You've spent too much time on the earth. You're too weak."

Seth's eyes burned as he sent a maelstrom of lightning blasts towards Zed. Zed deflected the blows, sending them ricocheting into the road, until it was filled with scorch marks and the scent of burning asphalt. But Seth's assault was relentless, until the air pulsed with a violent red hue and Zed's defenses began to weaken. A blast of lightning struck the ground at his feet, sending him hurtling backwards, until he landed in a heap of smoking rubble.

Tempest ran towards him, desperate to help, but Ixion held her back.

"No, you can't involve yourself in Stormchaser business. Seth will kill you."

Zed roared out as another blast of lightning struck him, sending angry red sparks racing through his skin.

"Stop it, please!"

Seth's eyes flickered to Tempest, like a predator turning to its prey. His cold laughter echoed through the street as peals of thunder.

"How cute. Your earth-bound pet has fallen for you." His eyes pulsed with a violent red energy as he gathered lightning in his hands. "I told you to stay away, earth-bound. I warned you that our world is no place for a mortal. Perhaps it's time you see the true power of the storm."

Tempest gasped and staggered backwards as he gathered power. But Dash and Ixion stood before her, joined by the Stormchasers still loyal to Zed.

"If you want her, you'll have to go through us."

Seth sneered at their defiance. "Very well."

A darkness spread through Seth's eyes, while red electricity raced across his body. Angry blasts of lightning flashed overhead, and the winds gathered strength until Tempest struggled to keep her footing. She gasped as Seth's feet left the ground, and he levitated in the sky.

"The Stormchasers have lost their way." His voice boomed through the streets, shaking the very foundations of the earth. "We've grown soft. We've become nothing more than a bunch of earth-bound sympathizers. But it's time for us to return to our old ways."

Lightning struck a parked car, shattering its windscreen and sending glass exploding across the street.

"We are the bringers of darkness, who strike fear into the hearts of every earth-bound."

A blast of wind tore through the street, sending flowerpots and store signs hurtling into the sky above. Dark clouds billowed overhead, until sheets of black rain descended onto the town below.

"We can destroy towns with a single sweep of our hand."

Another lightning blast struck the street, shattering the window of the library. Tempest cried out as the storm tore through the building, and loose pages scattered in the winds.

"It's time to return to our true nature." Seth's dark eyes turned to Zed. "And only the strongest can ride with us."

Zed staggered to his feet and faced Seth defiantly. "We both know you're not strong enough to finish me."

"Oh, I won't need to. Not all the earth-bound in this town are so willing to give you such a warm welcome."

Tempest's stomach lurched as several figures appeared behind Seth, clubs and pickaxes in their hands. She gasped as she recognized their ringleader.

"Mason, what are you doing?"

"Stay out of this Tempest." Mason's eyes narrowed at Zed. "I told you to leave this town."

Zed turned to Seth, his face filled with rage. "What is this? You're getting the earth-bound to do your dirty work for you?"

Seth smiled. "I have bigger things to focus on." The winds whipped around him, and he looked to the sky. "Starting with this town."

The storm gathered strength, until Tempest could feel its ancient power deep in her bones. The pressure built in her head, forming a migraine so strong she staggered backwards in pain. Blinding flashes of lightning blasted through the street, and the air became filled with the sound of shattering glass. She gasped at the savagery of the storm, as scorch marks lined the streets and cracks formed in the roads. Seth had unleashed the true power of the storm. And it would destroy everything.

Mason yelled out to the miners, and they attacked at once, surrounding Zed like a pack of animals. Zed roared out in fury, but fell to his knees at their assault, his power drained from his fight with Seth. He was outnumbered, and Tempest knew he wouldn't last long.

As fighting broke out across the yard, Tempest forced her way past the warring Stormchasers and raced to Zed. She made a fist and landed a blow on one of the miners, before she pulled at Mason's shirt.

"Get off him! Mason, what are you doing?"

"Stay back, Tempest."

Tempest fell to the floor as he pushed her away and cried out as a sharp pain shot through her arm. Zed roared out, desperate to help her, but the miners pulled him backwards. Tempest turned to Mason in fear as he loomed over her, and cradled a baseball bat menacingly in his hands.

"This biker has poisoned your mind, Tempest. He's made you think you can leap for the skies. But someone needs to put an end to these ridiculous dreams of yours."

Tempest's eyes widened with horror as he swung the bat. But she realized she wasn't his target, nor Zed. Mason had found another way to destroy her. The sound of shattering glass and dented metal filled the air as he struck her mother's dirt bike. Her screams echoed through the street as he hit it over and over again. Each blow destroyed the dreams she once had, until nothing was left.

Mason turned to her with a sneer, as the dirt bike lay in a crumpled, smoking heap before him.

"It's for your own good, Tempest. Maybe now you'll remember to keep your feet on the earth, where you belong."

He nodded to the miners, who hauled Zed to his feet. His nose was bloodied, and he swayed as he battled with unconsciousness.

Tempest staggered forwards and called for help, but cursed as Ixion and Dash remained locked in battle with Seth's men.

"It's time to teach this Stormchaser a lesson." Mason's lips curled into a smile. "Something that ensures his kind will never return to this town again."

Tempest cried out and charged towards the miners, desperate to stop them. But before she could reach them, Seth raised his hands to the sky, and a blinding flash filled the street. Tempest's feet left the earth as she was sent flying backwards, before she landed in a pile of rubble.

She staggered to her feet, and searched for Zed in the chaos that raged around her. But as the lightning cleared, she felt her stomach lurch.

Zed, and the miners, were gone.

23

— · —

L ightning tore through the sky, illuminating the carnage that unfolded below. Broken glass and debris filled the once peaceful streets, while the skies raged above with a battle of light and shadow. It was as if a rift to hell had been opened over the town. And Tempest had found herself firmly in the center of it all.

She ran to the library, her feet splashing through puddles of dark rainwater. She raced past books that lie sodden and strewn on the ground, and through glittering shards of glass that reflected the chaos above. This was her fault. It was all her fault.

Tempest gasped as she entered the library. It looked as though a hurricane had torn through it and swept everything in its path. Bookcases lay toppled, black rain poured through the broken windows, and loose pages scattered in the winds. She looked in bewilderment at the devastation before her, then cried out as she saw a figure trapped beneath a fallen bookcase.

"Arthur! I'm coming!"

Tempest leaned against the bookcase, trying to free him. But under the weight of the books, it was impossible. She called out for help, her pleas echoing through the street, before trying to shift it once more.

The sound of running footsteps and the scent of wildflowers filled the library as Mary raced to help her. Together, they pulled the books from the shelves, then leaned against the bookcase once more, lifting it enough for Arthur to crawl out of the narrow space beneath.

"Arthur! Are you okay?"

Arthur dusted down his tweed suit before he looked in dismay at the library. "My books! Oh, the first editions are soaked!"

"We've got more to worry about than just your books. If this storm gets any bigger, it will destroy the entire town." Mary turned to Tempest, her eyes wide with fright. "Can't Zed do something about this? The storm is out of control."

"He's gone. Mason and the miners attacked him and took him somewhere." Tempest felt her heart wrench in her chest as she thought of Zed. He had given up everything for her. He had chosen her over the skies. And now, because of her, he was in danger. "We have to find him."

Arthur yelped out in surprise as a flash of lightning illuminated the library, and Ixion and Dash appeared. Tempest looked at them expectantly, but they shook their heads.

"We've searched everywhere. Wherever those miners have taken him, it's nowhere we can find."

Tempest's heart sank as the storm raged above the town. She searched for a flash of golden lightning and listened for the sound of his thunder call, but there was nothing.

Ixion followed her gaze, and her scowl deepened. "I've ridden through the darkest of storms, but this beats them all." She turned to Tempest gravely. "We need to evacuate the town until the worst of the storm passes."

Arthur's mustache quivered in anger. "Absolutely not. I won't let that madman destroy my books."

"You have more than just your books to worry about. Seth won't stop until this entire town is destroyed. I've never seen him so angry."

"Could he really destroy the town?"

Ixion's scowl deepened, and she nodded. "You might be an earth-bound, but you've scared him, Tempest. Stormchasers are stronger with their fated mate. And he's done everything in his power to stop Zed from finding his. Seth would rather destroy this entire town, and you, than risk letting Zed become powerful enough to overthrow him. And there's nothing we can do to stop him. We have to run while we still can."

"No." Tempest summoned all of her strength and fixed Ixion with a scowl that rivaled her own. "This is my fault. I didn't make the leap because I listened to the doubts in my mind, when I should have listened to my heart. Zed was willing to give up everything for me, and I'm not going anywhere until we save him."

"But it's far too dangerous out there. None of us has the power to stop Seth."

"Perhaps not. But if what you say is true, then Zed does." Tempest looked at Ixion pleadingly. "We need to find him. He's the only one who stands a chance of stopping Seth."

"But we have no idea where he is. The storm is gathering power by the minute, and he could be anywhere. There's no way we'll find him in time."

Dash parted his blue fringe from his eyes and peered thoughtfully at Tempest. "Well, there is one way."

Ixion bristled, and her scowl reached new depths of disapproval. "Certainly not. You saw what happened last time. And besides, Zed would kill you."

Tempest stepped forwards. "What is it? Tell me, I'll do anything."

Dash glanced out of the window once more, towards the eye of the storm.

"You need to complete the Trials. It's the only way."

Tempest turned from him to where the storm raged in the sky, and her eyes widened. "Are you crazy? The storm is the strongest I've ever seen. Not to mention the bike you gave me shattered into a million pieces when I crashed."

"You could use one of our bikes."

"No way. They're both far too big for me to handle. I wouldn't know how to ride them. I'd fall off at the first hurdle."

Ixion nodded. "I agree with the earth-bound. It's far too dangerous."

"But it could work. If you're his fated mate, you could find him using your thunder call."

Tempest glanced at the sky uncertainly. "But Zed taught me his thunder call, and I can't hear it anywhere. This storm is too powerful."

"Of course you can't hear it with your earth-bound senses. But if you become a Stormchaser, your powers will be amplified. You'll be able to hear him, no matter how powerful the storm."

Tempest drew a shaky breath, while Ixion shook her head.

"It's too risky. No Stormchaser could ride in this storm, let alone an earth-bound."

But Tempest peered at the skies where the storm raged. She knew Zed was out there somewhere. He had been willing to give up everything for her. And she had to do the same for him. She wasn't sure if she believed in fated mates, but she had to take a leap of faith.

She glanced at Arthur, knowing that after last time, she didn't want to leave on bad terms. But he turned from her, to the storm that raged outside.

"Please, Arthur."

He shook his head, and the air filled with a stony silence before he left the library. Tempest's heart sank, but she felt Mary's hand on her shoulder.

"Tempest, you can't live your life for other people's approval. If this is what you want, then don't let anything stop you. Arthur will come around in time."

"But he's right. It's dangerous. I took the leap before, and I fell. What if the same happens again?"

Ixion directed her scowl towards Tempest. "Falling is a part of being a Stormchaser. We take risks. Sometimes we fly, sometimes we fall. What's important is getting back up again." She drew a deep breath, and her scowl softened. "I can't believe I'm going to say this, but I think Dash is right. You're our best hope of saving

Zed. But you must complete the Trials to stand a chance of finding him."

Dash nodded and grinned. "The storm is powerful, but you're more of a Stormchaser than most of us combined. If anyone can do it, it's you. You just need to believe in yourself."

"You need to choose, Tempest. Either you can stay here with the earth-bounds and hide from the storm. Or you can join it and become the person you're supposed to be."

Tempest looked out at the storm. She knew she had to do everything in her power to save Zed. But the memory of her fall flashed in her mind. She ran her finger along the edges of her necklace nervously. What would be so different this time?

A hammering noise filled the library, interrupting her thoughts with its incessant banging. Tempest glanced at the others uncertainly, before going to the door.

Illuminated by lightning, and soaked by the rain, she saw Arthur hunched over her mother's dirt bike, hammering out the bent metal and pulling the twisted wheel from the frame. She ran over to him, buffeted by the hurricane winds that tore through the streets.

"What are you doing?"

"What does it look like? I'm re-attaching your wheel. Now make yourself useful and pass me the tire irons."

Tempest looked in surprise as a toolbox sat next to him. She passed him the tool and watched as he used it to remove the twisted tire and fit a new one in its place.

"Since when did you know what a tire iron was?"

"Oh please. I grew up with your mother. Our house was filled with bike parts." Arthur shuddered as he recalled it. "There was bike oil everywhere."

Tempest watched him uncertainly as he fixed the bike, recalling their fight from before.

"You don't need to do this."

"Yes, I do." Arthur glanced at the stormy sky and sighed. "After your mother left, I thought my job as your guardian was to keep you safe. I tried so hard to keep you away from the storms. I forced you to work all those summers in the library. I confiscated your bike. I tried to convince you that all the adventure you needed could be found in books." He shook his head and smiled at her sadly. "But I was wrong. I'm not supposed to keep you safe. I'm supposed to help you fly."

"But you're right. The Trials are dangerous. I tried to do them and I fell."

"Falling is just a part of taking a risk. What matters is that you pick yourself up and try again." He smiled as he looked at her. "I might not understand the world of the Stormchasers, but what I know is this. You're special, Tempest. You always have been. And this is your chance to have the adventure you've always wanted."

"But what if it goes wrong?"

"Surely it's worth taking a risk rather than never knowing at all?"

Tempest couldn't help but return Arthur's smile. He was right. She needed to dust herself off, and try again. And this time, she wouldn't falter.

But as Arthur finished re-attaching the wheel of her bike, she shook her head at the state of it.

"This thing is a wreck. It'll take more than a new tire to fix it."

She turned as the others approached from the library. Dash clapped his hands and his eyes gleamed with mischievous sparks.

"Well, then. I guess it's time to turn this piece of junk into something road-worthy."

24

The storm gathered power. Violent flashes of lightning pulsed within the roiling clouds of darkness, while hurricane winds tore across the mountaintop. It was the worst storm Tempest had ever seen. And she would be riding straight into its center.

She smiled uneasily at the others assembled at Zed's cabin. "Well, I guess there's no turning back now."

Arthur looked at the sky uneasily as another lightning blast scorched the mountains. "Are you sure you can't wait until the storm has passed? Perhaps you could do this on a sunnier day?"

Tempest shook her head. "We need to save Zed, and we need to save the town. We can't wait any longer. And besides, it's good weather for a Stormchaser, right?"

Ixion smiled uneasily. "Even for a Stormchaser, this is suicide. But we'll ride with you, no matter what."

Arthur sighed and his mustache quivered. "Just be careful. I made a promise to your mother that I would take care of you, and I don't intend to break it."

Mary finished fixing a string of charms on Tempest's handlebars and smiled.

"It might not be much, but a few luck charms are the least I can do." She hugged Tempest, filling the air with her perfume of herbs and earthy scents. "Believe in yourself, Tempest. Use the strength of your feelings for Zed to guide you. Draw on it to give you the courage to take the leap."

Tempest smiled and drew in Mary and Arthur for a hug. Arthur adjusted his glasses as she released him, and his eyes grew watery as he shook his head.

"You've always had dreams bigger than this town. Be careful, my girl. We'll be cheering for you from down here."

"Thank you, Arthur. For everything. If I'm able to soar into the sky, it's because of you."

Tempest glanced at the town below, where the storm continued to wreak havoc. If she waited much longer, it would be reduced to nothing but rubble. She started the engine of her mother's bike and marveled as it roared to life. It was still bashed and dented beyond recognition, and it was no Stormchaser motorcycle, but it had been built by the love of her friends and family. And she knew how to ride it better than any other bike in existence.

She revved her engine, joined by Dash and Ixion. It was time. With a last wave to Arthur and Mary, she sped to the peaks and left her life behind.

The winds tore around her as she raced across the mountain and neared the eye of the storm. Ixion and Dash rode on either side of her as they sped towards the mountain ridge that would take them to the sky.

"Just remember to time the jump carefully. It's all about precision. Too fast or too slow, and you'll miss your shot. You only have one chance to make this work."

"Once you're on the track, just remember to ride fast and ride hard. Only those who believe in themselves can succeed in the Trials. Ignore your earth-bound instincts and don't pay any attention to your doubts..."

"... or the deadly thunderbolts..."

"... or the gale force winds..."

"... on second thoughts, is this really a good idea?"

Tempest turned to Ixion and Dash in exasperation. "We need to find Zed. And it's too late to turn back now. Come on!"

Tempest revved her engine and sped towards the slope. She observed the movements of the storm as she began the ascent, knowing there was no room for error. Her mind raced as she approached the mountain edge, and her brain screamed for her to stop. But she ignored her earth-bound instincts and revved the engine. It was time to listen to her heart.

She screamed out as her bike left the ground and soared through the air. The winds caught her and pulled her along their current, before she landed with a thud on the jetstream. A flash of turquoise and violet appeared next to her, before the group stared in horror at the track before them.

The jetstreams raced at breakneck speeds, twisting around hairpin bends designed to dismount even the hardiest of riders. Stray bolts of lightning struck the track, while hurricane winds threatened to throw riders off at every turn. But Tempest's chest tightened as she looked at the jetstreams further ahead. The storm had destroyed large parts of them, reducing sections of the track to small fragments of air that floated in the sky.

Dash let out a whistle of bewilderment while Ixion scowled at the track. "I've never seen anything like this. It's not too late to turn back."

Tempest shook her head. She'd had enough of turning back. But doubts crept into her mind as she looked at the broken jetstreams along the track.

"How do I complete the Trials if the track is broken?"

"You'll need to jump between the jetstreams to do it."

Tempest's stomach lurched as she glanced at the track. A cold dread swept through her as she thought of what had happened last time. But her eyes were drawn to the center of the storm. It glowed and pulsed with an ancient power. A power that could save Zed and the town.

A blast of wind raced through the sky, nearly knocking Dash from his bike.

"Tempest, I'm not so sure this is a good idea. Perhaps we could..."

Tempest revved her engine and narrowed her eyes. "I'm doing this, and that's final. Either you can race with me, or be beaten by an earth-bound."

She sped off at once across the jetstream, hearing Ixion and Dash's astounded laughter behind her. The jetstream pulled her along at breakneck speed, and her eyes widened as she struggled to stay on the narrow track. It was like racing a motorcycle on a tightrope. But as she drifted around the first series of corners, Tempest felt her confidence grow. She glanced at the center of the track once more, and felt a flicker of hope ignite within her heart. She could do this.

"There's a jump ahead. Brace yourself, if you…"

Ixion's words were cut short as Tempest revved her engine and threw caution to the wind. She took the first leap, and soared through the sky until she landed on an adjacent jetstream. Tempest cried out with joy as she sped along the narrow sliver of road and continued racing ahead. She made another jump, gaining confidence as she passed the first quarter of the track, and raced deeper into the storm.

The air grew colder as she sped ahead and the rain turned to hail that pelted the track. Tempest felt her wheels slide on the icy jetstream, causing her bike to drift as she took a corner too wide. She pulled sharply to correct herself, and breathed out as she zoomed along, thankful she was riding on her dirt bike. A larger bike would have been too bulky to make such a tight turn. She smiled and patted her mother's bike like a steed. Perhaps it wasn't such a piece of junk after all.

Tempest continued to race along the jetstream, weaving in-between blasts of lightning, while Dash and Ixion scouted ahead. Despite her fear, despite the danger, despite the peril she faced, a smile flickered across her lips. She'd never felt so alive.

A blast of red-hued lightning filled the air. Tempest cursed as the skies darkened and a red lightning bolt flew towards her. Her stomach lurched as she saw Seth's silhouette within it, until he raced on a jetstream alongside her.

"You should have stayed where you belong, earth-bound. The storms are my domain. And you don't belong here."

A blast of lightning struck the front wheel of her bike, forcing her to veer sharply from the jetstream. She gasped and pulled against the handlebars to keep herself from falling from the track.

"You'll never be a Stormchaser, you hear me? Never!"

Tempest stared in horror as Seth gathered electricity in his hands. She knew her bike was no match for his power. His eyes gleamed in the darkness while his taunting laughter echoed through the skies.

"There's no one to save you this time, earth-bound. Enjoy your trip back to earth."

A flash of turquoise and violet lightning bolts soared through the sky. They struck Seth's bike in an explosion of colorful sparks, knocking him off-balance. He roared with fury as his own shot flew off into the distance, until Dash and Ixion emerged and flanked him on either side.

More flashes of lightning filled the air, as dozens of Stormchasers arrived and waged battle against one another. Tempest looked in wonder as the sky became filled with colorful bursts of sparks as Seth's men battled against those still loyal to Zed.

"Just follow the jetstreams," called Dash. He veered his bike into Seth's, forcing him away from Tempest. "We'll take care of this bully."

Ixion's scowl eased, and she broke into a smile. "Just keep riding, Tempest. For an earth-bound, you make one mighty fine Stormchaser."

Tempest returned her smile and revved her engine as she raced across to the next jetstream. She braced herself against gale force winds and weaved between stray bolts of lightning that struck the track. She soared through the skies, taking leap after leap, as she sped towards the finish line.

The flashes and booms of the Stormchaser's battle began to fade as she neared the center of the storm. A small jetstream led to the glowing center, the air frozen solid to form a glistening bridge suspended in the air. Tempest felt her breath catch in her throat at the sight of it. She had nearly made it.

She raced up the jetstream and took the final jump, before landing on the frozen road. Her speedometer struggled to keep up with her as she sped across the bridge to the storm's center. The surrounding air crackled, and she gasped as electricity ran through her bike and into her hands. She was becoming one with the storm.

Tempest let out a cry of excitement as the light of the storm billowed around her. She was going to make it. She was going to become a Stormchaser.

A sonic boom blasted through the sky, and Tempest ducked as a blast of red lightning narrowly missed her. She turned to see Seth advance on her, a pulsing red specter within the darkness of the storm. His dark eyes radiated with power and red sparks flew from his wheels. He gathered electricity in his hands and sneered at her.

"You should never have tried to fly, earth-bound. People like you only fall."

Tempest braced herself as lightning flew from his hands. The bolt soared past her and struck the jetstream before her. At first, she thought he had missed. But as the road beneath her tires trembled, she realized his strike was right on-target.

Seth's laugh boomed across the skies as cracks raced through the frozen jetstream. Tempest looked in horror as fragments of the frozen road plummeted from the sky, until a gaping hole loomed before her. The finish line loomed in the distance, now cut off into a distant island.

Seth had destroyed her one chance of finishing the race, and with it, all hope of becoming a Stormchaser. And as Tempest raced at top speed towards the broken road, she knew it was too late to turn back.

25

—·—

Tempest cried out as she sped towards the broken road.

She called for Dash and Ixion, but cursed as the sounds of battle drowned out her pleas for help. Her mind raced as she thought of what to do. The road was too narrow for her to turn around, and she knew that using her brakes risked sliding off the icy track. No, the only way was forwards. Tempest glanced nervously at the jump before her. It was practically impossible. But she had to try.

The winds tore at her as she sped ahead, trying to hold her back like the doubts in her mind. She looked at the daredevil jump before her and felt her brain scream for her to stop. It pleaded with her to return to her life of safety in the town, to not risk everything over a leap of faith. But she thought of Zed and the golden sparks in his eyes. And she knew she was done listening to her head. It was time to listen to her heart.

Tempest revved her engine and raced forwards. She pressed herself flat against her bike as she hit the edge of the track and soared into the air. She held her breath as the other side of the frozen road inched closer, until it was within reaching distance.

But she gasped as her ascent slowed, and she began to fall. She hadn't gained enough speed. The jump was too far. And she knew that despite everything, she wouldn't make it.

Tempest's cries echoed through the heavens. She felt time slow as she began her descent through the sky. She called out for Ixion, for Dash, for Zed, for anyone to help her. But she knew no one could save her this time. As she fell, she wondered if it had been like this for her mother. Had she also come so close, only to fall at the final hurdle? She pressed her hand to her necklace and closed her eyes.

A faint breeze fluttered behind Tempest. It blew against the storm, a tiny whisper compared to the hurricane winds that raged within the storm. It held a warm wind, as if it came from a faraway place. And there was something else in it, too. Tempest breathed it in, and her eyes widened as she recognized the smell. It was her mother's perfume.

Mom?

Tempest gasped in surprise as the breeze grew. All those years she had sensed her mother's presence in the storms, all those times she had caught a scent of her perfume. It hadn't been her mind playing tricks on her, nor her nostalgia affecting her senses. She had always been here, in the storm, calling to Tempest. Her mother had beaten the Trials. And now, so would she.

The perfumed breeze gathered power, until it turned into a gale, slowing Tempest's descent and pushing her closer to the finish line. Tempest revved her engine and soared through the air, until the jetstream came into view. Her front wheel struck something solid, and she pulled the brakes hard, before she swerved into the center of the storm.

Tempest looked around, barely daring to breathe. Her hands, white from gripping onto the handlebars so hard, shook with fear and adrenaline. She had to pinch herself to believe it was really true. She was alive. And, against all odds, she had completed the Trials.

Tempest let out a jubilant cry as she realized she'd made it. The heart of the storm reacted to her presence, pulsing with a radiant beauty she had never seen before. The sky crackled with raw power, and Tempest gasped as a blast of lightning scorched the surrounding air. Another blast seared the sky, until Tempest found herself surrounded by the storm. And yet, despite its power, she knew she had nothing to fear from it.

This lightning didn't intend to harm. It intended to do something quite different.

Tempest looked up and saw a bolt of lightning form above her. It radiated with the power of the gods. A power that only Zeus himself could bestow. She drew a breath, sent a silent prayer to anyone who would listen, and braced herself as the bolt of lightning descended towards her.

The bolt struck her bike, sending sparks shooting through it, and upwards into her body. Its energy crackled through every bone and muscle, raced through every cell, and flowed through her veins. She gasped as her mind and body connected to the surrounding storm, and her senses heightened. The storm's sounds grew in clarity, until she heard the battle cries of the Stormchasers in every roll of thunder. Her vision adjusted to the blinding flashes of the lightning, until she saw the Stormchasers that raced within them, the colors of the electricity matched with the hues of their bike. And as sparks flickered from her fingertips, she broke into a smile. The storm was hers to command.

Tempest raised her hands, and the air stirred at her touch, the currents twisting around her fingers like strands of a tapestry. The wind raced towards her, tousling her hair, and lightning illuminated her against the storm. She watched the perfumed breeze longingly as it drifted away, and placed a hand to her necklace. Her mother had helped her make the leap. Somewhere in the world, she rode the storm. And one day, they would be reunited.

A jetstream spiraled towards her and two lightning bolts sped across it. Tempest waved to Dash and Ixion as they approached in their turquoise and violet hues, their cheers of jubilation echoing across the sky.

"I can't believe it. The earth-bound did it!"

"In all my life, I've never seen someone make a jump like that. You're a Stormchaser through and through."

"How do you feel?"

Tempest stretched her hands and felt the storm respond to her touch. She felt herself connect with every lightning bolt, every droplet of rain, every current of wind.

"I feel alive."

As she moved her hand through the air, faint marks appeared on her wrist. Tempest's eyes widened as a tattoo of chains snaked around her skin, a reminder of the Stormchaser's curse. It was faint, for now, but grew darker by the minute.

"We need to be quick. While your body is still adjusting to being a Stormchaser, you're not fully bound to Seth. It gives us an edge that he won't expect." Ixion looked across the skies where the sounds of the battling Stormchasers raged on. "It's time to test those new Stormchaser abilities. It's time to find Zed."

Tempest nodded and closed her eyes.

"Every Stormchaser has a unique thunder call. Try to pick them out, one by one."

Tempest focussed and detected the unique calls within the storm. She heard the booming calls of those still loyal to Zed, and the violent cries of Seth and his gang.

"Even in the darkest of storms, a Stormchaser can always find their true love. No matter how loud the thunder, no matter how strong the winds blow, our thunder call means we will never be separated. And if Zed really is your fated mate, you'll be able to find him."

Tempest concentrated on the surrounding storm. She stretched her mind across the skies and into the mountains. A cacophony of different calls filled her ears, of clashing booms and ringing peals of thunder. But within the noise, one call was missing. She couldn't hear Zed anywhere.

"I can't find him." Tempest opened her eyes and looked at Ixion and Dash uncertainly. "He's not here."

"Just focus. Reach out as far as you can with your mind. You'll find him."

Tears of frustration filled Tempest's eyes, and a sense of hopelessness settled into the pit of her stomach.

"What if I'm not his mate?"

Ixion took a step forward. "Take my word for it, earth-bound. You might have been from different worlds, but I've never seen a better pairing than the two of you. You're the earth-bound who stopped the storm. You just need to try again."

Tempest drew a shaky breath and closed her eyes. She listened for Zed's call once more, only to be met with silence. Panic spread through her body. Perhaps she'd been a fool to think a mortal like her could be fated mates with a god. What if she'd made the leap for nothing?

She called out to Zed again with her mind. She screamed for him. She pleaded with him to return her call. But as silence descended around her, her hopelessness turned into a deep despair.

Please don't leave me alone, Zed.

She'd ridden through the darkest of storms to find him. To save the man who had brought magic into her life, and had given her the courage to take the leap. She summoned him once more, using the power of her heart to strengthen her call. And as she listened to her heart, she realized she might not know much about fated mates, but she knew one thing.

I love you, Zed.

The winds stirred, carrying a faint whisper on the breeze. Tempest gasped as it called to her. It was a sound so familiar she could pick it out of a crowd anywhere.

"Zed!"

Another whisper. A faint boom of thunder that sent sparks racing down her body. He was alive. He was her fated mate. And she was his.

"Zed! He's alive!"

Tempest wasted no time and revved her engine, soaring across the jetstreams towards the sound of his thunder. As she raced, she didn't need to think about her balance, and didn't need to slow for the hairpin bends. Her fear and doubt had dissolved. She had become one with the storm. She leaped across the jetstreams with ease, embraced the winds as they helped her soar through the skies, and used the lightning to guide her way.

Tempest followed Zed's call, speeding away from the mountains and down into the plains. Onwards she rode, his voice guiding her, until she used her brakes to come to a screaming stop.

Tempest clutched onto her handlebars, her knuckles white, as realization struck her. She knew where Zed had been taken. Ixion and Dash pulled up beside her, and looked at her expectantly.

"Well? Where is he?"

A rage flowed through Tempest's body, and sparks flew from her hands in fury.

"He's in the worst place imaginable for a Stormchaser. They've taken him down there to die."

Dash and Ixion followed her gaze, and paled as they looked at the caves in the distance. The miners had taken Zed to a place beneath the earth itself. A place where he would never see the sky again.

26

— · —

Hurricane winds raced across the plains, while dark and violent energies twisted and flashed in the sky. The storm was gathering power, and Tempest knew she didn't have long. She needed to save the town. But first, she needed to save Zed.

She turned to the mouth of the caves before her, the entrance yawning wide like a jaw ready to devour them into the depths of hell. Seth had taken Zed there to die, to leave him trapped beneath the earth, never to see the sky again. It was the worst death imaginable for a Stormchaser. As sparks of anger raced across her skin, she vowed she would do anything to free him.

Tempest nodded to Dash and Ixion, before they followed her into the darkness. She listened out for Zed's call to guide her through the dark labyrinth of tunnels. But with each passing minute, his thunder call grew weaker. She had to hurry.

With each step into the caves, Tempest's skin tingled, then itched, then seared with pain as if aflame. The air was too close, too stale, and the further she descended, the more she gasped for breath. Beads of sweat formed on the Stormchaser's faces and their skin paled. Tempest shuddered as she wondered how long Zed had been down here. How much longer could he survive?

A grunt of pain filled the air as Tempest emerged into the cavern. Her eyes widened as she saw a figure in its center, illuminated by the glow of the crystallized stalactites. Zed.

He staggered to his knees as Mason wrestled him to the ground, their bodies slick with sweat and the dust of the mines. Zed roared out as Mason struck him, sending a blast of thunder rumbling overhead. The golden sparks in his eyes grew dim, and he swayed as he dipped in and out of consciousness. They were killing him. And from the looks of it, he had little time left.

A terrible rage flowed through Tempest, a violent anger that wanted to destroy everything in sight. She summoned the power of the storm to her hands and stepped forward, only to feel Ixion restrain her and pull her into the shadows.

"What are you doing? We have to help him!"

"We're outnumbered, earth-bound. You didn't ride through that storm, only to fall at the first hurdle. Look."

Tempest turned to where Ixion pointed and saw two of Seth's men stand guard, while a dozen miners prowled the cavern with pickaxes and baseball bats in hand. But despite their greater numbers, she met Ixion's scowl with one of her own.

"We should teach them a lesson. We should show them the true power of the storm."

Ixion shook her head. "They might be a bunch of ignorant jocks, but they're not killers. They don't understand Zed's powers, so they don't know the danger this poses to him. Besides, we're weaker down here, and completely outnumbered. We can't just go rushing in there."

But Dash ran a hand through his wind-blown hair and grinned as he looked at the network of tunnels before them.

"I have an idea." He rubbed his hands together and chuckled before turning to Tempest. "When I give the signal, focus on getting Zed out of here. Don't worry about the others. Ixion and I will take care of them."

"You're sure?"

He nodded as his eyes sparkled with a mischievous gleam. "This is going to be fun."

Together they disappeared into the tunnels, while Tempest remained shrouded in the dark. She gasped as Mason landed a punch on Zed and blood spilled across the ground. Sparks flew from her fingers, and she narrowed her eyes at Mason. It was about time someone taught that bully a lesson.

A sharp sound filled the cavern, causing the miners to glance warily at the tunnels. A whistle echoed through the air, joined by another from a different tunnel. The miners hung back, while Seth's men stepped cautiously into the darkness of the tunnels. A knowing smile crossed Tempest's lips as a low rumble filled the air, until something emerged from the gloom.

A cry erupted from one of Seth's men as a motorcycle zoomed past him, soaring through the cavern and into another tunnel. Another bike burst into the cavern, weaving towards the miners with a mind of its own. They leapt away from the danger, while Seth's men raced down the tunnels to find the mystery assailants.

Shouts of confusion and fear erupted as the bikes sped around the caves, while flashes of lightning filled the tunnels. The cavern descended into chaos as the miners scattered within the caves, their shouts and screams echoing along the earth walls as the bikes pursued them relentlessly. Tempest smiled at the sight. Somewhere deep in the tunnels, she knew Dash would be chuckling to himself at the chaos he'd caused.

As Mason fled from an oncoming bike, Tempest saw her chance. She ran from the shadows and through the pandemonium, until she reached Zed.

"Zed! We'll get you out of here. Just hold on."

Tempest's heart sank as she looked into his eyes. They were a dull gray, like a storm that had passed. Only the tiniest flicker of golden sparks remained within them. She tried to lift him to his feet, but he remained rooted to the earth, his breathing labored and slow.

"Zed?" Tempest looked deep into his eyes for any sign of response. She shook him and called to him again. "Zed, look at me. Zed!"

Tempest yelped as a stray lightning bolt struck the ceiling above her and turned to see Dash and Ixion emerge from the tunnels, locked in battle against Seth's men. As Zed's eyes grew more distant, she knew she had little time.

"We have to get out of here. Come on!"

She hauled Zed to his feet and turned to see herself surrounded. Mason and the miners gathered around her, clubs and pickaxes resting in their hands. Mason puffed out his chest and stepped forward.

"Leave him, Tempest."

"No, you don't understand. If he stays down here any longer, he'll die."

"That Stormchaser isn't your concern. He's bad news for you. He's poisoned your mind with dreams of adventure, and brought nothing but trouble to this town. And we're here to teach him a lesson." His eyes narrowed. "I could have given you everything, Tempest. And instead, you threw it all away, for *him*."

"No, you would have kept me prisoner in this town."

"What's so wrong with this town? What's so wrong with staying here, with settling down, with being happy?" Mason clenched his jaw and took another step forward. "People like us don't get to run off into the sky. We don't get to travel to faraway places and have a life of adventure. We should stay in this town, live our lives, and be content with what we have. Reach for the sky, and you'll just fall."

"Is that so?"

"Trust me, Tempest. The Stormchasers might seem exciting, but they're from another world. You'll never keep up with them. Sooner or later, they'll get bored with you and move on, leaving you behind." Mason stepped forwards, pickaxe in hand. "Now stand aside. It's time to forget about him and to forget about these ridiculous dreams."

A peal of thunder echoed through the caverns, reverberating through the very bowels of the earth. Tempest shuddered as she thought of the devastation Seth was causing above.

"Mason, you have to listen to me. That biker, Seth, is bad news. If we don't do something, he'll destroy the entire town. Zed's the only one strong enough to stop him."

Mason sneered. "Destroy the entire town? Let him try."

A deep rumble reverberated through the caves as another peal of thunder echoed in the town.

"You don't understand, Mason. The Stormchasers... they're from another world. They have powers you couldn't even dream of."

Mason snorted with derision. "This is why I don't like you reading those books. They fill your head with too many ideas. It's not good for you. Next you'll be telling me motorcycles can fly." The miners guffawed, and his lips thinned into a scowl. "One day, you'll thank me for this. Now stand aside."

Tempest sighed in frustration. Mason's hot-headedness was threatening to destroy the one chance they had of saving the town. Her hands clenched into fists as he stepped closer.

"Do you want to end up like that old witch, Mary? An oddball who doesn't fit in? Or like your mother? Drifting from town to town, raising a child alone?" Mason shook his head in disdain. "Too much dreaming isn't good for a woman. You need to accept the life you have here."

"And if I want a different life?"

Mason sneered at her. "What are you going to do? Fight your way out of here?"

Tempest smiled at the idea. She closed her eyes in concentration, until sparks flew from her fingertips.

"That's exactly what I'm planning on doing."

As she focussed, the sparks became bigger, merging together to form a pulsing lightning bolt. Silver light cascaded around the cavern, filling it with an ethereal glow that reflected from the stalactites above. A lock of her silver hair fell before Tempest's eyes, and she smiled. Of course her lightning was silver.

The miners yelped out in fright, while Mason turned to Zed in horror.

"What have you done to her? This is your fault!"

Tempest called to the heavens, and gathered electricity in her palms. The cavern crackled with energy and her feet left the ground, until she floated in the air. The miners, who had once looked so tall and menacing, now looked terrified, as jolts of electricity shot towards them.

"You men think you run this town. You keep everyone chained here, and crush our dreams. All so that this town remains your kingdom."

Tempest let a lightning bolt loose, which struck two of the men to Mason's left.

"You wanted to tame me. To control me. To shatter my dreams and chain me to the earth. And now I know why."

Another strike of lightning, and two more miners fell to the floor.

"Because you're nothing but a bunch of jocks, trying to cling onto your power. You're scared of change, scared of ideas, scared of anything that means you lose control. And nothing terrifies you more than the big wide world."

Tempest let loose another bolt, until only Mason was left standing. Terror shone in his eyes and he pointed the pickaxe at her with a trembling hand.

"You stop this now, Tempest. I command you to stop."

The winds picked up speed, and Tempest smiled.

"I won't listen to you anymore. I won't stand by while you control this town. And I won't repress the storm anymore. It's time to set it free."

Tempest unleashed her power until the storm tore through the cavern. Gale force winds knocked Mason to his knees, while icy rain pelted him, hardening into hail as it struck him. He struggled to his feet, but a thunderous boom shook the ground, forcing him to his knees once again.

Lightning flashed in warning as he staggered towards Tempest. His teeth were bared in an angry snarl, while he clutched the pickaxe tighter in his hands. Tempest froze as he neared, knowing that using the full strength of her powers would be too dangerous. She had to maintain control over the storm, and keep her humanity. But as Mason's eyes gleamed with a furious rage, she realized he'd lost his entirely.

Tempest gasped as Mason raised the pickaxe, and swung it towards her. A burst of lightning erupted as he went to strike her, striking him in the chest and sending him flying across the cavern. He landed sprawled on the ground, the pickaxe falling to the floor by Tempest's feet.

Tempest turned to see Zed standing with his hands outstretched, sparks flying from his fingertips. He gazed at Tempest and the golden sparks gleamed in his eyes once again.

"I never did like that guy."

Tempest breathed out with relief and threw herself towards him. Zed wrapped his arms around her and placed his lips to hers as electricity danced between their bodies. As sparks raced between them, she felt connected to him in a way she'd never experienced before. Every touch, every caress, every sensation was heightened until it sent tingles racing through her entire body. Like two wires connecting to complete a circuit, she felt whole with him.

"You... you became a Stormchaser. You completed the Trials." Zed's eyes shone with golden sparks that radiated in the cavern. But as he looked at her wrist, where the chain tattoo was nearly complete, the sparks flashed with concern. "But Seth will never accept you. Even as a Stormchaser, you won't be safe."

Tempest looked to the ceiling of the cavern where peals of thunder reverberated above them. "Well, luckily, I have a plan."

She whistled sharply until her dirt bike raced through the tunnels to meet them. Zed raised an eyebrow at the state of it.

"Do you really expect me to ride this thing?"

Tempest laughed as she jumped onto the saddle. "No one rides this bike but me. Now hop on the back. We've got a town to save."

27

— • —

The storm raged. Hurricane winds howled through the once-peaceful town, while blasts of lightning struck every shop window in sight, sending their wares hurtling to the skies above. Terrified residents huddled together, seeking shelter from the hellish nightmare that unfolded in the sleepy town. With no shutters left to hide behind, they clung to one another and looked at the sky in horror. The storm had arrived. And it wouldn't stop until everything in its path was destroyed.

Tempest watched as mementos of a former peaceful life flew into the dark vortex that raged above. She followed the residents' looks of bewilderment as Seth levitated in the center of the storm, his eyes glowing in the dark skies. He drew more power by the second, and if they didn't act soon, the entire town would be reduced to rubble.

Tempest returned to those gathered in the library. Ixion scowled menacingly at the storm, while Dash's hair grew more windswept by the minute. Arthur busied himself hauling the first editions to higher and safer ground, while Mary hung charms from the doorways and windows. Zed stood by the doorway, bathed in the storm's light, as he watched the chaos that unfolded.

"He's drawing on our powers to strengthen the storm. And he's growing more powerful by the minute. We don't stand a chance against him."

Mary shook her head, and her emerald eyes sparkled knowingly. "Seth might be powerful, but he's not invincible. A new alpha needs to rise. Only then will his command over your powers be broken."

"But I tried to fight him before." The light of the storm caught the scar over Zed's cheekbone. "And it didn't work."

"There's a reason Seth tried to keep you on the road for so long. A reason he forced you to live alone, and to never think about settling down. Because Stormchasers are stronger when they find their fated mate. And now that Tempest is a Stormchaser..."

"I'll be stronger."

Zed looked from Mary to his hands. He focussed, and a charge of golden lightning ran down his arms, crackling more powerfully than before. He drew a startled breath at the power at his fingertips, before turning to Tempest.

"What do you think?"

"I think we should fight him together. I didn't save you from the mines only to risk losing you again."

But Mary shook her head. "You can't, Tempest. The Stormchaser rules are clear. There can only be one alpha. Zed needs to do this alone. If there's any interference, we can't be sure that this will work."

Ixion scowled and turned to Zed. "I vote we find the nearest jetstream and make our way out of this town. Let Seth bring it tumbling down. Why risk our lives for these earth-bounds?"

"You don't mean that, Ixion. Besides, Seth would find us eventually."

Ixion ran a hand through her purple Mohawk and groaned. "I hate it when you're right."

"Dash?"

A mischievous grin flickered across Dash's lips, and he let out a sharp whistle. A revving sound filled the street as a bike raced towards them.

"I figure it's always useful to have a spare." Dash grinned at Zed and handed him the keys. "Take it. Just try not to destroy this one, okay?"

Tempest shook her head and took Zed's hand in hers. "Please don't do this alone. There must be another way."

"Tempest, I've spent my entire life never thinking about the future. I've drifted through life, only ever living for the present. But now I have something to fight for." Zed smiled as he held her gaze. "Let me build a brighter future, for both of us."

"But it's dangerous."

"No more dangerous than riding into the strongest storm we've seen in decades and completing the Trials. You took a risk for me. Now let me do it for you."

Tempest felt her stomach twist with worry. "What if Seth hurts you? What if you fall?"

Golden sparks burned in Zed's eyes. "But what if I fly?"

Tempest could feel the power within him. A strength they shared, that flowed through his veins. She sighed, knowing she couldn't stop him from reaching for his destiny. As dangerous as it was, the only thing she could do was give him the strength to fly. To help him soar, rather than fall.

She ran a hand through Zed's hair, and pressed her lips to his. It was a kiss that told him to fly. And as his lips met hers, he kissed her with a promise he would return.

Zed made his way to his bike, and flashed Tempest a reassuring grin as he revved the engine.

"It's time to end Seth's reign, once and for all." He looked at the jetstreams that spiraled into the center of the storm, where Seth lurked. "It's time for us to be free."

Without another word, Zed accelerated down the street, towards the dark vortex of the storm. His tires screamed as he raced down the road, leaving the smell of burning rubber and tire marks behind him. His body blurred with a golden light as he gathered speed, and the roar of his engine echoed along the street like a boom of thunder. This was it. There was no turning back now.

Tempest gasped as red lightning bolts descended from the sky, blasting the road where Zed rode. He weaved between them, before riding across an overturned car and leaping onto the nearest jetstream. He sped along it towards the center of the storm, his bike and body charged with electricity, and gathered a lightning bolt in his hand. It pulsed with a radiant golden light that pierced through the storm's darkness and kept the shadows at bay. He rode onwards, towards the eye of the storm, until he hurled the lightning bolt at Seth.

A sonic boom erupted in the heavens, and Tempest gasped as the earth shook beneath her feet. She watched with awe as the center of the storm exploded in a shower of golden sparks, sending dark clouds billowing across the street. As the winds died down, Tempest barely dared to breathe as she peered into the gloom. Had it worked? Had Zed succeeded?

As her vision cleared, Tempest saw something stir within the gloom. Two glowing lights that shone through the shadows. Her blood turned cold as she recognized them. They were no lights. They were eyes that watched her from within the darkness. Eyes that told her they had failed. Eyes that told her she would pay the price.

Seth's laughter echoed across the town like a peal of thunder. The winds howled with more fury than before, while red-hued lightning streaked across the sky. Seth floated in the center of the storm, untouched by Zed's assault.

"You are a fool to challenge me, Zed. The mines would have been a mercy compared to what I will do to you." He raised his hand and summoned a bolt of lightning. "You might be a strong Stormchaser, but you're nothing compared to a god."

Tempest cried out as Seth hurled the lightning at Zed. It caught his bike, knocking him from the jetstream and through the window of a nearby building. Screams erupted inside, and residents raced out of the building. Christie led the charge, her eyes wide with terror at the pandemonium that unfolded above.

A wicked smile crossed Seth's lips. He jumped onto his own bike before he sped into the building, hunting Zed like a predator. A flash of lights and an explosion of sparks erupted within, before another window shattered and Zed raced back into the sky, Seth following close behind.

Tempest's heart pounded in her chest as she watched them race along the jetstreams, sending gold and red sparks showering onto the ground below. It was dizzyingly fast, breathtakingly beautiful and dangerously savage.

A golden bolt struck Seth, followed by another. He roared out in rage and conjured a maelstrom of lightning, but Zed weaved through his assault with ease. Tempest felt her heart soar as another of Zed's blows connected, and Seth began to weaken. Seth might be strong, but Zed was faster.

Zed raced through the skies faster than she had ever seen him before, striking Seth with blow after blow. As smoke billowed from Seth's bike, Tempest knew Zed was just moments away from victory. She watched with bated breath as Zed gathered power, ready to deliver the final blow.

A shower of sparks exploded next to Zed as a lightning bolt struck the jetstream. Another followed, until the track was filled with an eruption of light and sparks. Tempest cursed as Seth's cronies descended from the sky like a swarm, each of them sending blasts of lightning at Zed as they joined the fight.

"He's cheating! We have to help Zed!"

"But the rules!"

Mary shook her head. "Forget the rules! The alpha has broken them, so we can, too. But you have to hurry. Zed can't last in this for long."

Tempest mounted her bike and revved her engine. "I'm going in."

The smell of hairspray wafted down the street as Christie raced towards her, her eyes wild, her hair ruined from the downpour.

"Don't be ridiculous, Tempest. You could be killed!" She shrieked with fright and ran a trembling hand through her hair. "That man, he can do things... impossible things. This isn't a fight for us."

"Stand there if you want, but I'm going to save this town."

Tempest revved her engine, but Christie placed a restraining hand on her.

"The Stormchasers are dangerous, Tempest. We need to hide and wait for the storm to pass. People like us don't get to fly into the sky."

Tempest looked at her friend. She saw the fear in her eyes. The desire to cling to the safety of life as she knew it. The other residents of the town huddled behind her, cowering at the sight above. But Tempest shook her head and gazed at the storm.

"You're wrong, Christie. We can achieve anything. All it takes is a dream and a leap of faith."

Tempest revved her engine and raced upwards onto the jetstreams. As she sped into the air, she glanced in her side mirror and smiled as Christie's jaw dropped in disbelief. The residents of this town had spent their lives looking at the earth. Now it was time for them to look at the sky.

The sound of revving engines filled the air as Ixion and Dash approached on a nearby jetstream. Ixion's scowl deepened, and she shook her head as she looked down at the residents below.

"I can't believe I'm going to risk my life for a bunch of earth-bounds. Are you sure we can't just ride a jetstream out of here?"

"And miss the biggest battle in Stormchaser history?" Dash shook his windblown hair and grinned. "You've got to be kidding!"

Sparks burst excitedly from Ixion's Mohawk, and she turned to Tempest.

"Dash and I will call in reinforcements and take care of Seth's men. You and Zed just focus on bringing down Seth."

Tempest nodded and raced towards Zed, dodging lightning bolts as the battle raged. Dozens of Stormchasers descended from the heavens to join the battle, until the sky shimmered with technicolor explosions. Tempest swerved on her bike, narrowly avoiding a missile of lightning, and came to a screeching stop next to Zed. His bike was scratched and charred, while thick smoke billowed from the engine.

"Are you okay?"

"I'll be fine." His eyes darkened as he looked at the center of the storm. "Now come on. Let's teach Seth what it means to be a real Stormchaser."

They revved their engines and took off, riding through the dark clouds above the town. As they neared Seth, Tempest gathered power in her hand. She marveled at the silver electricity that wove between her fingers and hurled it through the air. It shot through the skies like an arrow, crashing into Seth's bike and almost unseating him from the saddle. His eyes widened with rage as he turned to her.

"You? You survived the Trials? Impossible!" Seth's eyes narrowed, and he gathered a ball of red electricity in his hands. "Well, this is one storm you won't survive, earth-bound."

Tempest braced herself for the impact as the ball of electricity raced towards her. A shimmer of gold sped through the air as Zed shielded her from the blow, until he was engulfed in an explosion of sparks. Tempest's cries echoed through the heavens as he fell from the jetstream and crashed onto the asphalt beneath. Anger coursed through her, and a lightning bolt erupted in her hand.

"You'll pay for that Seth!"

Seth swerved gracefully through the air, avoiding her attack, and laughed coldly.

"I don't think so, earth-bound." He smiled cruelly as he gathered another bolt of lightning in his hands. "Enjoy your trip back to earth."

Tempest cried out as he struck her front wheel in an explosion of sparks. She gasped as her bike veered from the jetstream and she plummeted to the earth below. And this time, there was no one to save her.

She struck the road below like an angel thrown from the heavens, the breath knocked from her lungs by the force of the fall. Zed groaned next to her and staggered to his knees, the golden sparks in his eyes growing dim.

The residents of the town called to her as they took refuge in nearby shops, cowering with fear from the storm above. Tempest knew she could run to them, that she could hide and wait for the storm to pass. But she'd made her decision. There was no returning to that life now. She had to find the strength to continue.

Tempest coughed as she staggered to her feet, the world spinning before her. A painful throbbing seared in her skull, and blood trickled down her forehead. The clouds above darkened as Seth descended to the earth, his lips curled into an evil sneer. His eyes radiated with a godly power, burning with the savagery of the storm.

"You just couldn't leave it, could you, earth-bound? You couldn't just stay on the ground, where you belong."

A sharp blast of electricity sent her and Zed to their knees. The scent of burned asphalt lingered in the air and cloyed in Tempest's nostrils.

"You might have completed the Trials, but I'll never accept you as a Stormchaser. As long as I'm alpha, you'll never be welcome with our kind."

Another blast of lightning. A scream erupted from Tempest's mouth as the electricity ravaged her body, while Zed roared out in pain.

"I will bring a new age to the Stormchasers. A glorious return to our values. We'll bring destruction wherever we travel. We'll take what we want and leave a trail of devastation in our wake. The storm is something all will fear. And the earth-bound will know their place."

Another blast of electricity. Tempest heard Christie's cry echo across the street, and saw Arthur's eyes widen in fear.

"People like you don't get to fly, earth-bound. You fall." Seth turned to the townsfolk, and sneered at the frightened faces of those huddled in the shops. "Let this be a lesson to you all. This is what happens to those who dare to fly."

Tempest braced herself as Seth gathered electricity in his hands. She knew she couldn't withstand another blast. She turned to Zed and gazed into the sparks of gold that flickered in his eyes. Eyes that had kept her spellbound from the moment they had met. Eyes that had promised her a life of adventure. Eyes that she would jump into the darkest of storms for.

Seth roared with fury and hurled the lightning bolt towards them. It burst from his hands, filling the streets with a hellish glow. But Tempest continued to gaze at Zed, wanting his beautiful eyes to be the last thing she saw.

Tempest winced as she felt the heat of the lightning bolt scorch the air. Her eyes widened as it raced above her, narrowly missing her and Zed. To her surprise, a yelp of anger filled the air as Seth rubbed a lump on his forehead, while a sodden book fell to the ground beside him. He turned to the crowd with a furious gaze, before another book catapulted through the air and struck him on the head.

"Take that, you intolerable bully!"

Tempest looked in surprise as Arthur threw another book at Seth. The rage in his eyes was magnified by his glasses, and his mustache quivered uncontrollably.

Seth gathered electricity in his hands and turned to him with a sneer. "You'll pay for that earth-bound, you and your kind will bow before me..."

Another book struck him, and Mary cackled with glee as it hit its target.

"I've had enough of you thinking you own the place. You give the Stormchasers a bad name."

Seth looked at the pair incredulously. "I'll destroy your town. I'll reduce it to rubble until there's nothing left. People like you can't fight me." His voice rose to a thunderous boom that echoed across the skies. "You should cower before me. I'll show you what happens to mortals who dare to defy the gods. I'll show you the true power of the storm."

"Oh yeah?" Tempest watched as Christie picked up a book and glowered at Seth. "Well, I've had enough of the storms. They're destructive, they're dangerous, and... they're ruining my hair!"

Christie turned to the other townspeople, who cowered behind her.

"Tempest's right. We can't wait for the storm to pass. We need to fight for our future." Her eyes narrowed at Seth, and her fingers clenched the book. "Starting now!"

Cheers and defiant cries filled the air as residents armed themselves with books, flower pots, and anything else they could find. As Tempest watched them, she realized that the excitement she had always wanted had come to the town. And this battle would be the adventure of a lifetime.

28

⸻ ∘ ⸻

Tempest ducked as a flowerpot hurtled across the street, exploding against one of Seth's men in a thunderous crash of soil and terracotta. A hailstorm of books flew towards another, while a group of Seth's cronies yelped as they became entangled in a web of bunting. Her eyes widened as Arthur dueled a Stormchaser using an umbrella for a weapon, while Christie struck another with her handbag.

Pandemonium erupted within the streets. Despite the danger, Tempest couldn't help but smile in wonder. The storm had ignited a spark in the town. And things would never go back to normal again.

Seth eyed the chaos in bewilderment, and jumped onto his bike to escape into the sky. He might be a powerful demigod, but even he knew he was outnumbered. With a glance at Zed, Tempest whistled and mounted her bike, before they soared along the jetstreams after him.

Together they rode high into the sky, where dark clouds gathered and violent lightning whipped through the air. Tempest swerved to avoid a crackling bolt of lightning, and gasped as it exploded into a dark flame. Seth was aiming to kill. Like an animal who knew it was trapped, he would do anything to survive.

She revved her engine until she flew through the sky like a missile. Sparks of silver electricity flickered across her bike and her skin, and the air glowed with a silver energy. She became one with the storm, and raced with the speed of light as she closed in on Seth.

"You're a fool to fight me, earth-bound. I am the bringer of storms. I am the alpha."

The skies opened and blasts of lightning erupted from the heavens. Tempest pulled sharply on her bike, weaving dangerously along the jetstream to avoid being struck.

"People like you don't get to fly, earth-bound. You fall."

Another blast of electricity raced towards her. But Tempest's confidence in her powers grew. She called to the storm to guide her, and sped expertly between each blast, closing in on Seth.

"Your time as alpha is over, Seth. Zed and I have a power that you'll never know. We have each other."

He sneered at her. "Love makes you weak."

"You're wrong. Love gives us strength. It gives us the courage to leap into the darkest of storms. And it gives us the strength to stop you."

Tempest called on the power of the storm and watched as electricity danced between her fingertips in a silver hue. It grew in strength, and extended into a gleaming lightning bolt, as beautiful as it was deadly. She threw it like a javelin and marveled as it streaked across the sky, its aim sure and true, before it struck Seth's bike in an explosion of sparks.

Black smoke billowed from his engine and sparks flew from the fuel tank. Seth's eyes widened, knowing it would blow at any minute. And in his eyes, Tempest saw something she'd never seen before. Fear.

As Seth's curses filled the sky, Zed looked uneasily at the smoke that billowed from his bike.

"Tempest, I can't leave him here."

Her eyes widened in disbelief. "He tried to kill us, Zed. He wouldn't do the same for you."

"Becoming alpha means setting an example for the gang. Death and destruction might be Seth's way, but it's not mine. And it's not yours either."

Tempest glanced at Seth, who coughed and spluttered from the thick smoke that surrounded him. She groaned, knowing Zed was right.

"Fine. But let's make it quick. I'd rather not be around that thing when it explodes."

Zed revved his engine at once and soared across the jetstream. He raced to Seth and called out to him, his hand outstretched.

"Take my hand. It doesn't need to end this way."

Seth narrowed his eyes, and his lips curled with rage.

"I'm the alpha. I don't need your help."

"Seth, you'll be killed. Please, don't do this."

Seth snarled and accelerated along the jetstream before turning sharply to face them. A wicked gleam sparkled in his eyes as he glared at them from across the track.

"I will never recognize you as alpha. Never! And if I'm going down, then I'm taking you both with me."

Seth roared out and sped towards them, his face a mask of rage. Dark smoke billowed from his bike and the sparks ignited, until he became a trail of fire, racing along the jetstream like a comet.

Zed cursed and struck Seth's bike with a blast of electricity, but it continued to race towards them like a possessed steed. Seth's laughter filled the air as he sped closer towards them.

"You alone don't have the power to stop me, Zed. I'm still the alpha."

Zed turned to Tempest, fear shining in his eyes. "You need to run, Tempest. I might not have the strength to stop him, but I can slow him down."

"And leave you here? I don't think so."

Tempest drew a shaky breath as Seth continued to race through Zed's assault, the golden blasts glancing harmlessly off him. Seth's control over the Stormchasers still granted him too much power. And Zed still didn't have enough strength to defeat him alone.

An idea struck her, and she took Zed's hand in her own.

"What are you doing?"

Tempest called the storm to them, until the air shimmered with golden and silver hues. Electricity burst between their hands, weaving together in a tapestry of beautiful sparks.

"The Stormchasers are more powerful with their fated mate, right? So let's combine our powers." Tempest glanced at Seth, who continued to advance on them, his red eyes gleaming in the darkness. "Together, we might be strong enough to stop the alpha."

Sparks flew between them, uniting them until their powers flowed into each other. Their lightning combined before them, twisting and weaving into a ball of light that grew in strength and shape. The gold and silver electricity merged into a radiant platinum bolt of lightning that pulsed with a deadly beauty.

Tempest channeled her power until electricity poured out of her veins and the air radiated with a blinding light. The platinum lightning grew in strength, piercing through the darkness of the storm. They continued to strengthen it with their combined powers, until it shone brightly in the sky. She smiled at the sight of it. Love would always be strong enough to keep the darkness at bay.

Tempest glanced at Zed, who nodded, and together they let their lightning bolt fly. It burst through the sky like a shooting star, light streaming from it as it sped across the air. It landed against Seth's bike in an explosion of blinding light, sending a shower of sparks cascading into the heavens. Seth's eyes widened, and a cry escaped his lips before he was engulfed in the explosion of light.

A sonic boom erupted, and heat and fire scorched the sky. Tempest cried out as her bike left the jetstream and she plummeted downwards, towards the streets below, lost in a cloud of dark smoke.

She hit the earth with a thunderous crash, and the asphalt splintered beneath her. Dark, thick smoke coated the air, obscuring her vision in a veil of darkness. She called out for Zed, coughing and choking on the acrid fumes. But panic rose in her chest as she was met with silence, and she looked through the gloom fearfully.

Tempest drew a breath and summoned the storm, until her thunder call boomed across the town. She called for Zed again and again, barely daring to breathe at the silence that met her.

Tempest felt her heart stir as another boom of thunder echoed through the sky. Tears of relief welled in her eyes as it called to her and coursed through her veins. She mounted her bike and sped through the darkness, towards the sound of his call.

If you follow my thunder call, you'll be able to find me, no matter how dark the storm.

Tempest gasped as a pair of golden eyes emerged from the darkness. She jumped from her bike and into Zed's arms, until their bodies were entwined. Sparks flew between them, traveling across their skin, connecting their bodies and minds. She ran a hand across his skin and marveled as she felt the sensation on her own body. She pressed her lips to his and felt the intensity of the kiss race through her. Like two wires joined to complete a circuit, they were joined as one. And she'd never felt so alive.

Light burst around them as the dark storm clouds cleared. Residents looked to the sky in confusion, as night turned to day, and a glorious cloud-free sky emerged. The storm had passed.

Cheers erupted across the street, and Tempest found herself surrounded by Ixion and Dash, Arthur and Mary, and Christie. She watched in wonder as Stormchasers and residents of the town celebrated with each other as Seth's men fled through the skies, taking the last of the storm with them.

Tempest looked at the devastation along the street. Windows were smashed, cars were overturned, scorch marks blasted the road. But she smiled at the sight of it. After the darkness of a storm always comes light. And as town residents looked at the sky, Tempest knew that there would be new beginnings, not just for her, but for everyone.

The crowd parted as a group of miners approached, Mason leading the pack. He narrowed his eyes, and clutched his pickaxe tightly.

"The Stormchasers aren't welcome here." Mason glared at Tempest. "And that means you, too."

Zed sighed and shook his head. "I wouldn't talk to her like that if I were you."

"Oh yeah? And what are you going to do?"

"It's not what I'm going to do. It's what she'll do."

Mason scoffed. "Tempest doesn't scare me."

A breeze drifted through the street and gathered at Tempest's fingertips. She closed her eyes and her mind connected with the skies. She felt the winds, the rain, the storms from faraway places. And she realized they were hers to summon. She turned to Zed, to see him smile knowingly.

"The storms chose you, Tempest."

Tempest's eyes widened as the Stormchasers kneeled before her. Ixion's usual scowl was replaced with a look of awe, while Dash grinned as he ran a hand through his windblown hair. There was a new alpha in town. And it was her.

Mason stepped forwards, pickaxe at the ready. "I won't ask again. You need to leave this town."

Tempest turned to Mason and the miners. As she looked at the fear in his eyes, the storm winds whispered to her. And she realized the storm had one more job to do.

"We won't be the ones leaving." Tempest smiled as electricity flickered along her body. "But you will."

Mason laughed with disdain. "You can't tell us to leave. You don't have that kind of power."

"Oh, don't I?" Tempest summoned the storm to her. The skies darkened, and winds howled through the streets, while lightning flashed ominously above. "Your days of controlling this town are over, Mason."

Fear shone in Mason's eyes. Not just of the power she wielded, but of the terror of being made to leave the safety of the town. Tempest's power grew as she thought of how he had tried to tame her. Of how he, and others like him, had chained women to the earth. And she vowed that she would put an end to his reign.

"We can't leave." Mason's face paled at the prospect. "Where will we go?"

"You'll have an adventure." Tempest smiled. "You'll experience new things, see new sights, and meet new people. You'll learn to look at the sky, and not at the earth. And you won't return here until you've learned who you really are."

The miners looked at Tempest in bewilderment. She knew there was a goodness hidden deep within them. They just had to learn to dream again.

Mason gripped the pickaxe tightly and shook his head. "You can't make us change. I'm not going anywhere."

Tempest raised her eyebrows as a storm cloud bloomed over the miners. Ominous lightning flashed within it and it emitted a low growl that shook the ground beneath them.

"I thought you might say that. Hopefully, this will encourage you to take the leap."

The rumble in the cloud grew louder, until a blast of lightning struck the ground near Mason's feet. He sprang backwards as another followed, until he and the miners fled from the town. Their shrieks filled the air as the thunderbolts pursued them, forcing them into a strange hopping dance as they raced into the distance.

Tempest smiled to herself as the thundercloud playfully chased them, ensuring they kept on their journey. As the miners left their kingdom, the clouds lifted. The town was finally free.

Zed turned to her and smiled. "So where do we go next, alpha? The storm is yours to control. And wherever you go, we follow."

Tempest glanced at the Stormchasers who looked up to her, awaiting her command. She felt their powers connect to her, strengthening her, and intoxicating her with the power of the alpha. She could go anywhere, do anything, and they would be hers to control.

But as Zed placed his hand in hers, she saw the chain tattoo gleam on his wrist. And she shook her head. She knew what power did to people. And she refused to make the same mistake as Seth.

Tempest closed her eyes as she sent her wish to the storms above. A gentle breeze fluttered through the street, until the Stormchasers gasped in surprise. She opened her eyes and smiled as the tattoo on Zed's wrist faded, until the chains disappeared, leaving only the sigil of the Stormchaser. Tempest turned to the gang, who looked at her in wonder.

"When I looked to the skies as an earth-bound, I dreamed of freedom. And I thought no one was more free than the Stormchasers. But I was wrong. With an alpha in charge, you're not free.

240

You're bound to them, forced to submit to their will. And that ends today."

Ixion looked at her hesitantly. "But if we don't have an alpha, what will we do? Who will lead the storms?"

Tempest smiled. "You'll follow your own storms. You'll ride through the skies and journey wherever you wish. You'll be free."

Ixion studied her wrist, before a shower of sparks erupted from her Mohawk. A piercing whistle escaped her lips, and she jumped onto the bike that sped towards her. A flash of turquoise burst through the air as Dash joined her, until the two of them raced into the sky.

"We're free! Free to go wherever we want to!"

"I've always dreamed of riding the Westerly winds. And of going to Europe!"

"Oh yeah? Well, I bet you can't beat me there."

"You're on!"

Tempest laughed joyously as they sped into the sky, leaving a glowing trail of violet and turquoise sparks behind them. One by one, the Stormchasers raced into the air, filling it with technicolor sparks that burst over the town like fireworks. Zed smiled as he ran a finger along his wrist, where the tattoo faded.

"To relinquish that kind of power takes a strength that no alpha before you has possessed." Zed placed his hand into hers and his eyes burned with golden sparks. "You might have given up your position, but you're still an alpha to me. And I want to be by your side for every adventure." Zed gazed longingly into her eyes and broke into a smile. "So, where shall we go first?"

Tempest returned his smile. She wanted adventure. She wanted excitement. She wanted to travel the world. And she would have it. But she shook her head.

"Right now, I don't want to think about the future." She looked into his eyes and smiled. "I want to follow my heart, and live for the moment."

Tempest drew herself closer to Zed and pressed her lips to his. As their bodies united and the air crackled around them, she felt the world around her dissolve. The kiss swept through her like a storm, taking her breath away until she lost herself in its power.

Their feet left the earth as the winds soared around them, and their bodies intertwined, until Tempest didn't know where she ended and he began. A shower of gold and silver sparks erupted across the town below, illuminating it with the power of their love. Tempest smiled as she gazed at the town below. Once she had dreamed of taking the leap. She had longed for adventure. And now, she had finally found it.

29

The chime of the town clock rang through the valley, pulling Tempest from her daydream. She was late, as usual, and knew she couldn't risk Arthur's wrath. She revved her engine and called for the winds to guide her, until her bike left the ground and sped through the plains at an eye-watering speed.

Tempest couldn't help but laugh at the blood-curdling screams that cascaded through the air behind her. She turned to see Arthur cling on for dear life, his mustache quivering in the wind as they soared through the sky and up towards the mountains. Her wheels struck the ground, and she pulled on her brakes, skidding the bike perfectly through the narrow strip of road until she came to a stop.

Tempest smiled at the gasps of the crowd and shook her wild hair free from her helmet. Arthur cursed, his knuckles white from gripping onto the bike so hard.

"Were you deliberately trying to give me a heart attack?" He cried out as he clambered awkwardly off the bike, before taking off his helmet and brushing down his tweed suit. "I'll never understand why you need to drive so fast. It's reckless, and dangerous. And don't get me started on the noise! Dear me..."

Tempest stifled a laugh as she smiled back at him. "Well, we couldn't be late for the big day."

Tempest turned to the crowd assembled. She'd driven her bike straight through the center of the makeshift aisle, the pews crowded with a blend of townsfolk and Stormchasers. She took her place beside Arthur, and gazed at the view beyond. It seemed like a lifetime ago that she'd once stood on this mountain, dreaming of adventure. And now she'd found it.

The sound of revving engines echoed across the valleys, and more bikes approached. A flash of violet and turquoise sparks filled the air as Ixion and Dash sped down the aisle. Ixion's usual scowl was replaced with a nervous smile, while Dash's windswept hair was neatly combed for once.

Music filled the air as a third bike approached. Tempest smiled as Zed rode slowly down the aisle, his usual leather jacket replaced with a suit. And behind him, looking unrecognizable out of her usual black clothing, sat Mary.

Tempest felt her heart swell as Mary dismounted from the bike and took Arthur's hand. They looked into each other's eyes with the kind of love that had blossomed over the years. Arthur radiated with joy, and he gazed into Mary's eyes with wonder. He had wanted this moment for so long. And it had all been possible because he had made the leap.

As the ceremony began, Tempest marveled at how much had changed since the storm had arrived. From the darkness of the storm, new beginnings had bloomed. Change was in the air, and for the first time, people looked to the sky, free to dream of the life they wanted. Tempest looked among the crowd, and Christie gave her a small wave, a book tucked neatly into her handbag.

Cheers erupted as Arthur swept Mary into a kiss. Earth-bounds threw confetti into the air, while Stormchasers filled the sky with colorful bursts of lightning. Tempest called to the wind, until the confetti somersaulted through the air, swirling around the newlyweds like a storm of cherry blossom. Sounds of merriment and revelry filled the air as Stormchasers and townsfolk danced with one another, their once separate worlds now united.

Tempest smiled as a pair of arms wrapped around her, and she watched the scene before her with delight.

"You were right. After the darkness of a storm always comes light. A light that brings change, hope, and new beginnings. The storm was the best thing that happened to this town." She turned to Zed, and gazed into his eyes as they blazed with golden sparks. "And it was the best thing that happened to me."

Their lips met, and Tempest felt her heart flutter at the sparks that raced across her lips. Every time, it still took her breath away.

"So, have you given any thought to where you want to go next?"

Tempest gazed across the valley to the horizon beyond. "Any-where and everywhere. I want to see the world. I want to have a real adventure. And I want to see it all with you."

"And this town?"

Tempest watched as Arthur and Mary danced with one anoth-er, moving to the music in their own unusual jig. Dash and Ixion shot lightning bolts into the air, each one bursting like fireworks, while Christie danced with a Stormchaser under the shimmering light.

As the guests mingled happily, Tempest took Zed's hand in her own and turned to him with a smile.

"Something tells me they'll be fine. Now come on, let's go on an adventure."

EPILOGUE

Zephyr floated along the skies, drifting away from the small town below. He couldn't help but smile to himself as a flutter of confetti somersaulted in the breeze alongside him. He'd delivered not just one happy ending, but two. Even Aphrodite would be impressed.

Despite his reservations, he had to admit that Hera was right. After all this time drifting through life, it was good to have a purpose again.

"Ah, you've returned." Hera greeted him with a smile as he floated through the palace. "I trust all went well with the King of the Storms?"

"Apart from an entire town almost being destroyed by a power-hungry demigod, it couldn't have gone smoother. Although if I have my way, I'll never have to see a motorcycle again. Those things are obnoxiously loud."

"Well, your hard work was worth it." Hera turned and gazed at the hearth. "It would appear you've saved us from disaster."

Zephyr leaned closer to the hearth, where a small bluish flame flickered to life. He sighed with relief and basked in the warmth of his glory.

"Well, now that I've saved the world, I'm looking forward to a well-earned rest." He peered eagerly at the Heroes Bar, where an enchanting siren-song floated on the winds. "I'm sure the Muses will want to hear of my heroic deeds."

"Not so fast." Hera's eyes narrowed, and she placed a restraining hand on him. "The fires might burn once again, but they're a long way from being restored. Until the light of the fires shines bright, the darkness still closes in. Which means you have another Son of Olympus to meet."

Zephyr groaned. "So much for my evening plans."

"The wind never rests, and neither should you. And if you want your hero's license, you best be on your way."

Zephyr sighed and pulled the photograph from his rain-soaked cloak. "Can I at least go somewhere drier this time?"

Hera smiled and studied the photograph. "That can be arranged." She pointed to a man who stood next to Zed, with eyes that burned like embers of a fire. "How about the descendent of Hephaestus? The future King of the Forge and Fires?"

Zephyr looked at Hera suspiciously. "What's the catch?"

"Zephyr, you insult me." But a flicker of a smile raced across her lips. "How do you feel about dragons?"

"Dragons? You've got to be kidding me."

"Well, I mustn't keep you. You've a long journey ahead of you." Hera clapped her hands as if the matter was decided. "Remember, Zephyr. The fate of the heavens and the earth are counting on you."

Without another word, Hera burst into golden light and soared across the sky, until she twinkled with the constellations up above.

As the sound of the Muses gently drifted into the skies, Zephyr groaned and shook his head.

The Muses would have to wait. He had a dragon to catch.

The End

Thank you for reading!

If you enjoyed this book, please consider leaving an Amazon review - as a new author, it makes such a difference, and I love hearing from readers!

The adventure continues! Read on for a preview of Tempest and Zed's next adventure - STORM BREAKER. Grab your copy for **FREE** at:
www.EdenRoyale.com

Eden x

ACKNOWLEDGMENTS

Thank you to my wonderful ARC team for their amazing feedback, support and for adding a big sprinkle of magic to my day. I am SO grateful to each and every one of you!

Special thanks goes to Nancy G, Gill Travers, Kristin Rufe, Ally Doby, Liz K, Jenni Spalding, Dawn S, Rhonda B, Rachel Gibbs, Augustine E and Melony Staab, along with all my other readers in Team Royale. I'm so thankful for your support!

If you would like to join my ARC team, and receive all future releases for free, you can do so over at:

www.edenroyale.com/team-royale

SONS OF
OLYMPUS

BOOK 1½
STORM BREAKER

EDEN ROYALE

Three days to plan the perfect wedding, find my missing mother, and impress my snobbish in-laws. Sounds perfectly doable, right?

When **Zed**, the descendant of Zeus, came crashing into **Tempest's** small-town library, life was never the same again. Swept into a world where Greek demigods ride through the storms, Tempest joined the Stormchasers on a journey of excitement and magic. But now comes their greatest adventure of all. Planning their wedding...

With just three days to plan the big day, the world's most irritating wedding planner, and a mother-in-law from hell, Tempest soon learns even demigods aren't impervious to wedding stress. But when faced with an ancient curse, Tempest has only one option - to find her long-lost mother and prove she belongs in Zed's world, once and for all.

Together, Tempest and Zed embark to the Lightning Cup - a competition where Stormchasers from around the world meet to prove their mettle on the track. But when they discover a dark and dangerous secret, they find themselves in a race to save the world... and get to the altar on time!

Grab your copy for FREE at EdenRoyale.com and read on for your preview of the first four chapters!

— • —

1

T he storm returned.

Arctic winds whipped through the once peaceful skies, while a maelstrom of icy rain plummeted to the earth. As forks of lightning raced through the dark clouds, the mortals below fled to the safety of their homes, eager to take shelter from the ominous rumbles of thunder. But there were some who peeked through their curtains and looked to the skies knowingly. Those who knew what raced within the clouds. Those who knew that the return of the storm meant one thing.

The Stormchasers had returned. And so had she.

Tempest revved her engine and launched herself across the finish line of the daredevil racetrack. She filled the sky with a light show of silver lightning in celebration, before returning to the earth. Her motorcycle landed with a thud, gravel and sparks flying around her as she skidded to a chaotic halt.

"Quite the bumpy landing there, earth-bound."

"Hey, some of us still have to get used to our powers." She flexed her fingers as silver sparks shot out of them haphazardly. "I count that another win for me. If my powers grow any more, you'll be no competition for me."

Zed cursed, but couldn't help but smile. "I can't believe it. Beaten by an earth-bound."

"*Former* earth-bound. And I always gave you a run for your money, even then."

A grin flickered across Zed's face, and Tempest drew herself into him as the storm surrounded them. She thought back to when they had first met. When he had swept in, like a storm, and helped her make the leap into the unknown. She pressed her lips to his and marveled as a flicker of electricity ran between them.

"Look, Tempest."

The storm cleared, the thick clouds replaced with glorious hues of the golden hour. As she took in its beauty, her eyes widened at the sight before them.

Nestled between the mountains, surrounded by a vast expanse of plains, stood a small town. She gazed at the identical streets of clapboard houses, at the immaculate gardens, at the library that sat proudly on a picture-perfect street. It was a town she would recognize anywhere. She was home.

She followed Zed's eyeline to the mountain, where a cabin sat, bathed in the sunset. He revved his engine and smiled once more.

"Race you there."

In a flash, he was off, speeding across the sky. Tempest cursed and took off after him, a silver streak of lightning gleaming behind her as she rode the currents of air towards the mountains. Together they raced above the town, through their shared memories, until they reached the cabin. As their bikes struck the earth and the last of the clouds cleared, she smiled at the view below. It was good to be back.

"This was where it all began."

Tempest drew herself into Zed, but felt his heart thunder in his chest. She looked up at him and saw the golden sparks in his eyes flicker nervously.

"Is everything okay?"

He drew a breath, and looked at her uncertainly.

"Actually, there's something I've been meaning to—"

"Tempest?"

Tempest turned as a nasal voice cut through the clearing. A waft of hairspray filled the air, and a torrent of blonde hair raced towards her.

"You're back!"

Christie's shriek of delight blasted across the valley, threatening to burst Tempest's eardrums.

"Oh, we've got so much to catch up on! Let's go for a drink at Mary's. I won't take no for an answer!"

Zed stepped forwards, and his eyes darkened. "Actually, I was hoping we could—"

"Tempest!"

Zed groaned as another voice rang through the clearing.

"Great, the welcome party's arrived."

A couple emerged from the woodland, merrily bickering with each other as they approached.

"Arthur! Mary!"

Between Mary's long black robes and Arthur's tweed suit, they looked as wonderfully mismatched as ever. Tempest ran towards them and wrapped her arms around them both.

"How did you know I was here?"

"Mary sensed a powerful storm was coming. And when we saw the streak of silver lightning, we knew it was you." Arthur took Tempest's hands in his, and his eyes shimmered in the light. "Look at you. You're all grown up. You look like you've been on wonderful adventures."

"It's been incredible. We've traveled the world, seen so many sights, met so many people. We once raced in a storm that took us straight across the Bermuda Triangle."

Tempest glanced at Zed, eager for him to share their tales. But dark shadows crossed his face, and he stood apart from the crowd, like a brooding storm against the surrounding joy.

"You always said you wanted adventure. And now you've found it." Mary smiled at the two of them, oblivious to Zed's darkening mood. "So, what brings you back here?"

"I was hoping to ask Tempest if—"

Another flash raced through the air as violet and blue lightning struck the earth. Arthur gasped as two figures emerged, one with a menacing Mohawk that shot purple sparks into the sky, and the other with a mischievous grin that flashed beneath his windblown turquoise hair.

"Hey, are you having a party without us?"

"Ixion, Dash!" Tempest raced towards them and drew them into a hug. "I haven't seen you since we rode the storm to London."

Ixion's face deepened into its usual scowl. "That's because this idiot took a shortcut."

"It wasn't my fault that we ended up in Scotland. And how was I supposed to know we'd disturb a dragon's nest?"

"Well, you should have known better than to ride one. You nearly burned down a castle."

Tempest felt her smile falter as she saw Zed's glare deepen, his mood darkening like thick clouds spoiling a sunny day.

"Zed, are you sure you're okay?"

"Can we go somewhere quieter?" Shadows bloomed in Zed's eyes as he glanced at the merry crowd of well-wishers. "There's something I want to talk to you about."

Tempest's breath faltered as the sparks flickered in his eyes once more. Something was wrong.

Dash scratched his head, and glanced at the group in confusion. "So, what's the party for?"

"There is no party. That's what I've been trying to tell you all." Zed clenched his jaw, while sparks flashed ominously in his eyes. "Now, if you don't mind, I'd like to speak with Tempest. Alone."

Dash's cheeks blushed, and he glanced at Zed awkwardly. "Well, about that..."

Zed groaned as the valley filled with the roar of motorbikes.

"How many Stormchasers did you bring here, Dash?"

"Oh, not *too* many. Just some of the gang... and their friends... and their friends of friends..."

Zed looked at the sky with horror as hundreds of motorcycles descended from the clouds. He turned back to Dash, his eyes ablaze with fury.

"This was supposed to be private. A moment for the two of us..."

Christie clapped her hands, oblivious to Zed's anger. "This is going to be the party of the century! I'll let everyone in town know."

Mary joined in with the joviality. "A welcome back party! What a wonderful idea, Zed." But her face paled as she looked at him. "Oh dear...."

Tempest's stomach lurched as she turned to Zed. His eyes blazed with anger and sparks erupted from his fingers as he looked at the crowd assembled. The sky above him darkened as thick storm clouds gathered, and lightning forked across the plains.

He was mad.

Really mad.

"I had planned this for months. This was supposed to be perfect." Zed drew a breath as he gathered power. "I've asked you all politely. And now I'm done asking."

The heavens parted, and lightning forked in the sky. The bright sunny day vanished, replaced with a thunderstorm that raged through the mountain.

"Zed, what's wrong?"

"I'll tell you what's wrong! I had everything planned. I waited for the perfect time, for the perfect day, for the perfect moment. And you all ruined it. All I wanted was a moment alone with Tempest, so I could ask her..."

Tempest turned to Zed, her heart pounding in her chest. "Ask me what?"

He roared out, and a flash of lightning struck the earth. "To ask you to marry me!"

Tempest gasped as a peal of thunder reverberated through the valley. Zed sighed, and the air grew still as the power of the storm faded. He got down on one knee and pulled a ring from his pocket.

She heard Christie gasp, saw Dash's face turn a deep shade of beetroot, and Arthur's eyes widen behind his spectacles. But Zed held her gaze, his eyes shimmering with golden sparks as the rain poured down around them.

"I'm sorry. I just wanted it to be perfect."

Tempest looked in wonder at her surroundings. The storm raged across the mountains, the sky filled with hundreds of motorcycles, and her friends and family gathered on the mountain. She took Zed's hand, and smiled.

"It *is* perfect."

The golden sparks in Zed's eyes glowed with warmth, and he drew a breath.

"Tempest, you were the earth-bound who stopped the storm in its tracks. The moment I laid eyes on you, I was spellbound." Zed smiled as he held her gaze. "I want to race by your side forever. To guide each other through the darkest storms. Being with you has been the adventure of my life. And I'm ready to take the next leap, if you are."

Tempest looked deep into Zed's eyes. Eyes that sparkled with the power of the storm. Eyes that had swept her away with the promise of adventure. Eyes that had changed everything.

"Yes."

Zed roared out and swept her into his arms. A boom of thunder echoed across the valley, accompanied by the cheers of those around her. Tempest pressed her lips to his, as peals of thunder ricocheted above, and the sky flashed with silver and golden streaks of lightning. And as he placed the ring on her finger, she knew that their love for one another was more powerful than any storm.

Tempest took his hand and smiled as she looked at her family and friends. She watched as the Stormchasers descended from the sky, and residents ventured out of their homes, drawn by the spectacle of lights above.

"Well, I guess it's time for that party, then."

2

The party swept through the town like a storm of its own. Tempest watched as revelers danced in Mary's bar, the Stormchasers and townsfolk united under a cacophony of thumping metal music. Life here had certainly changed.

Her eyes lingered on Zed as he laughed raucously with the Stormchasers and swapped tales of their travels. His eyes met hers, and sparks flew in the air as they connected. This man, this stranger, had changed her life. And now they would be together forever.

"I always knew you two were perfect for one another."

Tempest reluctantly pulled her gaze from Zed, and drifted back to her conversation with Christie.

"Actually, you did everything you could to stop us from being together. You called him a good-for-nothing biker, if I remember."

Christie shrugged and poured a pitcher of beer from behind the bar. "Well, a lot's changed."

"You work here now?"

"Yup. Mary needed the help, and it's decent money while I finish college. Besides, this place needs a spruce up. Just because it's a dive bar doesn't mean it can't be classy."

Tempest glanced at the bar, and saw the signs of Christie's touches everywhere. Small vases of delicate flowers, cocktail menus, and splashes of pink paint stood in stark contrast to the worn decor of the metal bar. It looked less like a dive bar and more like a nail salon.

"It's... it's..."

"Beautiful, I know! What can I say? I have a gift for these things."

Tempest stifled a laugh and smiled at her old friend.

"I guess you're right. Things have changed."

She watched as the townsfolk and Stormchasers mingled, old rivalries now long forgotten. She thought of Seth, of the fateful day he had called the storm to the town. And she realized he had done the one thing no one else had. He'd brought Stormchasers and mortals closer together than ever before. The thought made her smile as she took a seat with Christie and Ixion.

"I've seen my fair share of engagement rings, but I've never seen a rock like that. I'm surprised you can even lift your finger." Christie peered closer at Tempest's finger. "Wherever Zed got that ring from, it certainly wasn't from any shops around here."

"That diamond is ancient, and immensely powerful." Mary arrived at the table, her black skirts billowing behind her. "It's made from a fragment of Zeus' thunderbolt."

Tempest's eyes widened as she looked at her engagement ring more closely. Small streams of electricity danced through the diamond, like a storm caught in the precious stone.

Ixion leaned forwards, spellbound by the ring. "The fragments of Zeus' thunderbolt are incredibly rare. They're said to contain the most powerful storms created by Zeus himself. Storms that could destroy entire nations. Storms that could reshape the earth."

"It's also a giant battery for our powers." Dash grinned as he approached the table. "The fragments were once used to seal away powers of dangerous Stormchasers. They can store an immense amount of energy, enough to power a small continent."

Tempest looked at her ring uneasily. "Is it dangerous?"

"Once it would have been. But it's dormant now. See?" Dash let loose a small spark of lightning that was absorbed into the ring. "Nothing to fear. It would take the power of an entire nation's electricity grid to open it again."

"And let's pray that day never comes." Ixion turned to Tempest, her usual scowl softened into a smile. "Being entrusted with a shard of Zeus is an honor. And I can't think of anyone better suited to it."

"Okay, enough of the magical talk. We need to get down to business." Christy rifled through her bag and pulled out a wad of documents. "We have a wedding to plan."

Tempest's eyes widened at the thick files. "Christie, do you always carry a wedding planner?"

Christie shot her a look of incredulity. "Don't you?"

"Sure, I pack it right next to my kitchen sink." Tempest saw Ixion smirk, but Christie continued to rifle through the folder, seemingly oblivious.

"There's so much to think about. Music, flowers, color schemes..."

"We don't need anything extravagant."

"Nonsense, it's your wedding, Tempest. We'll go with a nice brushed silver for the color scheme. It's the perfect complement to your eyes, and it just screams elegant refinement. We'll use it for the flower arrangements, the ribbons, the marquee..."

"But I'm not sure I need a—"

"Forget refinement." Ixion leaned across the table and scowled. "What you need is a decent band. And there's no one better than The Furies."

"The Furies?"

"Sure. They don't usually do weddings, but they owe me a favor. Trust me, you can't go wrong with their heavy metal. They play so loud it'll make your ears bleed. It's awesome!"

"Maybe something a little more traditional would be—"

"Nonsense." Mary shook her head and adjusted her black robes. "The only thing you need at a wedding is each other."

For the first time, Tempest smiled. "Thank you, Mary."

"That, and the blessing of the earth mother."

"The... what now?"

"Oh, it's not much. Just a few charms to keep the spirits away. And the shaman. He would have to be nude, of course..."

Tempest looked at the three of them in bewilderment. "So we need Christie's elegant silver color scheme, Ixion's heavy metal band, and Mary's pagan charms—"

"Don't forget the light show." Dash grinned and ran a hand through his windswept hair. "You can't have a Stormchaser wedding without it. Just leave it to me. I can summon the best lightning storm this side of the hemisphere."

Tempest's eyes widened as she looked at the group. "And you want all of those things. In *one* wedding?"

The earnest nods at the table made her brain spin. She'd never expected that people would have so many opinions about her wedding.

A feeling of dread swept through Tempest as Christie continued to flick through the folder. What could possibly be next? Circus performers? A miniature petting zoo? She shook her head, knowing she shouldn't give Christie any ideas.

"Okay, now for the big one. Your dress..."

"Can't I just wear this?"

Christie looked at her with horror. "You want to wear your Mom's old leather jacket and a pair of oil-stained jeans?" She shuddered at the mere thought. "Absolutely not."

"But I like it. I feel like myself in it."

"Tempest, this is your wedding, not some bike ride. No, no, no, we'll need to find a dress." She ran a hand through Tempest's hair and tried to tame it into something more presentable. "Remind me to get you booked into the salon sooner rather than later. And then there's the guest list..."

"I just want something small. Just close friends, that's all we need. I don't want anything over the top."

Christie raised an eyebrow and scribbled something in her notepad. Tempest sighed, wondering when Christie had appointed herself as the wedding planner. With every scribble, she knew her dream of a small wedding was growing further away. But with the turn of a page, Christie paused and chewed her pen.

"What is it? What's wrong?"

"Well, it's just... what about your mother?"

The table fell silent, and all eyes turned to Tempest. She clutched the heart-shaped locket around her neck and sighed.

"We still haven't found her. It's been months of searching, following new leads, trying to track her down. But we can't find her anywhere."

"She's out there, somewhere."

"That's what scares me. So much time has passed. What if she doesn't want to be found?"

"Nonsense. Something is stopping her from finding you, I'm certain of it. And she'd want to be there on the big day. She's your mother."

Tempest wasn't so sure. A storm brewed inside of her as she looked at the bridal magazines in Christie's files, the brides and their mothers smiling happily for the camera. She closed the folder and tried to shut off the conflicting emotions that raced through her.

"Okay, now for the venue."

Tempest smiled. At least this was an easy decision.

"We'll have it here, if that's okay?"

Mary's eyes widened and gleamed with happiness. "Of course! It would be my honor."

Even Christie looked happy with the decision. "That's perfect! With the right eye, and a good lick of paint, this place could be transformed." But a frown formed as she flicked through the folder in front of her. "Although finding a date might prove challenging. We're booked out for months."

"The sooner the better."

Tempest felt a pair of arms wrap around her waist and turned to see two sparkling eyes meet her own. Zed smiled and pressed his lips to hers, melting away the tension that had formed during Christie's wedding planning.

"Well, it'll either have to be in two years' time..."

Zed shook his head. "That's far too long." He flashed a smile at Tempest. "What if she changes her mind?"

Christie paused as she flicked to another page. "Or in three days' time."

"Three days? To plan a whole wedding?"

"I'm sorry, that's all we have."

"It's impossible." Tempest shook her head, but faltered as she saw the grin on Zed's face. "You can't be serious."

"Haven't you learned by now that nothing is impossible?" He drew himself into her, intoxicating her mind with his scent of motorcycle oil and fresh rain. "Like I said. The sooner the better."

Tempest looked at Christie uncertainly. "What do you think?"

Christie frantically flicked through her wedding folder. "Well, we'd need to simplify the color palette, the dress would have to be off the rack, and invites would have to be sent immediately."

"But is it possible?"

Christie looked up from the files, her eyes gleaming. "Say the word, and you'll have the wedding of a lifetime."

Tempest laughed in bewilderment and turned back to Zed. "Then let's do it!"

She leaped into his arms and felt him spin her around while the others cheered. They shared a kiss as the music blared around them, and sparks raced between their lips. Tempest gazed into the eyes of the man who had changed everything, the man who would become her husband. But as she glanced at Christie's wedding folder, her smile faded.

"I never realized how many other people are involved in a wedding."

Zed nodded and grimaced. "About that... I think it's time we made the trip. For you to meet my family. Before the wedding."

"You don't need to look so worried. We've survived an alpha who tried to destroy us and the entire town. I'm sure dinner with your family will be a walk in the park in comparison."

"You haven't met my mother."

Tempest laughed, but nodded. "Let's do it. Although we'll have to go soon. Three days doesn't give us much time."

"How does tomorrow sound?"

Tempest couldn't help but smile. Life with Zed was always driven at one speed. Fast. A surprise proposal. Dinner with his family tomorrow. A wedding in three days. She wondered what other surprises he had up his sleeve.

"Tomorrow it is." She kissed him once more, but sighed as she looked back at the party.

"What's wrong?"

"It's silly, but with all the celebrations, I've hardly seen you today. And with the wedding preparations Christie has planned, we won't get much time with each other until the big day. I suppose I just want you to myself for a moment."

Zed broke into a grin, and his eyes flashed with golden sparks.

"That can be arranged."

With a flash of lightning, Tempest felt herself disappear from the bar, and reappear somewhere else entirely. Zed clicked his fingers and a bolt of electricity raced from them, igniting dozens of candles that filled the space. Tempest looked around in wonder as they emerged in his cabin, where a bottle of wine lay in wait and a fire leaped into flame.

"This was what I'd planned. Before the others sabotaged our night."

"It's beautiful." She smiled and ran a hand through his hair. "You changed my life when you came here. You taught me to take risks. You helped me take the leap into the unknown. And I'm so grateful I got swept up in your storm."

"And you taught me that the storm is only worth riding if someone is by your side. I was lost before you, aimlessly drifting like a storm with no purpose. You freed me, and the others, and showed us what a true Stormchaser is. And although you gave up your alpha powers to free us, you'll always own me, and my heart."

As the storm brewed outside, Tempest pressed her lips to his and marveled as sparks leaped between them. She drew him to her, lightning racing through their bodies as she became lost in the power of the kiss. Zed's hands roamed her body, and hers across his, sparks leaping at their touch. Their bodies entwined, skin on skin, until Tempest didn't know where he began and she ended.

She looked deep into the golden sparks that burned within his eyes, at the man who had swept her away with the power of his storm. And as she pulled him to her, she knew she was ready to be swept away once more.

"Just relax. I can feel your nervousness in the storm."

"I'm not nervous, I'm fine."

Zed raised an eyebrow as sparks leaped from Tempest's fingers and the air crackled around her.

"Okay, I'm nervous. It's not every day you have dinner with the mother-in-law thousands of feet in the sky."

"You have nothing to worry about. She'll love you."

"It's not just that..."

"Tell me."

"You're from a long line of Stormchasers, descended from Zeus himself. But me... I have a runaway mother, and grew up in a library. I just worry that I won't be good enough for your family."

"None of that matters. I'm lucky to have you. Trust me."

Tempest smiled, wanting to believe him. But the wedding had brought her family into focus like never before. She placed her hand on her locket and looked across the skies, wondering where her mother might be.

"Maybe I should stay in the town. To help Christie with the wedding planning."

"And spoil her fun? This is a dream come true for her. You know how much she loves to plan a big event."

"That's what I'm afraid of."

"Besides, it's too late to turn back now." Zed shot her a grin. "We've arrived."

The storm cleared, and Tempest gasped at the sight before her. A beautiful city sat nestled in the clouds, its buildings of white-washed stone reflecting the golden hues of the surrounding sky. Picturesque homes with domed roofs dotted the landscape, scattered along the clouds like they were built into the slopes of a mountain.

"Welcome to Olympia."

But Tempest's eyes were drawn to the city center, where the largest building stood, surrounded by large stone columns that gleamed against the backdrop of clouds.

"You never told me you lived in a temple."

Zed shrugged sheepishly. "It's not as impressive as it looks…"

"Well, it's a world away from a cabin in the woods."

"Don't be nervous." Zed broke into a reassuring smile. "Now come on, they're expecting us."

He revved his engine, and they raced ahead, following the jet-streams down into the city. Tempest's eyes widened at the temple's beauty. Statues and friezes adorned the building, while frozen jetstreams arched from its steps, glittering like diamonds in the sunlight. It was from another world entirely. A world that Tempest wasn't sure she belonged in.

A shimmer of movement in the sky caught her attention. Her eyes widened as she took in the shape. A pair of giant wings beat the air, glimmering with golden scales, while a long and vicious tail whipped behind its reptilian body. It was impossible, it couldn't be real, but it looked like a...

"Dragon! Look out, Zed!"

The dragon roared and swooped down from the sky, snatching Zed in its talons. Tempest summoned a bolt of lightning in her hands and hurled it at the beast. She cursed as her shot went wide and sparks flew from her fingers.

"Dammit, what's the point of having these powers if I can't use them?" She shook her hands like she would to a television remote with empty batteries. "Come on!"

Another blast flew from her hands. The howl of the dragon told her this time her aim had been true. It staggered backwards into the temple, before a thunderous crash filled the air and a plume of dust erupted out of the arches. She raced over the threshold, to be met by a scene of chaos. Tables lay overturned, smoke billowed from the bookcases, while tapestries lay torn and pulled from their hangings. And in the middle of it all, Zed brawled with the golden dragon.

"Zed! Zed, are you okay?"

She raced towards him and gathered more electricity in her hands, ready to shoot again. But as she glanced at Zed, she faltered. The sparks in his eyes burned, not from the adrenaline of the fight, but from the joy of it. A smile flickered across his face, followed by a laugh. She looked at him uncertainly. What kind of crazy person laughed as they fought a dragon?

The beast howled once more, before it sent a plume of fire towards Zed. Zed roared out jovially and sent a blast of lightning in return, their powers exploding on impact. Tempest drew a breath as realization dawned on her. They didn't fight to kill. This was nothing more than a game.

The dragon threw Zed into the air, sending him sprawling into the rubble of what had once been a statue. As he emerged, Zed glanced looked at the lightning that crackled in Tempest's hands and shook his head.

"No, don't shoot! He's not an enemy."

Zed charged at the beast, and the two wrestled, Zed's arms bulging while the dragon's hind legs tensed. Tempest watched with an expression of incredulity. She'd thought Zed was about to be eaten alive. She rolled her eyes. This was just so typical of men.

"So what? Is this your pet or something?"

Zed roared out with laughter while the dragon glared at her.

First you electrocute me, and then you call me a pet? This is why we used to eat your kind for breakfast.

The beast swung its tail, trying to trip Zed. But Zed pounced onto it, before digging his feet into the ground and pulling backwards with all of his might. His biceps bulged as he lifted the dragon into the air, before he threw it across the room. It struck a dining table, sending a deafening boom ricocheting through the temple as it landed in a pile of splinters, cutlery and rubble. Zed roared out victoriously as the dragon groaned and slumped onto the ground, bested by his strength.

Tempest took in the destruction across the temple. Antique vases lay smashed, tapestries smoked and burned, and scorch marks lined the marble walls. She'd never seen so much chaos and carnage in one place.

Footsteps echoed behind her, the sound of high heels on marble floors. An older woman approached, her arms crossed and her lips pursed. Her eyes blazed with something that Tempest recognized instantly. A flash of warning before the storm.

"You haven't even been here for five minutes, and you're already destroying the place." The woman batted a flaming tapestry with a torn pillow, sending feathers everywhere as she tried to control the blaze. "This is an antique from the Byzantine era! And you've destroyed the dinner table." Her eyes narrowed at Zed and electricity surged within them. "Give me one good reason why I shouldn't send you to Tartarus."

Tempest expected Zed to fight back, to argue, to explode with his inner rage. But the light in his eyes dimmed, and a look of apology crossed his face.

"I'm sorry, Mom."

"*Mom*?"

It's then that Tempest saw the similarities between Zed and the woman. The inner power that radiated from them. The hint of danger within the curve of their smile. The eyes that sparkled with the power and beauty of the storm.

"Why, oh why, did Hera have to curse me with an entire line of boys?" The woman turned to Tempest and drew a long breath to summon her patience. "He was always like this, even as a child. We never could get a babysitter to stay for more than a week." But the woman's eyes softened, and she broke into a smile. "You must be Tempest. I've heard so much about you."

Tempest returned the smile, but before she could respond, heard a groaning sound from the remnants of the dining table. Zed's mother rolled her eyes before turning to Zed.

"Get this place tidied up before your brothers arrive. And for goodness' sake, get cousin Ash off the dining table."

"Cousin Ash?"

A blinding light surrounded the golden dragon, as it changed its form. Tempest shrieked out as a man stood nude before her, clutching a fruit bowl to cover his modesty.

"You're Zed's cousin?"

He rubbed a bruise on his forehead and frowned. "Do you plan on electrocuting every family member you meet?" But within his eyes of fire, there was warmth. "I can see why you want to marry this one, Zed."

As laughter rippled through the room, and the sound of motorcycle engines signaled the arrival of Zed's brothers, Tempest looked around in wonder. She watched as Zed welded the dining table back together, while Ash lit candles with a touch of his finger. And she marveled that life had become so strange and magical, that she would have dinner with demigods and a dragon in a temple that floated in the sky.

— · —

4

S ome people might expect a dragon crashing onto the dining table to affect dinner plans. But Zed's mother wasn't one of them. Tempest had returned to the dining room to find the rubble cleared, the tapestries hung once more, and a gleaming spread laid out, as if by magic. Then again, Tempest reminded herself, it probably was.

Zed gave her a reassuring squeeze of his hand as his brothers continued to bicker amongst themselves. She couldn't help but smile as they argued. Despite their powers, they were just like a normal family.

"You'd think I'd have offended Hera in a former life. Seven sons and not a single daughter." But Zed's mother glanced at Tempest's ring and smiled. "Although that's set to change soon enough. I see he used the shard of the thunderbolt."

Ash narrowed his eyes at the ring, and smoke billowed out of his nostrils. "That thing was a nightmare to use in the forge. It kept zapping me every time I tried to fit it into the ring."

"You... you made this?"

He nodded and grinned. "You're looking at a descendant of Hephaestus, Greek god of fire and forge."

"Thank you, it really is beautiful. And I'm sorry again for the..."

"Unprovoked electrocution?" He shrugged as he jabbed a bit of steak with his fork, and seared it with a flame that burst from his fingertip. "Don't worry about it. But you should be careful with that ring. It might look pretty, but that thing has enough power to reduce a city to ashes."

Zed's mother smiled. "Try a small continent, and you'd be correct. But you have nothing to fear from the ring. It's been dormant for years. And I must say, it looks good on you."

A flickering of light in the sky drew Tempest's attention, and she glanced outside, wondering what else might come through the door. A deafening roar of motorcycles filled the air, and Zed's mother cursed as the cutlery shook on the dinner table.

"My apologies for the light show outside. It's like this every year."

"What is it?"

One of Zed's brothers smiled, sparks gleaming in his eyes. "Only the best race in the world. The Lightning Cup."

Another brother nodded eagerly. "You have to visit it while it's in town. Everyone who's anyone will be there. It's the one time of year every Stormchaser meets to test their speed against each other. There's nothing else like it."

Zed's mother shook her head. "It's also run by a power-mad criminal who tried to claim your father's throne. He's a gambler, a cheat, and a madman."

"He's also a genius. There's no better inventor in the world."

"His machines and gadgets violate the natural order, and are an affront to the old gods." Another growl of bikes, and the dining table continued to tremble. Zed's mother's face filled with rage, and her voice echoed through the sky like thunder. "And every year he ruins the peace of this city with his Lightning Cup."

Tempest braced herself as Zed's mother's eyes lit up with rage. A gigantic lightning bolt whipped through the air outside, followed by a monstrous boom of thunder. The air grew silent, the motorcycle noise ceased, and Zed's mother sighed, before she smiled serenely as if nothing had happened. Tempest made a mental note to herself to ensure she was never on the receiving end of one of her tantrums.

"So, we must talk about the wedding. Three days to plan a ceremony doesn't give us long, but I think we can arrange it in time."

Tempest glanced at Zed. Apparently, Christie wasn't the only person who fancied herself as a wedding planner.

"I've spoken with the council, and they've agreed that you can use the temple for the ceremony." She narrowed her eyes at Zed's brothers and Ash. "Providing everyone is on their best behavior."

"Thanks Mom, but we have a venue lined up already."

"Zed, please. No other venue compares to the temple. Only the direct descendents of Zeus himself can marry there. It's an honor to be offered it."

"Actually, we're getting married where Tempest grew up."

Tempest sensed the hesitation in Zed's voice, and his mother looked at him questioningly.

"Oh, and where's that?"

"It's just a small place. A little further out from here..."

Tempest's eyes widened as she realized why Zed was being so vague. She lowered her voice to a furious whisper.

"You didn't tell her."

Zed's eyes flashed with apology, and Tempest felt her stomach lurch. His mother looked between the two of them in confusion.

"What didn't he tell me? What's the matter?"

"He didn't tell you that when we met... I was an earth-bound."

Silence fell over the table. A plume of smoke billowed from Ash's nostrils, while Zed's brothers exchanged awkward glances. Zed's mother's eyes blazed with sparks before she fixed Zed with a glare.

"She's an earth-bound?"

"Mom, don't start."

Tempest turned to Zed in exasperation. "Why didn't you tell her?"

But as she saw the looks of shock amongst his family, she knew why. He was embarrassed.

His mother's face paled as she chewed her food, as if an unpleasant taste had just filled her mouth.

"Goodness, this is a surprise. I suppose this means you'll have to get married on the earth." Even saying it made her shudder. As she spoke, Tempest saw her mind whirring, mentally striking off the rich and famous guests she had planned to invite. "We'll have to scrap the first dance in the clouds, and we can forget about the Muses Choir attending..."

"This isn't your wedding, Mom..."

Zed's mother placed a trembling hand to her chest. "My goodness, how will I convince the elder to conduct the ceremony? I don't believe his feet have ever touched the earth."

Tempest glanced at Zed and his brothers. Something told her that melodrama over the dinner table wasn't uncommon.

"But the blessing." Zed's mother's eyes became wide and watery. "How will you get married without it?"

"What blessing?"

She spoke through gasping breaths and half sobs, a handkerchief pressed to the corners of her eyes. "It's an ancient tradition, where the newlyweds are showered with the lightning of their two families. I believe you earth-bounds have something similar, where you throw..."

"Confetti?"

Zed's mother nodded, but looked positively nauseous at the thought. "When Stormchasers marry, both families combine their powers over the couple. It grants them protection, strength, and Zeus' blessing. Without the blessing, a marriage is cursed."

"Mom, that's enough."

Silence returned over the table. Tempest gulped and glanced at Zed's mother. Of all the disastrous meetings with the mother-in-law, this had to set a record.

Without the blessing, a marriage is cursed.

Tempest looked at the temple she sat in. At the antiques and extravagant furnishings that surrounded her. At the mythical beings and gods that sat at the dinner table. And she realized she had been right all along. She didn't belong here. Where Zed had a long and rich family history, she had none. Where Zed had grown up in a palace in the sky, she'd lived in a town no one had heard of. And where Zed could marry in a temple of the gods, she could hire a dive bar on earth.

She caught eyes with Zed's mother and saw what they reflected. Disappointment. And despite everything Tempest had done to get her powers, she knew that she still wasn't good enough.

The air crackled with tension as Zed and his mother exchanged hostile glares. A storm was brewing, and Tempest didn't want to be around when it erupted. His mother turned to the brothers, who cowered under her gaze.

"Make yourselves useful for once, and clear the table."

They leaped into action, as if they couldn't get out of the room fast enough. Tempest rose from her chair to help them, wanting to be as far away from Zed and his mother as possible.

"Tempest, wait..."

But Zed's words died out as Tempest left the dining room. The air around her crackled with electricity as a hot flash of anger raced through her, like a violent storm gathering strength.

Without the blessing, a marriage is cursed.

Zed hadn't told his family about her. He was embarrassed by her. Thick storm clouds billowed in the skies as her anger grew. An ominous flash of silver lightning burst above, while a peal of thunder echoed through the temple. Darkness bloomed across the city as the storm fed from her anger. It called to her with its primal desire to lash out. To destroy.

No. She mustn't.

Tempest shook her head and leaned against the marble walls. She knew firsthand that no good came from getting swept up in the storm's darkness. She had to control her powers. And besides, the last thing she needed was to give Zed's mother even more reason to disapprove of her.

She took deep breaths to compose herself, until the storm clouds dissipated and the clear skies returned. She braced herself, and tried to gather the courage to return to the dining room. But as the sounds of an argument drifted through the air, she hovered by the doorway.

"You didn't think to tell me she was an earth-bound?"

"What does it matter, Mom?"

"It matters plenty! Like it or not, one day you'll take my place as our leader. You'll be the King of the Storms. And so, you must uphold our reputation." Zed's mother shook her head and took his hands into her own. "Tempest seems like a lovely woman. But you're from two different worlds. And her kind doesn't belong here."

"You're being a snob."

"So what if I am? How will this look to the council? An earth-bound for a daughter-in-law... it's an embarrassment."

Tempest felt the anger flicker through her once more.

"None of that matters to me, Mom."

"Well it should. You might not care for our traditions, but you'd be a fool to marry without the blessing. The curse is all too real. I've seen it. And you'll be doomed without it."

Silence fell across the table. Zed's mother rose to her feet and sighed.

"I'm sorry, Zed. But there's a reason earth-bound and Storm-chasers don't mix. Without the blessing, this marriage will be cursed."

She left the room, leaving Zed alone. Tempest watched him as his shoulders slumped and the golden sparks in his eyes dimmed. A deep sense of shame spread through her, and hot tears of frustration filled her eyes. Their relationship had been against the rules from the very beginning. And it was still no different.

Tempest placed her hand to her necklace, feeling the edges of the broken heart in her fingers. She wished she could find her mother. She wished she could come to the wedding and perform the blessing. She wanted it like she had wanted nothing before, until it burned through every fiber of her being. She sent her wish to the heavens, and opened her eyes to see Zed look at her, regret hanging in his eyes.

"Tempest, wait. Please."

She drew a breath and blinked back her tears.

"You didn't tell her."

"I'm sorry. I should have told her. I didn't think..."

"She's embarrassed of me. And so are you." The anger boiled within her, and the surrounding air sparked and crackled. "And now, our marriage will be cursed, apparently."

Zed stepped forwards and took her hands into his own.

"I don't care what anyone thinks. I don't care about rules, I don't care about curses, and I don't care about traditions. I only care about you."

The silver sparks crackled in warning, but Zed continued to hold her. He looked deep into her eyes and drew himself closer.

285

"Please, Tempest, believe me. None of this matters to me. The only thing that matters is you."

She looked into his eyes, at the golden sparks that flashed with concern, and felt her anger fade. The air returned to normal as he held her close, and stroked the silver streak in her hair.

"Don't let what my mother said worry you. It's just an old myth."

But Tempest shook her head. "If there's one thing I've learned, it's that myth and make-believe should be taken seriously. Your mother is right. If we're going to get married, I want to do it properly. No more breaking rules, no more curses. I want a *real* marriage." She looked at the beauty of Olympia and sighed. "And I want to feel like I belong here."

The wind blew through the open arches of the windows, bringing with it the scent of a faraway storm. She closed her eyes and inhaled, sensing the fragrance of her mother's perfume. She was out there, somewhere. And Tempest knew what she had to do.

"I want to find my mother. She's the only one who can perform the blessing for me." Tempest held Zed's gaze, and felt her resolve strengthen. "It's the only way for us to have our wedding. A real wedding, with a real future together. "

Zed wrapped his arms around her and held her close. "I want to find her, too. But we've looked everywhere, and asked everyone. And our wedding is in two days."

But Tempest smiled as the breeze carried the sound of revving motorcycles and cheering crowds.

"Well, luckily, I know where to look. The one place every Stormchaser is bound to go to."

She looked into the distance, where the storm burned brightest, and the sounds of racing roared through the sky.

"It's time to go to the Lightning Cup."

STORM BREAKER

OUT NOW

Claim your FREE copy at
EdenRoyale.com

ABOUT THE AUTHOR

Eden Royale is a paranormal romance / urban fantasy romance writer whose books add a sprinkle of magic to a reader's day.

A fan of trouble-making heroes and heroines who save the day, Eden's books are known for their light-hearted action, magical adventure, feel-good happily ever afters, and several laughs along the way.

Eden lives in a tiny rose-covered cottage in London, England, with their husband. When not daydreaming about magic, you can find Eden exploring London's coffee shops, and gardening with a glass of wine in hand.

Add a sprinkle of magic to your day by joining Eden's newsletter:

EdenRoyale.com/newsletter

Add a sprinkle of magic to your day!

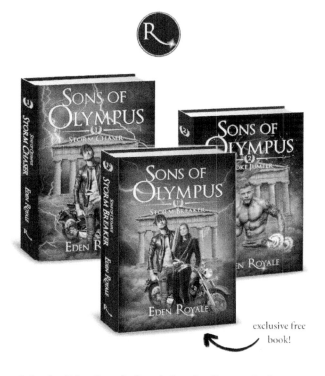

exclusive free book!

Join the Eden Royale fan club to be first in the know about future releases, book promotions and to claim your free book!

www.EdenRoyale.com